Sleeping Beauties

Sleeping Beauties

SUSANNA MOORE

ALFRED A. KNOPF

NEW YORK

1993

THIS IS A BORZOI BOOK
PUBLISHED BY ALFRED A. KNOPF, INC.

Grateful acknowledgment is made to the following for
permission to reprint previously published material:

New Directions Publishing Corporation: Excerpt from poem
xxxvii by Marichiko from *One Hundred More Poems from
the Japanese*, translated by Kenneth Rexroth, copyright ©
1974, 1976 by Kenneth Rexroth. Reprinted by permission.
University of Hawaii Press: Excerpt from "The Prince's
Words to the Princess" from *The Echo of Our Song: Chants
and Poems of the Hawaiians*, translated and edited by Mary
Kawena Pukui and Alfons L. Korn, copyright © 1973 by
The University Press of Hawaii; excerpt from "Minamoto
No Morotada" from *Japanese Poetry the 'Uta'* by Arthur
Waley, copyright © 1976 by George Allen & Unwin Ltd.
Reprinted by permission.

Library of Congress Cataloging-in-Publication Data
Moore, Susanna.
        Sleeping beauties : a novel / by Susanna Moore.—
1st ed.
        p.   cm.
    ISBN 0-394-58280-2
    I. Title.
PS3563.0667S57   1993
813'.54—DC20   93-12335
                                                     CIP

Manufactured in the United States of America

FIRST EDITION

For Ale Kaiser

Sleeping Beauties

The paths were matted with leaves. Long black seedpods from the monkeypod trees lay on the rotten garden benches and Clio thought at first that the seedpods were centipedes. The pond where a raft once floated for summer dancing was dry, its banks papered with fluttering strips of frogs' eggs.

Thief palms, yellow snake trees, and betel-nut palms from Malaysia grew around the house, leaning on it and hiding it, and the buildings of downtown Honolulu so surrounded it that even at midday the garden was in shadow, and inside the house it was as dark as a tomb.

The dry branches hanging from the palms looked like grass hula skirts. Sometimes the rats that lived in the trees wandered onto the porch and into the house. At Christmas, when Clio and her cousin Mamie were invited to tea, the girls ate damp Ritz crackers and watched the rats play in the knotted wisteria vines. "Don't trouble them," Emma Fitzroy once said when she noticed them staring at the rats. "They're just bent-over old-man rats."

Emma must have seen Clio from one of the rooms in which she was still able to live, for she appeared on the verandah as if by magic.

"What is it, child?" she asked, as if she saw Clio every day. "You're pale." As if it were Clio who was the ghost.

Clio held her hands behind her back. She did not want her aunt to see that she was trembling. She was hungry and she had scratched herself on the branches piled against the gate. Clio wiped her face on her cotton sleeve, glancing without self-pity or even surprise at the small dots of blood that blossomed on the cloth.

Having brought nothing with her, she imagined that she asked for nothing as well. Unexpected and uninvited, she hoped only that the mysterious ties of blood of which she had heard so much (Clio saw these ties not as mere symbols but as strands of red sinew stretched taut between families and houses, island to island) would wrap their strong tendrils around her and bind her so that she would not be forced to return to her father and stepmother.

She looked up at the house and considered whether it would collapse with the weight of her bare foot on the verandah step. The very walls, mapped with leafless vines, seemed inconsequential to her, as if the web of vines alone held them upright.

"I want to live with you," she said.

Emma came down the steps. "Come inside, child." She took Clio by the hand and led her into the house, and Clio was relieved that the house did not fall on them.

"Wait here," Emma said, "I will fetch you some water."

For a moment, Clio thought she saw someone, a woman, standing in the doorway of the music room. Clio had learned to recognize the many spirits of sky and land, and she seemed to carry her own water spirit deep within her, the tides rising and falling with the rush of her blood. She was not afraid of spirits. There were gods and lesser gods, and she knew them. Every manifestation of nature—rocks and headlands, trees, streams, reefs—had its own guardian spirit. There were gods of districts, bays, and shallows; gods of priests and commoners, sharks, lizards, birds. There

were deified ancestors. They had been there at the beginning, in the volcanic green beauty, before the reckless ad-
venturers from the south landed with their women and
dogs and children, their seeds and rootstock wrapped in
damp *kapa*. They had been there before the coming of the
white man—before Contact, as Emma would say; before
the explorers and the shrewd merchants of timber and
sea biscuit, and the pious, vigorous missionaries. Clio was
descended from all of them. The spirits, as well as the
seafarers, were her ancestors.

Clio considered for a moment asking the ghost if she
might stay. It was not dread or fear that made her hesitate.
She knew that she would stay at Wisteria House whether
the spirits wanted her there or not.

"I would like to change my *'aumakua*," Clio said quietly
when Emma returned with a glass of water.

Clio's *'aumakua*, her family totem, was the lizard. She
had always hoped for something more symbolically powerful for her *'aumakua*, like the shark, although she would
have been very happy with the short-eared owl or even the
plover. Clio was ashamed to admit it, but she disliked being
under the protection of a lizard. She worried that she, too,
was a changeable, timid thing.

"The lizard is adaptable, modest, small, nocturnal,"
Emma answered carefully. She handed Clio the glass. "He
demands very little and he does a great service. He is an
amiable, useful creature. He eats flies and mosquitoes."

Clio drank the warm water. She suspected that she was
a lizard who couldn't even perform the service of eating
insects. She was not even sure that she was amiable. She
had sat in bed night after night and watched her lizards
move fitfully, usefully, across the ceiling. The one trait of
the lizard that she did admire was its ability to grow a
new tail. Her brother, Dix, liked to eat the discarded tails.

She wondered if she could become a lizard with a new tail. She would send Dix her old tail with the other delicacies she mailed to him at boarding school.

"You may pick another 'aumakua if you wish," Emma said. "I, too, as you know, am protected by the lizard. I like him very much. As you know, the giant lizard god, Mo'o, can change at will into different shapes. I myself have seen it."

"You have seen it?" asked Clio, not in disbelief but in awe.

"Yes," Emma said. "I myself have seen it."

Clio decided, for the moment, to keep her 'aumakua, not least of all because she did not want to miss the chance of seeing Mo'o herself.

In 1871, Clio's great-grandmother, a princess of full Hawaiian blood, married Redmond Clarke, a shipwrecked Irish sailor who won favor with the king. Included in her dowry was a coastal plain on the island of O'ahu that was one day to become the city of Honolulu. Wisteria House was Redmond Clarke's gift to his bride, and the princess used it as her town residence. Emma, who was the granddaughter of Princess Ruth, had inherited Wisteria House. The princess had been a shrewd, temperamental woman, rather large, and Emma's mother always liked to say, quite unfairly, that Emma had inherited the princess's character along with her house.

Clio used to imagine that nothing had come off the ships in Honolulu harbor that did not pass through the rooms of Wisteria House: the first grand piano ever seen in the islands, the first refrigerator, the first carriage and pair, the first Brazil nut. By the time Clio arrived at Wisteria House, faded red and yellow capes from the time of Kamehameha I, woven from the breast feathers of thousands of birds, lay stiffly over dusty *koa* tables. The capes looked like the crepe paper animals on abandoned carnival floats. Carved idols with abalone-shell eyes and mouths of sharks' teeth leaned disconsolately against the walls, their upraised arms bound in clotted webs, their shoulders powdered with the dried wings of bats and birds. The *koa* chests, full of folded layers of *kapa* cloth, were kept open so that the fragrance of dried *mokihana* flowers, like anise, could seep through the house, but even so, the rooms smelled to Clio as if damp towels had been kept in them for years.

The rooms where Emma lived, however, were clean and fresh. The wood floors were kept bare. The big *koa* calabashes and bowls were polished every day with bags of flannel dipped in *kukui* oil. The walls were covered with *lau hala* matting. There were pale, ghostly rectangles on the walls, lighter in color than the rest of the matting, where there once had been paintings, and Clio, years later, found a photograph in an old auction catalogue of a Gauguin that had once belonged to Emma.

Emma kept her heavy black hair in a chignon, held at the back of her neck with jade hairpins. She wore a white piqué shirtwaist dress and brown-and-white, sometimes navy-and-white, spectator pumps. It was an old-fashioned way to dress, without variation and even without color, but Clio thought it daring in its simplicity and its deliberation. There was not much that Emma had not considered. There was little that surprised her, and although she had a ready understanding of how she wanted things done, the dereliction of others did not call forth her alarm or even her displeasure. She did not need much, not in the way of things, not even in the way of people.

Like her native ancestors, Emma believed in the power of dark forces. All of the ancient *kapus* had once had practical usages—the king's excrement had been borne away by his most trusted chief and destroyed in secret not because of modesty or shame, or even hygiene, but because an evildoer might use it for sorcery. If you were so reckless as to raise your head as the big calabash was borne past, you were taken to the *heiau* and strangled to death. During periods of mourning, no fires could be lit. Cats were muzzled and chickens were thrown into covered calabashes to keep them silent. At the death of the king, the people broke all the rules with exuberance. They burned, looted, and murdered, and the women joyously offered themselves as prostitutes—but only until the decomposition of the king's corpse was complete, when social order, with its system of *kapu*, was effortlessly restored.

A taboo existed in order to be transgressed. Violence, ritualized violence, had lain deep at the center of things. To be an ancient Hawaiian was to be terrified most of the time. It is a modern idea that to live in a subconscious state is poetic. It is also a sentimental idea, and Emma would have been the first to agree.

The thirteen-year-old child and the childless, solitary woman fell into an easy routine of study and domesticity. Clio liked very much that time of the evening, after their early supper (cooked by Emma, served precariously by Emma's servant, Lester, cleared and washed by Clio), when Emma would ceremoniously invite her to the library to talk-story. Emma drank a bottle of San Miguel beer and when she finished it, she banged loudly on the floor with a Maori war club for Lester to bring her another.

Emma talked to Clio of the things she had come to fear would be lost: the long songs without rhyme or metre called *meles*; the hulas and oral genealogies; the very history of her passing race: "Sandalwood was once plentiful in the mountains of the islands. It was of no commercial value to the Hawaiians—they used it only to impart fragrance to their *kapa*—but the Chinese needed sandalwood, and soon a commerce began between the foreigners and the agents of Kamehameha, one of whom was your great-grandfather Redmond Clarke. The Hawaiians readily, even heedlessly, gave away the trees in exchange for nails and rough cloth, and later for muskets and ammunition. As a consequence, by 1840 there was little sandalwood left in the Hawaiian Islands."

It was sometimes difficult for Clio to stay awake during the lessons. They worked steadily, surrounded by books and papers, until Clio would finally be sent to bed with a book that Emma had chosen for her, perhaps Isabella Bird's nineteenth-century travel letters. Clio would try to read the book that Emma had given her, but it would not be long before she succumbed and reached under her bed to pull out the books that she had been waiting all day to read, books that she found in her aunt's library, Rumer Godden and Somerset Maugham and Katherine Mansfield. She would read through the night. She kept the book that Emma had given her close by, so that she could open it if Emma came to her room, but Emma never disturbed her. It was not her way.

If Clio succumbed so easily, so willingly, to Emma, it was because Emma enabled her to wipe away her own small past. It was an extraordinary gift that Emma gave her. Clio was relieved to exchange the story of her own childhood for the vision that Emma conjured up for her. The myths that Emma told her, the legends that she whispered to Clio, became confused with Clio's dreams, and even her recollections, so that eventually Clio came to believe, willed herself to believe, that Emma's stories were her own memories. Because of Emma, Clio grew convinced that she'd come from the ocean, born of the marriage of earth and light. All cultures, all genealogies, begin with the marriage of earth and light, Emma said. "I myself have seen it."

Emma's servant, Lester, had come to Wisteria House in 1922 as Clio's grandfather's chauffeur. He was of Chinese and Hawaiian descent, and he had left the islands only once, the time he accompanied the Rolls-Royce sedan to Scotland for Mr. Junior's golf holiday.

As a young man, Lester had fallen in love with a Japanese girl whose father worked in the cane fields of Hale Moku. The girl had lived with her family in one of the small wooden houses in the workers' camp, a half mile from the plantation house. In the evenings, Lester would walk to the camp to watch her tend the vanda orchids in her mother's small garden. One night he found the courage to speak the few short sentences he had memorized as he walked down the beach. He stood in the road and persuaded her to take a walk with him.

Two days later, when he returned, the garden was empty. The girl's father came out of the house and shouted at him to go away. Lester walked through the camp every night for weeks until Emma told him what she had heard at the mill store. The morning after her walk through the camp with Lester, the girl had been sent to her grandparents in Japan. A romance with a man who was not Japanese was considered impossible, a shaming thing, and the girl had been sent away for the good of her family and even, some might have said, for the good of the community.

Lester had a collection of blues and jazz recordings that was unusual to find in Honolulu, a city where there were few places to hear or to buy such music, and few people who listened to it. Lester would invite Clio to join him in his room at Wisteria House, often on a weekend evening when she did not have schoolwork and Emma had gone to call on friends, where he played records for her, very loud. He smoked a Filipino cigar, his bad-tempered face dark against a frayed hand-me-down chair, and the cigar smoke filled the room as they listened to John Coltrane play "What's New?" Sometimes if Emma returned early, she would bring a bottle of beer from the kitchen and stand in the doorway and listen to the music. Emma liked the later Billie Holiday, those recordings in which the singing was a little dissolute, a little slurred.

It was during these evening sessions with Lester that Clio realized with both elation and fear that there was something in the world that might be there for the taking, something that she came to think of, perhaps unwisely, as romance. The world itself, she thought then, was romance.

Sometimes Lester would arrive soundlessly at her door or suddenly appear ahead of her on one of the garden paths and hiss morosely, "You want to see things, missy?"

Then he would take her into the attic, into the empty stables and carriage house, into rooms that had not been used for fifty years. He wore a heavy ring of keys attached to his stained waistcoat with a gold watch chain that had belonged to Redmond Clarke. He would unlock the doors of the rooms with deliberate, malicious ceremony, hunched over to catch the dust-filled light, taking his time. He never condescended to try the key in the lock, but insisted on finding each key by sight. Once inside, he opened the shutters with a clatter, flinging them back with impatience. He did not allow Clio to spend much time in the rooms. The dust made her sneeze, and this upset him. He thought it impolite, and even disruptive, as if the sudden noise might disturb one of her great-aunts, dead for years, bending over her embroidery.

One afternoon, Clio noticed a small animal trotting down the center of the second-floor hall. She thought it might be one of the rats that sometimes slipped inside the house and she stepped back calmly to let it pass. To her surprise, the door behind her fell open.

A large *koa* bed sat heavily under a swag of faded striped damask. Festoons of dusty yellow feathers were tied to the top of each bedpost, an adornment, Clio knew, once allowed only the nobility. There was a slender chaise, its covering of gray sprigged silk faded and torn. There was a dressing table made of mother-of-pearl. She knew of the table; Lester had described it to her, a wedding gift to her great-grandmother from the ambassador of China. There were large mirrors in gilded frames, the glass blind with rust. There was a chamber pot under a tall *koa* chest.

She opened the chest. Hundreds of feathers floated to her feet. White doves, she thought in astonishment. And then she saw that they were not birds. They were shoes. Shoes sewn with feathers and lace and tiny rosettes of seed pearls, shoes with soles of thin white leather and the words Madame d'Espina, Rue Cambon embossed in gold in the faded satin linings. She sat on the floor and gathered the shoes into her lap.

A light fragrance of dusting powder rose from the shoes. Some of them had never been worn. She tried to pair them, delicately tucking her fingers into the toes so as not to soil them or injure the brittle velvet ribbons. She hesitated for only a moment, then slid her foot into a shoe that looked as if it had once been the color of lavender. She walked up and down the room, arms aloft, toes pointed like a ballerina.

Clio did not tell Lester that she had discovered the secret of the unlocked doors, nor did she fidget or otherwise give herself away while he slowly searched for the key to the nursery. But she did avail herself night and day of the rooms that her ancestors had left open for her.

Lester pointed out to Emma that if Clio were staying, she would require new clothes. Could he put her into something of Miss Clara's?

Emma, who was frowning with the effort of rendering a name-chant into English, a chant that had never before been written in any language, looked up absently and said, "Good heavens, Lester. You must be mad."

Miss Clara had died in 1937. Lester looked at the floor, his face pinched with anger.

"They wouldn't fit the child," Emma said in explanation.

Clio exhaled with gratitude. It was the first time that her stay at Wisteria House, permanent or not, had ever been acknowledged, and she had thought for one moment that Emma's chastisement meant that she would not be staying long. But neither Lester nor her aunt were thinking of that, nor was her presence at Wisteria House ever mentioned, not in all the years that she lived there with them.

Later that afternoon, after she had finished the translation, Emma took Clio to Stant's Department Store. Emma parked her black Buick in front of the Stant building on Fort Street, only four blocks from Wisteria House. Clio had not been to the store for many years, not since her mother moved to Australia. Few people still patronized Stant's, preferring instead the big mall at Ala Moana, even though their families had been dressed by the Stants for generations. The merchandise at Stant's was not very fashionable.

There were no other customers in the store that day. Emma and Clio took the wrought-iron cage elevator to the second floor, the Children and Foundations floor, where they were greeted ceremoniously by Mrs. Okamura. Mrs.

Okamura proudly told Clio that she had helped her mother to order her first trousseau from *Harper's Bazaar*. Still looking a little dazed, Mrs. Okamura said that Kitty had not thought the selection at Stant's quite right.

She neatly laid out for their approval all of the things deemed essential for a thirteen-year-old girl, including, to Clio's delight, a white cotton brassiere. Emma pronounced brassiere the French way, exaggerating the consonants and giving Clio a moment's shame. Clio's happiness, however, was so complete that she didn't even blush when Emma went on to ask Mrs. Okamura if she advised the wearing of nylon slips, as if nylon were more lascivious, more tending to corruption, than cotton. Mrs. Okamura thought that nylon would do very well.

Clio's stepmother, Burta Yamada, had enforced stringent economies of dress, as well as of food. She thought it important that her stepchildren learn the principle of cause and effect—or perhaps it was supply and demand, Clio could never get it straight. Clio had been made to wear Burta's old clothes, dresses fitted with extra panels of cloth to accommodate Clio's height. She was given four pairs of underpants and two nightgowns each September at the start of the school year, and she wore them until they were gray with use. She often went to school so oddly costumed that her friends gave to her clothes the name Paris-Frocks, which revealed as much about island standards of taste as Clio's wardrobe. So no young girl in the world could have been happier than Clio when Mrs. Okamura ran her competent fingers under Clio's breasts to ensure that the brassiere was a good fit. Mrs. Okamura even called it a training bra, but it was fine with Clio.

Their many packages, Clio's many packages, were to be sent to Wisteria House, but when Emma saw the dismay on Clio's face when she realized that the pleasure of laying the new clothes on her bed and looking at them would be delayed, she allowed Clio to pick three things to carry home. Clio happily lugged the packages after her, banging them awkwardly against her legs as she followed Emma down to the Men's Department. Emma needed to buy socks for Lester, who'd been complaining of cramp.

Clio waited patiently, thinking of her new things, while Emma chatted with Mr. Day, the salesclerk. As her aunt and Mr. Day discussed the decline of sugar prices, Clio noticed a woman putting dozens of bow ties into a straw bag. Without looking around, the woman moved confidently to a table laden with men's bathing shorts. She examined and discarded several pairs before she found a few to her liking. She put them into her bag.

Clio was astonished. It was not just the thievery that confused her, but the idea that a woman who seemed so respectable, a person so like her aunt, was a thief. The woman wore a *lau hala* hat with a feather band, and a flower-printed dress, and laced white summer shoes chalky with polish.

Clio was so mesmerized that she did not hear Emma call her name. She jumped as if it were she who was filling the straw bag. She realized that Emma, too, had seen the woman, but Emma did not seem surprised or even concerned. She certainly said nothing to Mr. Day, who, Clio noticed, allowed his eyes to flicker for only the briefest moment to the woman clumsily wrestling with the torso of a mannequin, the better to remove its terry-cloth beach jacket.

Emma's car was still in front of the store, undisturbed, although a line of cars was backed behind it. Drivers pushed their horns, and a Chinese man in a van swore furiously at them as he swerved around the Buick. Clio was embarrassed, but Emma was unperturbed.

When they were in the car, Clio asked Emma if she had seen the woman in the store.

"Yes," Emma said, pulling confidently into traffic. The car behind them was forced to change lanes, and the driver made an obscene gesture with his finger.

"We were at school together," Emma said.

"Did you see what she was doing?" Clio was suddenly unsure that she had seen anything, so extraordinary did it seem.

Emma signaled to turn into the back gate of Wisteria House with her arm held stiffly out the window. "Her name is Alice Stant," she said as she turned, both hands on the big steering wheel. "I'm afraid she has not been herself for some time. Her mother sees that everything is returned the next day, of course. Stant's has always had wonderful delivery service and I've often wondered if there were any connection." She stopped at the rusted iron gate laced with chicken wire and dead palm branches. She smiled at Clio as if Miss Stant were only a little eccentric, as if Emma herself were only a little eccentric. She set the heavy hand brake, making her point. "She was unhappy in love."

Clio nodded in agreement, not understanding but wanting to understand, and jumped out to open the gate.

Clio often wondered if Emma had asked her father, John Lynott, to allow her to stay at Wisteria House. She liked to think that he had at least inquired about her, but she knew that it was possible that he and Emma had never spoken about her at all. He certainly never spoke to Clio about it, and the few times each year that she saw him, he never mentioned Emma's name. There was a tradition in the islands of taking the child of a relative or friend to raise, a *hanai* child, but Emma did not adopt Clio. There were legal considerations.

After he divorced their mother, Lynott had not allowed

Clio and her brother, Dix, to see their mother's family except for formal calls at Christmas and Easter. John Lynott did not like his sister-in-law, perhaps because he knew that she had never been fooled by him. It is true that she didn't admire him, but she did not dislike him. It would not have occurred to her to dislike him. It wasn't because he was a newcomer to the islands, Emma wasn't a snob; he just did not interest her. But he mistook her reserve for haughtiness, and it made him resentful.

Emma was careful not to appear to supersede the tentative, even questionable, authority she had gained in regard to Clio, and it was she who suggested that Clio visit her mother, Kitty, in Australia. Arrangements to visit Kitty and her husband, Rory Armacost, had been made and broken many times in the years since Kitty's marriage. Kitty would suggest a time, but it would be in the middle of the school term. Lynott would ask Kitty to take Clio at Christmas, but since the seasons were reversed and it was summer in Australia, Kitty would be at her fishing camp in New Zealand; no place for a child, she said.

Every so often, Kitty sent Clio a stuffed koala bear, sometimes a windup bear that played "Waltzing Matilda." Clio had seven of them. Kitty also sent her alligator handbags with broken clasps and bed jackets with stains that might have been crème de menthe. Kitty seldom wrote, but when she did, it was to ask that Clio return something that Kitty had sent her. Clio particularly remembered an ermine muff that looked as if bites had been taken out of it, which Kitty wanted to use to line some bedroom slippers.

While Clio still lived with her father and stepmother in Nuʻuanu, the arrival of one of Kitty's letters would fill her with alarm. Sometimes Clio had lost Kitty's gifts or given them away, and she would spend days composing letters of apology. Even if she managed to retrieve from one of the maids the shoe with the ripped ankle strap, she still had to make up the package. She needed someone to take the package to the post office. She needed help to fill out the customs form. Burta would catch Clio making arrangements with the gardener to mail a badly wrapped box, and Burta would gloat for weeks over Kitty's bad behavior. "Well, your mother never asked for you back, did she?" Burta would say.

To be fair to Kitty, she had been obliged to establish a small trust fund for Clio and Dix. Kitty was discovered mishandling, selling really, some ranchland that had been left to Clio and Dix by their grandfather. A check for seven hundred dollars was deposited in each of their savings accounts on the fifteenth of each month by Kitty's lawyer in Sydney. Clio used to study the monthly statements as if they were diaries or atlases. Clio was always flattered to see herself addressed as Miss Cliome Meliaokamalu Lynott, which was, after all, her name. It was as if the formality of her mother's legal obligation conferred on her not an insult but an honor.

Kitty Clarke would have been surprised at the distress she seemed to cause. She had had a life so full, it had been impossible to find the time for even a moment's reflection. She prided herself on her impulses. They were everything to her. If she suddenly felt she should be killing sheep in the Yukon, she was gone the next day, on her way to the Northwest Territories. She once decided that her maids should wear uniforms copied from a nineteenth-century engraving. Unhappy Filipino girls wore hot black bombazine frocks with piqué collars and cuffs for three days until they finally buried the dresses in a cane field and disappeared back into the workers' camp. Kitty was without servants, uniformed or not, for months. She demanded one very dry summer that the missile base at Dry Sands use its nuclear reactor to provide desalinated water for her garden. When the Navy declined her request, she'd stamped her foot and predicted that we'd lose everything to the Japanese. That she had money certainly helped, although she claimed, completely disingenuously, that money had nothing to do with the way that she lived.

Impulse led her to marry Kimo Danforth straight from the schoolroom. They spent their days going from ranch to ranch, as they all did, and plantation house to plantation house, until Kimo was killed in a fall. Kitty had insisted that he pick ginger for her one moonlit night. He had been drinking all day and lost his footing at the edge of the cliff. It took a week for the cowboys to find his body and to hoist it, bouncing it against the rocks, back up the mountain.

Kitty moved across the island to Honolulu, where she met John Lynott, a lawyer from the mainland. He'd first come to Hawai'i in 1955 with the Stanford varsity crew, and after two weeks at the Outrigger Canoe Club, he vowed to return. He had never seen anything so promising as Honolulu. It was a small town even then, just beginning to change, easy and provincial. He knew that he would do well.

He was not interested in the disturbances of the past, and this was to his benefit. He began with a small business, making T-shirts. He sold the shirts in a booth at the International Market Place in Waikiki. The T-shirts had slogans like *Maui No Ka 'Oi* and SPAM and Love's Bakery Makes Jelly Rolls and Remember Pearl Harbor. All the while, he was studying law and waiting on tables at the Pacific Club, where the important men of the city and state had their chicken sandwiches every afternoon after a game of squash. He was taken up by the wife of a senator, who engaged him to give tennis lessons to her teenage children and, some said, although Emma never believed it, some lessons for herself as well, although she had won the club's women's singles championship three years in a row. Emma did not believe that John Lynott was ever the lover of the delightful Mrs. Irwing not because he was incapable of seduction or betrayal, but because he did not need sex to make his way. He needed Senator Irwing, not his wife. And it was Senator Irwing for whom he went to clerk during his summer vacation. Lynott was too clever, and too practical, to settle for pleasure. He was in too much of a hurry. By the time Kitty met him, at a dinner party given by Clare Boothe Luce, he was thought to be one of the most promising, most interesting young men in Honolulu, even taking into consideration the fact that six years earlier no one had ever heard of him.

Impulse led Kitty to Lynott, just as it led her to a rather too young and too beautiful beach boy named Bunny Mendonca, with whom Lynott found her one afternoon shortly after Clio's brother was born. Kitty was not one of those women who lose years of their lives to pregnancy and the raising of children. She liked to say that if you saw her from behind, eight months pregnant, in a bikini, you'd never have suspected that she was *hapai*. So although her newborn son Dixon had not even shed the pig's tail of his umbilical cord, she followed her impulses. Not maternal, although Emma said admiringly that Bunny Mendonca had been young enough to qualify. It may not be true, but Lynott told everyone that he'd found Kitty and Bunny naked in the bottom of a canoe after the July Fourth regatta.

Kitty did not hold herself responsible. Her little wishes and desires existed outside herself, supernaturally, like spirits who playfully led her on for good or ill. In a pleasant and even mischievous way, they were beyond her control, beyond even her wish to control. She was not particularly upset to be thrown out by Lynott, who was by then bored to death with her. He was playing golf every Thursday afternoon with Mrs. Yamada, a Japanese woman who worked in his office. He didn't need Kitty anymore.

Dix and Clio were sent to San Francisco to attend their mother at her marriage to Mr. Rory Armacost. They stayed only two days, as Kitty and Mr. Armacost had been eager to be alone. Mr. Armacost had not known that Kitty had two young children. Although she told him about Clio and Dix only a week before the wedding, he was very nice to them. He took them to watch the sea lions at the Cliff House when Kitty went to Elizabeth Arden.

Kitty moved with Rory Armacost to a ranch in Australia that was larger than the state of Colorado, and Clio's father married Mrs. Yamada, a woman of such envy and cruelty that it was a wonder to everyone that Dix and Clio grew up at all. Their mother was gone, riding on her million acres, swatting black flies and sleeping with the hands, and their father was busy defending gray whales and Cambodian refugees in preparation for running for the state senate, and their stepmother hated them so much that she tried to starve them.

Clio had her brother, Dix, but Dix was like Kitty—full of a tireless, excitable vanity. Later there was her half-brother, Steamy, who really did love her, but by the time Steamy might have done Clio some good, she was nearly grown, flirting awkwardly with the boys who came in the summer to surf and take classes at the university. And she had Emma. You would think that having one or two people to love you would be enough, but the heart really wants more. Not all that it can get, at least not in Clio's case. She was not greedy. But she wanted more than Emma, a woman, and Steamy, a boy, could give her.

Clio was eight years old the summer that her mother moved to Australia. It was the summer that she invented the Love Contest. She and Dix would round up their animals—two poodles, three cats, an old gray-haired dachshund, a Chinese pig, a mynah that lived in the rafters of the garage—and herd the excited animals into the center of the lawn. The mynah, tempted by the fruit in their hands, circled above them, screaming and diving at their heads as the animals raced back and forth in frenzies of joy. Clio and Dix whooped and shouted at them, trying to lure the animals into their arms, for the child who gathered the most animals was the winner of the Love Contest.

One morning, Dix and Clio awakened to find that the dogs were not in their accustomed places at the foot of their beds. The cats were not on the lanai. Even the mynah was gone. They went from room to room looking for them, calmly at first, then more and more worried as they went through the house. They ran into the garden and into the rain forest, but the animals had vanished.

Burta Yamada was waiting for them when they came out of the forest. "I did it while you were asleep." She lighted a small black cigar and shook out the match. "I decide who lives here now."

Clio turned back to the forest.

"It won't do any good," Burta said. "Hide in the forest, Clio. Hide in the bushes if you want. No more Love Contests."

A few weeks later, there arrived at the house two King Charles spaniels. Burta had read that the breed was admired by the Japanese royal family. Clio and Dix would have nothing to do with the dogs, which suited Burta just fine. The dogs were devoted to Burta, and she to them.

Working late at night in his room with a hammer wrapped in a beach towel, Dix spent weeks grinding a bathroom glass into tiny splinters. Burta caught him putting the ground glass into the dogs' food bowl, and two days later, as soon as his trunk was packed, he was sent to boarding school on the Big Island. Then he, too, was gone. Burta decided who lived there.

Clio told Emma that she did not want to visit her mother and Mr. Armacost in Australia. Emma said, as she was to say hundreds of times, "You are an island girl. You know how to do these things. Island girls are not afraid." She wiped the tears from Clio's face and sent her to Melbourne more terrified of being a frightened island girl than she was frightened of her mother.

The visit wasn't as bad as Clio had expected. The good thing, it turned out, was that her mother was exactly the way Clio had remembered her. Clio realized that she had a mother who was meant to be very far away. Not a mother to hold Clio in her arms and caress her, to talk to her, to calm her and praise her, but a mother who came to dinner in taffeta capri pants holding an amber cigarette holder; who frowned in distaste at Clio's short fingernails; who told Clio that she was lucky to have breeding, as she hadn't the good fortune to have money. Clio saw from the start that Kitty was incapable of being interested in any child. It had nothing to do with Clio. She was relieved. It was not that she had failed her mother—Kitty was simply thinking of other, more fascinating things. Kitty wasn't even particularly interested in Rory Armacost. Clio thought that she liked him better than Kitty liked him.

Uncle Rory, as her mother insisted that she call him, was the first man, other than a teacher, to put a book into Clio's hands and say, read this. In Rory's case, he put twenty books in her hands, small paperbacks happily, and said solemnly, "These may change your life, Clio. They did mine." The books were the adventures of Napoleon Bonaparte, a mission-educated aborigine who had risen

through his gifts of Socratic deduction and primitive in-
stinct to become the most feared detective-inspector in
Australia.

Clio saw right away that the books might provide her
with the kind of light conversation that her mother seemed
to enjoy at dinner. Clio read two of the mystery books the
first night. Luckily, she did not see much of her mother,
and this gave her the time that she needed to memorize
the more interesting details of the dry, serious plots.

"I am going to move to Australia when I grow up,"
Clio announced at dinner.

"Oh, are you?" Kitty asked, peering down the table at
her.

"Perth sounds enchanting," Clio said. It was the first
time that she had ever used the word "enchanting."

"Good sailing off Perth," Rory said.

"What about your aunt? Unless I'm misinformed, Clio,
you are my sister's hope. You can't live in Australia! Emma
won't let you leave the islands. You are the next keeper of
the flame, poor child. Perhaps you'll dance a hula for us
after dinner. I'm surprised Mother and Emma allowed you
even to visit your own mother."

"It was Emma's idea that I come," Clio said, startled by
her mother's tone.

"Oh?" Kitty raised her eyebrows. "Is that so?" She pretended to be puzzled. "Emma considered *my* feelings?"

"First-rate fish tonight," Rory said, laying his knife and
fork side by side on his plate.

"Emma was thinking of me?" Kitty asked again. "I can't
begin to count the number of times I've asked you to come
to stay." There was melancholy, and grievance, in her lovely
voice. The butler reached around her to remove a plate,
but she waved him away. "Both you and your brother,
Dixon. Countless times." She was offended just thinking

of the injustices she had suffered on behalf of her children. "And you say that you wish to live here!"

"The child merely said she was interested in Perth, darling. Lovely city, Perth. *The Mystery of Swordfish Reef*, I believe?" Rory asked, turning to Clio.

"*I* wouldn't know," Kitty said. "I wouldn't know any of it." With a sigh, she waved her chiffon handkerchief, and the butler removed her plate. She sighed again and gazed sadly out the open terrace doors. There was no more conversation.

Rory and Clio went quietly into the library after dinner. He made himself a brandy and soda and smoked a cigarette of uncut Turkish tobacco that he folded inside thin slips of paper. Clio drank chamomile tea, the only drink her mother allowed her before bed. They sat in leather chairs before the fire, their feet on the fender. Rory's dogs yawned in happiness as Clio and Rory discussed in low voices some of Inspector Bonaparte's more confounding cases. Clio could hear her mother in the next room. Kitty sat at a card table in the salon and listened to records of Broadway shows as she filled leather albums with her clippings and photographs. Now and again, she would forget that her feelings were supposed to have been hurt, and Clio would hear her singing gaily to the music.

Clio was sent home a week before she was due to leave with a suitcase of books from Rory and an unmatched pair of riding boots, both right feet, from her mother. When Kitty gave Clio the heavy boots the night before she left, Clio knew that her small wrapping skills, although improved, would not be adequate to the task of one day returning them. And then she remembered that she was going home to Emma. Emma would know what to do with the boots.

And she did. When Kitty's letter arrived at Wisteria

House, asking not for the boots but for a large organdy hat she'd given Clio as Clio was getting into the car to go to the airport, Emma said calmly, "You're not to do it. Stop returning things and she'll stop sending them to you."

Clio understood that it would mean an end to their scant correspondence, but she knew that her mother really had very little to say to her, and even less to give her. Clio did not return the hat.

Although Emma was able to take care of their needs, Clio did not have much pocket money. She was not yet allowed to use the money that her mother put into the trust, and she did not receive money from her father. She convinced a man who owned a camera store in Waikiki to give her a job.

The store offered many courtesies to tourists. In the front of the store, a Chinese boy sat on a barstool in a red *malo*, a silk flower behind his ear, waiting for customers who wished to take a picture of a native. Clio was embarrassed watching him, especially after she realized that he had chosen to sit on the stool in the hope that something would escape from his loincloth. She was relieved when the manager moved her to a tiny room with blacked-out windows where customers could view their film as soon as it was developed. It was Clio's job to thread an old Bell and Howell projector and run the film. She sat in the dark all day with strangers, usually men, and watched the reels of film.

As a child, Clio had wondered why tourists came to Hawai'i, excluded as they seemed to be from the world that she knew, the world that Emma worked so hard to preserve, and she was made uncomfortable by the ease with which the visitors were so easily satisfied. They seemed to get so little. Clio wondered if it were simply a matter of taste. She was confused by the difference between what people seemed willing to accept and what more there was for the taking.

She would see, over and over, unlikely images of her island home, Filipino dancers in pink cellophane hula skirts and Japanese children waving in front of the cement memorial at Pearl Harbor and *haole* girls swimming with sedated porpoises in hotel lagoons. After work she would go home to Emma and she would listen to Emma's stories of leisurely visits to other islands by schooner, and descriptions of the mountain houses and cattle ranches of her friends and cousins, and their hospitality. Emma would hum verses of the lovely music that had been composed in her honor.

Each evening when Clio put the projector away for the night, covering it with its plastic hood like a bird in a cage, she would grow more and more furious at Emma. By the time Clio reached Wisteria House, she wanted to shout the truth she'd discovered about Emma's beloved islands. But she did not say anything.

Clio knew that Emma wondered why she was so intent on working in the camera shop when she could have had a summer internship at the Bishop Museum. Clio explained to Emma that she liked Waikiki. She liked the bright fluorescence of it. She liked the good-natured college boys from Oregon in their Sex Wax T-shirts. Emma didn't discourage Clio from working in the camera shop, she wouldn't have, but Clio knew that it depressed her, and after the first month she left to work as a research assistant at the East-West Center at the university, tracking tidal patterns in the Marquesas. It was not so much fun as being in Waikiki, but she knew that it pleased Emma more. She was, at least in the area of ocean currents, staying closer to home.

At the head of the garden path was a young tamarind tree. It was rare to see a tamarind in the city. Emma thought the tree uncouth and she feigned displeasure at its unexpectedness, as if the little tree were to blame for wandering into the dying garden. Clio thought that the tamarind's bright orange flowers resembled the tiger-claw jewelry once worn by the women of her family. Each growing season the tamarind shed all of its leaves, and for that reason Clio liked to think it capable of bringing itself to life each spring.

For generations, ferns had been brought by hand to Wisteria House from the rain forests of Koke'e and the Big Island, the black clotted roots held carefully in damp towels, to be planted beneath the verandah. The ferns had grown sturdy and dense, less dependent on the sun than the other plants in the garden. They pushed their way through the gaps left by the missing floorboards, and through the splintered fretwork of the verandah railings.

Emma knew the origin of each fern and its genus, of course, but she was also learned in the medicinal and magical uses of the ferns. In the evening, she and Clio would water them with leaking hoses, the water slowly soaking their legs. Emma sat on the steps with her skirt tucked between her knees, the canvas hose held loosely in one hand. Clio was entrusted with the weeding, and her arms and face would become dotted with orange pollen as she bent among the slender leaves.

"You have found the chest full of slippers," Emma said one night.

Clio straightened and stood with her hands on the small of her back, as she had seen Emma do many times, the scant weeds clutched in her fists. "Yes," she said. "And they fit me!"

Emma tapped her empty beer bottle on the porch railing and Lester appeared as if by magic with another bottle. He looked at Clio, then disappeared along the verandah.

Music suddenly came from the house. It was Dinah Washington, singing "All of Me." Emma moved her foot in time, her garden slipper swinging lazily from her toes. "Your great-grandmother used to go to dances at Iolani Palace. Just down the street. She would dance all night and walk home carrying those satin slippers to keep from ruining them in the mud of the unpaved roads." She took a drink of beer. "That was only eighty years ago."

"We have the same size foot," Clio said proudly. "Great-grandmother and I."

Emma nodded. "I'm not surprised."

The dying trees seemed to draw the heat of the day into their leaves and bark, straining to find a little light for themselves. Clio thought it foolish of the trees, for the garden was lovely at night. The darkness hid its shame. The lights left burning in the big office buildings high above them shed a chill sheen on the garden, and sometimes when Clio looked up at the buildings surrounding them, it seemed as if she and Emma were on a stage.

Clio gently plucked spiders from the ferns and put them inside a glass jar to release later by the pond. She had lost the top. She used one hand to cover the jar, and the spiders danced across the palm of her hand, tickling her.

Emma turned off the water and they sat on the steps, leaning against the loose rail posts. Clio lay a wet rag over the top of the jar.

There was something outlandish about Emma, something that Clio felt even then. If Emma had too much to drink, it only showed in her use of language. A story would often begin with the words "In the indefinite past . . ." Clio eventually came to see Emma's meaning, but in those days, the past seemed to Clio to be very definite. Emma spoke as if to convey a literal truth, as if she believed what she said: "Namaka was skilled in the art of war as well as sport. He was particularly adept at backbreaking. When escaping from his enemies, he would spread his strong arms like wings and fly away. All of these things," she said, "he learned at Kahuku, not far from our house, Hale Moku. I myself have seen it."

She banged on the porch for Lester. "Have you ever noticed, child, how little there is here in the way of worldly things? There is no architecture left, not that there ever was much. A few plantation houses. Two or three coral churches. Some wooden chapels, barely standing they're so full of termites. There is very little literature, very little art. All that we have is nature. The ocean that you love so much. The air—that lovely air that doesn't even belong to us. And the ginger and the *pua kenikeni* and the *'opihi.* The native mountain apple." She gazed into her dying garden. "Do you remember how surprised you once were to find me paying the water bill?"

Clio had not realized that water was a thing, a commodity, that could belong to someone who would charge for the use of it. She understood that the conveyance of the water must be recompensed, and the purification and storing of it, but she had imagined that water was held in trust, that all people owned the water and contributed to its maintenance and distribution. In her mother's house in Nu'uanu, rainwater had been collected in big wooden tanks and Clio had bathed, and washed her hair, in water turned red by the rust that grew on the iron bands of the tanks. She herself benefited, albeit indirectly, since her mother and Emma belonged to a family who had profited from the selling of water. It was a discovery, this ownership of water, that had caused her to recognize both her privilege and her naiveté—a naiveté, or ignorance some might say, that was the result of that very privilege.

"The irony, Clio, is that the disappearance of everything is just what has allowed us to see the worth of it. When my husband, Johnny Fitzroy, asked me to fly away to Tahiti with him, to leave my family, I came from the ranch on Moloka'i here to Wisteria House to ask my grandmother's consent. The yellow monkeypod trees that once lined the drive were in bloom as I turned in the gate, and the smell of them was overpowering. It seemed as if all the nights of my life had been scented." She looked around in surprise. "I could not bring myself to ask her consent. And here I still am! And the monkeypod trees are gone."

She leaned forward to see Clio's face in the dark. "Fitzroy was wrong to leave me here. And I was wrong not to go."

She turned toward the house and called, "Lester! Come talk-story with us! It is lovely out!" She rested her head on the railing, waiting for Lester, but he did not appear, and when she spoke again, her voice was full of sadness. "I was not in love with Johnny Fitzroy, even though I married him. I knew it and he knew it, and no one minded. We got on. We liked horses. He taught me to play the guitar. We were compatible—even in matters of love we were compatible. And we thought that was enough. And it might have been. But when the great weight of things fell on us—this family, this place, even Mother"—Emma nodded her head politely at the garden to signify that it, too, was included—"Johnny Fitzroy was overcome by it. You know the feeling very well, Clio. It is this feeling that causes you to take flight, too."

Clio looked at Emma. She was surprised. She had not imagined that Emma knew so much about her.

"Mabel wanted us to live at Hale Moku," Emma said.

"To give parties and build municipal swimming pools. She didn't believe me, that the money was gone. She still doesn't believe me." She gazed up at the dark house. "If you do not know what it means to be in a family, and in one so interfering as ours, it can be a terrible thing." She reached out to take an album from a table on the verandah, and when she opened it, thousands of insect wings fell into her lap. "I have believed that the conscious experience of the past was everything. I have collected the past, as if it, too, were an artifact." She sighed. "This afternoon I told you that in the old time the victor in a hand-to-hand struggle often consumed the heart of his opponent. I myself have seen it. It was a gesture of reverence, taking in the strength of the enemy." She brushed the thousands of translucent wings from her lap and set aside the album. "What do you think about that?"

"Heart-eating?" asked Clio warily.

"All of it."

Clio paused. She did not know if she would be able to say what it was that she felt. "When I used to hide from my father and stepmother, I would go into the forest, in order to be myself again. I have that feeling now, here with you, of being myself, whoever that is. But I don't know what to think about the past. I don't know if I want it." She was embarrassed. "Like Johnny Fitzroy."

When Emma did not speak, Clio leaned forward to find her face in the dark. "But I could try," she whispered.

"You have suffered more than anyone knows," Emma said quietly.

She held out her hand and Clio pulled her to her feet. "If you give me your heart, Clio, I promise I won't eat it."

Clio nodded solemnly as they found their way into the house, nodded her acceptance, but Emma did not see her, and she did not ask again.

Clio was asked by her cousins, Mamie and Claire Clarke, to come to stay at Waimea, on the island of Kaua'i. Their father, McCully, had drowned in a tidal wave, and their mother, Mary, ran the sugar plantation. In 1841, a king grateful to be absolved from the sin of polygamy had given the land to an obliging, even enterprising, missionary named Asa Clarke, but Mary Clarke was from the mainland, and although she was already an accomplished gardener, it was with envious surprise that her Clarke relatives watched her manage the plantation. She was not an island girl, and although she won the family's gratitude, she did not win their affection.

Mamie and Claire met Clio at the airport. They drove through the dark fields to home in an open Jeep, the radio turned loud. Claire, who was thirteen, a year younger than Mamie, sat in the back, smoking marijuana. She leaned on the back of Clio's seat, her arm around Clio's neck.

"Gertrude is back," she yelled in Clio's ear. "She works days now. She had a baby and Mother pretends that Gertrude and Benjie are married."

Mamie laughed. "She asked Gertrude what china pattern she had picked."

"And Gertrude didn't know what Mother was talking about," shouted Claire. "Until Mamie said to Gertrude, 'The plates, not the place.'" She screamed with delight.

Clio was elated by their independence, their mischief, the cool blackness, the speed with which they moved through the night. She had friends at school in Honolulu, but she had not often brought them to Wisteria House. Her work with Emma did not leave her much time for play.

"Claire gives kissing lessons now," said Mamie. "It's her summer job."

Clio turned around to look at Claire.

Claire nodded and passed Clio the joint. The sparks from the cigarette flew out of the car, bouncing behind them in the dirt road. "I charge three dollars a lesson. Two kisses a lesson. More for French," she said.

"I have to kiss *you*?" Clio asked, taking a drag on the cigarette.

The sisters screamed. "No," Mamie said, both hands tight on the steering wheel, leaning forward to see the road. There were no streetlights. "She has an assistant. Claire just supervises. She's the make-out manager."

"Do you remember Orval? Orval Nalag from the camp?" Claire asked Clio. "He is my assistant. He does it for free."

They laughed all the way home, the sound of their high, light voices weaving through the swaying stalks of cane.

At Clio's request, made that first night, Claire arranged a lesson for her.

On their way through the garden to the old banyan tree, Mamie said to Clio, "Don't mention this to Mother."

Clio looked at her. Claire had told her mother that they were walking to the library to see a slide show on New Guinea. "Don't go through the camp," Mary had said, reading a book on rose culture.

"I mean, don't say that you even know Orval. Mother doesn't like us seeing local boys."

Clio promised not to mention him.

"You know about kissing, right? You're seventeen," said Claire as they settled themselves into a fork high in the tree.

There was a strong odor of resin and sap. It reminded

Clio of the smell of earwax. The insect tracks on the leaves glistened like dried sugar water. "Of course," she said to Claire.

"I don't think she should have to pay," Mamie said to her sister.

"I want to," Clio said, and Claire did not demur.

There was the sound of a bicycle, its salt-rusted tire chains squeaking rhythmically. Clio looked down through the leaves. The top of Orval's black head, greased with pomade, shone up at them. "Why does your mother mind?" she whispered to Mamie.

"She's prejudiced. Like everyone here. They all mind someone."

Clio watched him climb up to them. She felt a quick tightening between her legs, and she put her hand there.

"You can go first," Claire said to Clio.

Clio looked at her.

"We all get a turn, even the teacher. But you're paying, so you can start."

"I'd rather go second. Or last maybe. To see how it's done," Clio said.

"How it's done?" Claire asked, as if she'd been misled about Clio's qualifications.

"I mean how you guys do it. You know, the lesson part."

"I'll go first," Mamie said with a sigh, sliding down a branch. "Hi, Orval," Clio heard her say in the darkness.

Clio could see the porch lights of the house. She could smell his hair.

"Hi, Mamie," she heard him say. "How's it?"

Mamie had her turn, about ten minutes, and then Claire took her own turn, a bit longer and a bit livelier, Clio could tell by the shaking of the tree, and then Orval hoisted himself up onto the branch where Clio sat alone in the dark and said, hanging from the limb like a monkey, "I'm kind of worn-up."

She thought that he was canceling the lesson. She was so disappointed that she felt tears come to her eyes. "Okay," she said. She saw a large green lizard sitting on the branch beneath her. Motionless, unblinking, it looked as if it had been sewn into its bright green suit, the badly stitched thread knotted roughly up his back.

Orval shimmied along to her, straddling the branch. She wondered if it were painful, if it hurt his testicles, or his penis. It cannot hurt, she thought, or he would not do it.

"Okay what?" he asked, smiling at her. His skin was dark.

"Okay, you can stop if you're tired."

He reached out and touched her breast.

Her nipple grew hard and she was embarrassed that he would know it, as if her excitement made her suddenly vulnerable.

"Where's my cousin?"

"She went."

"Where?"

He shrugged. "She said she'd be back. After."

"After what?"

"The lesson."

Drawn by expectation and desire, she was docile.

"Stand up," he said.

She stepped lightly along the branch and stood where he told her, in a fork in the banyan. He leaned her against the tree. The dense, drooping limbs, thick with leaves, fell around them.

He took her hand and pressed it against his jeans and she felt him get hard.

He stood on the branch and opened her shorts, his hand caught between her body and his body, pressing against her. He licked his fingers and put them into her vagina.

She watched him. She knew that if she closed her eyes, she would grow dizzy and she would fall out of the tree. His eyes were closed, the corners raised elegantly, the lids paler than his face, the lashes thin, disparate, as if they'd been combed. She wondered idly if his greater experience in trees enabled him to shut his eyes. She felt separated from her body, as if she were watching both the boy and herself in the crook of the tree.

His face in her neck, breathing into her neck, not over-come, her body swollen, enlarged, slow. She thought at first that he must be searching for something inside of her without knowing what it was that he sought, without knowing that it caused her pain, or if she minded or did not mind, but when he found it, to her surprise—surprise because she realized that he had known what he was seek-ing all along, and more than that, she had known, too—she succumbed into his hand, flooded into his hand, and he succumbed, too.

Not long after Clio's return from Waimea, the slate roof on the third floor collapsed during a summer storm, dam-aging some of the furniture that had been stored in the attic, furniture that Emma, to her own surprise, had for-gotten she owned. The structure of the house was precar-ious with damp, termites, and age, and a cousin of Lester's, who owned an exterminating company, advised Emma to leave the house as quickly as possible. She told him that she valued his concern, but she hoped to stay a while longer. He shook his head in disapproval and left without sub-mitting a bill.

The rare gardens of Wisteria House, planted in 1871 for Clio's great-grandmother, Princess Ruth, fared no better in the storm. Those trees that had not perished from lack of light finally surrendered—not to darkness, but to damp.

The legislature—composed of members whose names Emma had never heard before, most of them Japanese—quickly voted to condemn the house. They requisitioned the land for a city park.

There was a fuss in the newspapers, one of them owned by Emma's aunt, and the final vote to take the land was indefinitely delayed. Or definitely delayed, as Clio said. There were offers from developers, but Emma refused to sell. Editorials were written, and letters to the newspaper, but Emma did not read them, not even the ones that defended what her critics called *haole* imperialism.

Clio dreamed that the house was being taken away from them because she had left Emma for the month that she spent at Waimea. She told no one of her dream, and she worried in secret that she had somehow caused the ferns that grew under the verandah to die.

Lester was of no help to her. His gloom turned to belligerence. He seemed to seek out Clio to harry and chastise her.

"I am not going with you," he said. "I am not leaving you anything."

"Good," she said. "I don't want anything."

"Good. Good for you, too. You thought you were getting Mr. Redmond's watch. But I've hidden it. Only Mr. Redmond knows where."

Clio, who had been brought up by people so firmly placed in the past that she might be said to have been raised by ghosts, did not gainsay him. He wearied her, but she said nothing. She loved him.

"She has no one to blame but herself," Lester said fretfully, walking up and down the verandah, sidestepping the loose boards out of habit.

"Blame?" Clio asked, sitting on the porch steps.

"I told her. She should have gone years ago. Years ago. We all should have." He stopped to look at her, squinting in fury. "And you! What are you doing here?"

"I don't know," she said, trying to soothe him. "The same as you perhaps."

"You seem different, girlie," he said, standing so close to her that she could smell the tobacco on his breath, and the Crème de Singapore that he used on his still-black hair.

"Like something happen to you."

"I am different."

"You going away now? You going to the mainland to school?"

She shook her head.

"You're a stupid girl."

"I'm staying with Emma."

"You think I don't know that?" he shouted.

"Why are you so mad at me, Lester?"

He looked down at the brown spots that made his hands look like tiger lilies. "I'll give you the Coleman Hawkins," he said. "And McCoy Tyner." He looked up. "Might be the Coltrane." He threw his cigar over the railing and she saw that he was crying.

"Come with us," she said to him.

He waved her away and disappeared inside the house.

A few days after Lester's departure to live with his grand-niece on Maui, Emma and Clio went to live with Clio's grandmother, Mabel Clarke, on the north shore of O'ahu at the plantation house known as Hale Moku. To Clio's surprise, Emma took only the few pieces of furniture and decoration that were in her private rooms, leaving the rest to be packed and stored in warehouses downtown. Clio took all of her things—books, childhood souvenirs, clothes, trinkets—and a fern from Kaua'i, the *Lawai* fern, that she had carried by hand from the mountains of Koke'e to plant under the verandah steps.

Mabel Clarke stopped receiving guests the day that her second husband drowned. Except for those rare hours when they could escape Mabel's bad-tempered vigilance to run into town to flirt with the cowboys, her young daughters, Kitty and Emma, had grown up with women. Their brother, McCully, was away at school. Miss Mabel only allowed Japanese women to work at Hale Moku, and year after year, the women wandered through the rooms in which they dreamed at night and malingered through the long hot days. By the time Kitty and Emma were sent to boarding school on the Big Island, only a few of the old servants were still alive. When Mabel reluctantly asked a former employee of the telephone company to do long-neglected repairs, he became famous because of it, and was known after that as the Hale Moku Man.

Sometimes tourists found their way down the drive, drawn perhaps by the red *huapala* vine considered unlucky by the Hawaiians, the vines enflaming the smooth gray trunks of the trees. The intruders were astonished to come suddenly upon the house, shrouded as if under an enchantment. The eaves and balustrades were so thickly netted with jasmine and Chinese honeysuckle that the very house seemed made of flowers. The trespassers were further startled to see old and hobbled Japanese women in kimonos and *tabis* come stumbling along the verandah shouting curses at them as if the intruders were Koreans.

The treasure and detritus of six generations of collectors filled the house, the possessions not of scholars or anti-quaries, but of ordinary people who simply could not throw away anything: quilts, hymnals, the weightless skulls of owls, shell-and-rattan maps, netted calabashes, chipped Venetian glass, *koa* bedsteads, *makaloa* mats, paintings on velvet, crates of black China tea, jawbone fish hooks, cloaks and capes and helmets, *ukiyoe*, tenth-century wedding ki-monos, lacquer boxes, bolts of Thai silk, rusted swords, conch-shell tea sets, opium pipes, Buddhas, poison arrows, stained satin ball gowns, sea nets, rare *tifaifai* from Tahiti, stovepipe hats, *lau hala* sails, polo mallets, one stuffed *nene* goose (an endangered species in the Hawaiian Islands), and every proclamation of Queen Liuliu'okalani's court from 1891 to the day of her bitter abdication.

Clio's *haole* great-grandfather had been aide-de-camp to the last queen of Hawai'i. Clio's Hawaiian great-grand-father was the son of the last chiefess of the sacred island of Kaua'i. Clio belonged to a family whose fortune had come from the ownership of land. With that ownership came privilege, of course, but also responsibility. Her family was proud of its generosity. There were few places in the small town of Kaikea on the windward side of O'ahu that did not bear her grandmother's name: the Clarke Ele-mentary School, the Clarke Library, the swimming pool, the clinic.

As a child, before her mother Kitty went away, Clio had sometimes sneaked away from Hale Moku to sleep with the housemaids in the small workers' camp that was part of the plantation. At first light, the fishermen would take her out with them to catch tuna for the new hotels. Days would go by before Kitty, who was spending the winter in a cottage in the garden of Hale Moku, would realize that she had not seen Clio in some time. Kitty would only realize it then because she needed Clio to assist her in some way; needed Clio to put on a smocked dress and shoes if Aunt Cliome were coming to tea, lest Aunt Cliome, after whom Clio was named, decide to leave her black Tahitian pearls to a niece in San Diego. Kitty thought it important to have her daughter at her side, if only for a few minutes, even if Clio flinched involuntarily when Kitty stroked her with tense, soft fingers.

Hysterical maids would be sent to find Clio, bringing her back just in time to make her bathe and dress before her aunt's station wagon came slowly up the grass driveway. For years, Cliome had promised the pearls to Kitty, then taken them away whenever Kitty displeased her. Although Cliome never went anywhere without them, she did not wear them. They were enormous, and she thought them a bit vulgar. She carried them in her handbag. She had last taken back the pearls when Kitty married John Lynott. Emma used to say that although Kitty claimed to spend the months at Hale Moku waiting for her divorce from Lynott on behalf of her reputation, it was really on behalf of the pearls.

Kitty did not understand that the old woman would not have noticed whether her namesake, Clio, were present or not, so deeply was she lost in dreams. She was far out to sea with her own fishermen—not the teasing, rough-skinned Filipino men who'd taught Clio to bail with a rusty coffee can, but princely men, Hawaiian men—long since dead. It was difficult for Miss Cliome to accept that the old ways were lost forever. Enthralled to the past, she understood just enough to realize that the world had not changed to her advantage.

Kitty did get the black pearls eventually, but Clio could not recall them. It is unlikely that Clio never saw the black pearls, which were as big as brussels sprouts. She had trained herself to put certain things out of her mind, things that did not, at first glance, seem worthy of such a banishment. It was not lack of curiosity, or disinclination, but a kind of necessary unconcern. She spent her time in reflection—not in thought, not in remembrance. Years later, when Emma spoke of the pearls, a little enviously, Clio could say in wonder that she did not remember them.

As Mabel Clarke was not interested in the same things that interested Emma, Emma did not torment her mother with passages from *A Journal of a Residence in the Sandwich Islands*. Clio's book might be David Malo's *Hawaiian Antiquities* written in Hawaiian, which she was still trying to learn, or a monograph on the one hundred and forty-seven pieces of Hawaiian sculpture left in the world, nine pieces of which were owned by her family, two of which were on a table in her blind grandmother's dining room.

More often, Mabel recited Japanese poetry from the *Man'yoshu*, especially the work of Izumi Shikibu, whom she loved more than any other poet. She began reading Izumi in middle age. "Clio," she used to say, "Izumi Shikibu is to blame for everything," and Clio would agree.

Emma and Clio spoke as if the old woman were still able to see, still able to reason. This did not in any way impede conversation. Even on her worst days, Mabel took their meaning. There were people in the small town of Kaikea who for years refused to believe that Mabel was either sightless or mad. She was confined to a chair. Her legs were swollen to the size of palm trunks. Her hands looked like gingerroot.

While Mabel was going blind, she built a moon-viewing pavilion in the garden. It was copied from a Hiroshige print in *One Hundred Views of Edo*, and the architect from Japan lived in the guest cottage, the same one that Clio used, for the year it took to build the pavilion to his and Mabel's liking. Mabel composed poetry in the Japanese style, using the *waka* or haiku form. The poems were published in a small but handsome edition by the University of Hawaii Press. She was not untalented. Clio was not very talented, especially not in composing thirty-one-syllable poems about the dew on plum blossoms. She had tried, to please Mabel, but even Clio had known that the poems were not very good. Too much feeling.

Mabel had decorated the library at Hale Moku to resemble a ten-mat Japanese room. There were *tansu* chests in which to hide rolls of Scotch tape and staplers and the telephone, all of the totems of the twentieth century which would have spoiled the illusion that they were sitting at the foot of Mount Hiei, outside the old capital city of Nara. It was somewhat impractical, this room that was a manifestation of Mabel's bitter fantasies. Each time one of them needed to wrap a package or find an envelope or writing paper, they had to remove everything from a *tansu* and, because there were, of course, no tables of the right height, lay everything on the tatami mats until the twine, or a ballpoint pen, was finally found. It was a reminder to Clio that too strong an interest in the past, even if it were only an aesthetic interest, required patience and a willingness, even an eagerness, to do things the hard way.

Mabel's grandfather had been the son of a chiefess, so she could not deny her Hawaiian birthright. Although Mabel knew many secrets—the location of the 'ape'ape herb found only in the damp mountain gullies of east Maui or the recipe for the love potion made from the last remaining stalks of red cane—she pretended that she had forgotten them. Emma would ask, "What was the prayer of the *kapu* chief when he wanted to put aside his dread exclusiveness so as to mingle with his people?" and Mabel would answer with vagueness, "What *kapu?* Whose people?"

Emma had counted on her mother to give her these gifts—her story and the story of her ancestors—just as she counted on Clio to receive them. She had counted on a more capacious truthfulness, or rather, because Emma understood that there were countless degrees of truth, a more capacious accuracy. Mabel was one of the few people left who could speak with any certainty. She knew that Emma had spent her life memorizing and recording, at first in large notebooks and later onto tape, the lore of her race, but Mabel would not help her. "She doesn't care," Emma said. And Mabel didn't care. Although Emma understood why Mabel was so intent on denying the past, and was even sympathetic to her mother, Emma had chosen, unlike her mother, knowledge over revenge.

Mabel kept secret the chief's chant as a way of repudiating her rank and her blood. As a married woman of forty, she had fallen in love with a prosperous orchid grower named Shiro Kageshiro whom she'd met one afternoon buying rootstock in Hilo. They saw each other over many months and many orchids and finally planned to travel in secret to Kyoto, separately, desperate with love, to sleep together for the first time. Although he was a widower, and Mabel would have given up her husband and Hale Moku and even her children for him, she was not permitted, in the end, to give up her past. They did everything to keep her from him—her husband, her mother, her lawyer and banker, her cousins and aunts, her maids and gardeners, even the old house—everyone and everything, except her eldest daughter, Emma, who implored her to go to Mr. Kageshiro. Mabel hadn't the strength, in the end, to prevail against their combined power. She did not go to Kyoto, and she never forgave them. She did not even forgive Emma, especially not Emma, who had been so generous.

Her family treated her, a grown woman, as if nothing had happened. They did not even give her the gift of condemnation. And so in retribution Mabel forgot overnight how to dance a hula, the way to weave *haku* lei, the verses of the birth chant. She became interested in Japanese lacquerware. She studied Buddhism. She practiced calligraphy. When her husband drowned one summer evening at Polihale, she did not run straight down the dirt road to Mr. Kageshiro's orchid farm, but shut herself even deeper into Hale Moku, as if her refusal to claim her belated happiness was just punishment for those who had deprived her of it in the first place.

Every Monday morning before the house was awake, until he, too, died, Mr. Kageshiro left a wheelbarrow full of orchids and fruit at the kitchen door of Hale Moku; fruit that Emma only took in her hand at breakfast, so bitter did it taste to her, who had implored her mother to spend all for love. Emma told Clio that Mabel always ate the fruit greedily, as if it were her due, as if she had traded Mr. Kageshiro himself for the sweet fruit and the rare Madagascar orchids. And perhaps she had. In Hawaiian, Hale Moku means Island House. But the word *moku* may also mean to cut or to sever. To break in two.

"I'm going over!" screamed Mabel.

Clio lifted her head to look at her grandmother. She wondered, not for the first time, if Mabel made so much noise when she ate—smacking and gulping; ripping apart the Portuguese sweet bread with her old jumbled teeth as if it were a struggle to the death—because her sightlessness had in some sympathetic way diminished her hearing. It was supposed to do just the opposite, Clio knew. No one who retained the gift of hearing would make so much noise as did Mabel when she ate. As an affectation of childishness, she pretended, or perhaps did not pretend, that the Rice Krispies spoke to her. "They're crying, 'Ouch, ooh, that hurts! I'm going over the falls! Ahhhhhh!' " Her shout would fall to a horrified whisper as the last of the cereal was swept over the Akaka Falls of her throat into the pool of her stomach.

"Do you think the word 'schooner' is best rendered *moku kia lua* or *kuna*?" Emma asked Clio one morning at breakfast. She was working on a new Hawaiian translation of Mark Twain's letters from the South Seas.

Clio rolled her eyes in mock exasperation and let her head fall forward onto the table. "What is the good of an oral tradition, Emma, if it cannot even tell you where you have come from? No one knows where the first Hawaiians came from—even they didn't know!"

"The Hawaiians came from the Marquesas," Emma said calmly.

Clio picked up the morning newspaper. She did not want to think about Mark Twain's letters. Lately, she had felt exhausted by their work—her work and Emma's work. Her tiredness was moral, not physical. She was, for the first time, unsure of their effort.

Emma glanced over Clio's shoulder as she came to what Emma called the society page. "Once I would have known all of those faces," Emma said. "We were related to most of them."

Once Clio would have known all of the faces, too. Once there would have been no one on the beach at Makapu'u whom Clio did not know. But now when she went to the beach or back into Nu'uanu Valley to pick ginger, there were Japanese and Chinese and Filipinos shooting down the mud slide into Jackass Ginger Pond, and pale *sansei* girls in gingham bikinis at Sandy Beach. The girls were still very Japanese with their neat ponytails and baskets of sunscreen and lip salve. They had that particular precision of movement that Clio so admired. They still kept apart, but the very fact that they were sitting at Makapuʻu Beach watching their boyfriends in the surf made Clio wonder where they had been all those years, even before the servicemen and the tourists had found the beach at Makapuʻu, all those years when Clio and her friends had been the only ones on the beach. Perhaps the Japanese girls had been in sewing class or Japanese language school. She could not imagine what their grandmothers thought of them now. It could no longer be said that the most sensual part of a Japanese woman was the nape of her neck.

Clio had discovered the conflict of democratization. If there were twenty Japanese girls in bikinis lying on the beach at Makapuʻu, there were twenty fewer Japanese girls who still wore kimonos and *geta*, who knew how to play the *samisen*, how to prepare tea, and arrange cherry branches in a way no *haole* girl could ever devise, no matter how many *ikebana* classes she endured.

Clio knew that the *samisen* was an instrument already unknown to these girls' mothers and grandmothers, women who would not have had the time or the training or the inclination to play difficult court music after twelve hours in the pineapple fields, their fingers too horribly slashed to play anything. It was a wonderful thing, in the end, to walk in jeans and sneakers rather than a hobbled silk robe and awkward, even dangerous, elevated lacquered clogs.

But the old ways were lovelier. The world was less full of beauty, even if it were bursting to good effect with equality. Clio knew that it was easy enough for her to lament. It was desirable, preferable, that Japanese girls be at Makapuʻu Beach.

"Clio, child, put me in the orchids," Mabel said, looking like an owl who has suddenly found itself in the light. Clio rose and pushed her grandmother's chair onto the lanai.

The descendants of the flowers once left on the kitchen steps by Mr. Kageshiro were planted in black sand in old Chinese pots—white *Macroplectrum* and fragrant cattleya and lilac *Spathoglottis* and the beautiful *Odontoglossum* with its heavy, petulant lip like a pouting girl.

"Did you really save Emma from a tidal wave by throwing her into a tree?" Clio asked as she placed her grandmother among the orchids.

"The Buddhist painter Jakuchu was famous for his love of chickens," Mabel said, nodding. She sucked *ume*, sour pickled cherries, fishing them from a glass quart jar.

"Will you play 'Net of the Moon' with me?" she asked. The big jar wobbled precariously and Clio reached out to steady it, but Mabel deftly slapped away her hand.

The light of the moon was necessary in order to play the hand game correctly, but as Mabel could not see the moon, she could play whenever she pleased. It had confused Clio to play a game that required the light of the moon without any moon at all, but over time she had grown used to playing it, like so many things, Mabel's way.

Mabel's fingers were sticky with syrup. Clio held her hand to Mabel's hand, and as they tried to trap the absent moon in the skein of their fingers, Clio thought that her grandmother had not outlived her memory, after all. She knew everything.

C lio saw Tommy Haywood for the first time in 1983 at the volleyball court at the Outrigger Canoe Club in Waikiki. She was twenty-seven years old. It was late afternoon. She had left the museum where she worked as a historian in the Department of Oceanic Myths two hours early in order to watch her boyfriend, Puna Silva, win his match. Puna's partner was Clio's younger brother, Dixon. It was not altogether a true victory, taking the club title, as the day before Dix had been suspended from the club. He had not paid his bar bill in eight months, or rather, Emma had not paid it. She was no longer able to pay his bill at the Outrigger Club. No one, except Clio and Puna, knew that Dix was not eligible to compete. Among other things, Dix used to keep a shoe box full of souvenirs from the war in Viet Nam, photographs of female genitalia turned inside out and a sealed bag of ears he'd bought from a door-gunner who'd apologized that the best ears, the ears from the right side, had already been removed by the time he reached the bodies. So competing in a state championship when he was disqualified was not a particularly serious lapse for Dix. He made the winning spike, as Clio would expect of him.

Mr. Haywood was in town making a movie about Japanese gangsters, and although Clio recognized him, she pretended not to know who he was. She was not trying to get his attention, although that is what she did. She sat on the damp sand in the shade, while Tommy Haywood and his bodyguard did stretching exercises. There was a pretty girl with Mr. Haywood. Clio recognized her. She was the daughter of the director of publicity at the Kahala Hilton. The girl rubbed oil on Haywood's back, and Clio noticed that he had acne scars on his shoulders.

She was introduced to him on the Hau Terrace by Dix, who was buying drinks for everyone. The Chinese barman, Ching See, didn't like that Dix was charging the drinks, and Clio would not have liked it any better had she known that Dix put the many, many drinks and orders of sashimi, and T-shirts from the Beach Shop that he gave to the girl with Tommy Haywood, on her account, but by the time Dix was signing the last of the chits, Clio had left the terrace to take a night swim with Puna and Tommy Haywood.

Two weeks later she married him. Tommy Haywood, not Puna.

The first night that Clio spent with him, he'd moved her aside with both hands and asked if she'd mind touching up his hair.

He had a cover interview with *Aloha* magazine in the morning. He usually had his hair color done in L.A., he explained, but he had prolonged his stay in Hawai'i in order to be with her and he had missed his last hair appointment. Not that he regretted staying. He said that he'd never met anyone like Clio, and he meant it, but a few gray hairs were beginning to show around his ears. Clio cheerfully got out of bed to dye his hair with the bottle of L'Oréal Brasilia he'd asked the bell captain to send to the room. Clio knew the bellboy who brought the bottle of hair color. He was in her hula class. His eyes opened wide when he recognized Tommy, and even wider when he saw Clio, but he pretended not to know her. "Hi, Galen," she said before she'd realized how pleased he was by his own discretion. She regretted her haste in speaking to him. He blushed as he pulled the door closed behind him.

"I can date you by your bra," Tommy said, looking away for a moment from the television when she walked across the room from the bathroom.

"You mean *for* my bra." She looked down at her brassiere. She'd thought it quite glamorous when she ordered it from a lingerie catalogue.

"No," he said. "*By* your bra. Older women wear bras that hook in back. I haven't seen one in years."

"An older woman?"

"Not you, babe. Not you." He winked at her and turned his handsome head back to the television. "Relax. I like you. I even like your family."

"My family?"

"I don't know from families," he said, patting his knee for her to come and sit. He was wearing the terry-cloth hotel robe and it fell open across his lap. "You're related to everyone on the island."

"Not really," she said. "It only seems that way. It's a form of snobbery."

"Whatever. It's cool. Power is cool." He grinned with pleasure at his own wisdom.

The sound of the surf rose from the little beach far below. She could see the lights of Waikiki. The glare of the lights diluted the black of the sky, and made the stars disappear.

"You don't talk much," he said, watching her. "I like that."

The telephone rang, but he did not answer it. When she turned to look at him, wondering if he wished her to answer it, he said, "It's that girl from the other night."

"The one you were going out with?" she asked.

He laughed and she blushed in embarrassment. "I don't date, babe," he said.

She turned back to the night sky.

"It's kind of a relief," he said. "Takes the pressure off. You know, having to pick her up in a car or telephone a hundred fucking times before she'll have dinner. You don't seem to mind about that stuff. You don't mind not going to restaurants."

She smiled. "My grandmother thinks it's common to eat in public."

"Common?"

"She thinks that we are in the nineteenth century. I mean, she really thinks it."

He shrugged. "Whatever."

The telephone rang again and he picked it up in irritation. "I told you to clear the calls, hon," he said to the operator. "No calls unannounced. No visitors. I've talked to security about this before." He grunted and put down the receiver. "Come sit, babe."

He looked down at his legs and patted his thighs. "You know, if my legs had been six inches longer, I'd have been famous six years sooner."

"And if they'd been six inches shorter?"

"I'd still be parking cars."

"And dating."

She went to him, and he pulled back his robe and she sat on the thighs that had belatedly made him a star.

The day before they left Honolulu, Tommy Haywood bought Clio a Bentley sedan. She had never had her own car. For years she had been driven around Honolulu by

Lester, both their lives at stake because she was afraid to offend him by refusing to ride with him. Tommy had the beautiful car wrapped in flannel and shipped to California.

Tommy saw the car more as an investment than as a gift, and Clio realized this, but she was too proud, too inexperienced, and too far gone in the details at least, not in the passion, to change her mind because of a 1954 dark green Bentley. "I know that he is not in love with me," she said to Emma, "and that is all right, but I refuse to be jealous of a car." Clio knew that although Emma did not, could not, admire Tommy Haywood, she would never speak against him.

"Sensible of you," Emma said. "About the car, I mean."

"It wasn't until I read *The Sun Also Rises* a second time that I finally understood the meaning of the word 'impotent.' I'd thought it meant ineffectual; a man who had trouble getting taxis or the attention of a waiter. These lapses had seemed perfectly good reasons for a woman's discontent."

"One has suffered for less."

"I suppose it is an unfashionable idea, but I've always liked the way that men are different from women. I am not aroused by sameness, but by the very way that a man is different from me. That is what interests me. The hair on his arms. The thickness and the smell of him. I like that penis."

"You are more old-fashioned than I even imagined."

"And you?"

"Oh. Me. I don't remember what I like. Yes, I liked the maleness, too. I did." She sounded sad.

"I used to feel guilty for liking it so much."

"I think," Emma said slowly, "that the great thing is the discovery, hardest for a woman, of the chasm between expectation and reality—the profound want of means—

oh, I don't mean penises and I certainly don't mean money and privilege, but the want of ramification. One is thrown into the ocean almost at birth and a girl is deceived into thinking that because she can hold her head above water, she will stay afloat."

"Oh, we are a different thing altogether. We have been *trying* to swim out of the current. Although you and Grandmother never seem to tire, it has been a difficult thing for me—to stay out of the current. I long to be in the current and it frightens me because you have taught me to want to stay out of it. You've taught me that to be in the current is to drown. Lester tried to get me into the current, with his music."

"And did he succeed?"

"Perhaps Tommy will pull me into the current," Clio said quietly. "He doesn't have to love me. He just has to know how to swim."

Clio had convinced herself that if she could leave the islands, if only for a little while, perhaps she'd be able to figure out just what she was meant to do with all of the secrets, all of the chants and songs and legends that so filled her head that she could no longer distinguish what was real from what was myth. She could no longer separate what had happened a hundred years earlier from what she had dreamed in the night. She used to say laughingly that she knew the ritual ceremony for wrapping the bones of a chief, but she could not divide fractions. She could steer an outrigger canoe through rough seas, but she had never learned to iron. Emma had kept her busy all those years, and Clio had been a good student. She had worked hard, and she was tired.

Emma, who was always so sensitive to Clio, misjudged her meaning. She thought that Clio was simply overwrought, preparing for her departure and her new life, and she did not pay too much attention to Clio's warning.

"You're too good in the water to ever drown," she said. But Clio knew better.

Tommy Haywood lived in Malibu, California, above the Pacific Coast Highway in a steel-beam and redwood house that looked like a big land crab. Its rusted metal legs extended stiffly in the scrub as if it had been dropped there to guard the dry fields and to keep the dirt and rock from spilling into the narrow canyon below. There was a swimming pool, and a chain link fence at the bottom of the steep terraced yard in case someone tripped on the ice plant and slid down the rocky slope to the highway. There was an electric gate and television monitors so that overeager fans would not be sitting in the kitchen when Tommy came down to breakfast each morning.

Tall stands of pine surrounded the house, hiding it from the road. There was a smell of mesquite and dust. Brush fires ignited spontaneously in the brush and Clio worried that they would be trapped in the house and burned to death. She asked if they could replace the louvers with screens or casements, but Tommy wouldn't hear of it. The opaque glass louvers kept people from seeing inside the house. The week before they returned from Honolulu, two teenage girls with binoculars had been found in an eucalyptus tree.

Emma had told Clio, years earlier, that she'd known everything she'd ever need to know about Clio's stepmother once she'd seen Burta's favorite painting, a view of Mount Fuji done in crushed coral and seashells. Clio had laughed and said, "If she were only just that bad." So although Clio understood aesthetic snobbery and she could see the fairness in the remark that her husband's house looked like a Mexican flying saucer on stilts, she did not laugh. After all, now it was her house, too.

Tommy had a cook named Bobby whom he had met at a health food store in West Hollywood. Bobby had advised Tommy on colonics and herbal cleansers and Tommy had asked him to work for him. Bobby did not sleep at the house. Tommy did not like his crew, as he called them, to be in the house at night. There was a young secretary, Judy, who came each morning. There was a gardener and a pool man and a security guard who sat at the gate. The pool man also sold drugs. There was an exercise trainer and a business manager, a press secretary, a lawyer, and an agent. It was difficult for Tommy to get around town without being recognized. His business was done at home.

Tommy was the sort of man who, before he became famous, bought postage stamps from a machine at the drug store, one packet at a time, as he needed them. If he had a headache, he asked if anyone had an aspirin. It is unlikely that he'd ever owned a pair of scissors or a pencil sharpener before Judy, his secretary, came to work for him. Judy tirelessly interviewed and hired the stream of Mexican maids who flowed serenely through the house. Tommy was convinced that the women, who did not speak English, would sell information about him to the newspapers, and the women were seldom allowed to stay for more than a few weeks. Judy bought bed sheets, magazines, after-shave lotion, hanging plants, compact discs, light bulbs, razor blades, athletic socks, and the occasional present that Tommy needed to give—in other words, everything. She was never upset by Tommy's demands, even his more eccentric ones. He insisted that she leave a new box of Tucks sanitary wipes on the back of the toilet each morning. Clio discovered a cabinet full of unopened green Tucks boxes.

Devi, the girl who gave Tommy a massage twice a week, told Clio that she often did girls up at the house after she did Tommy. She also did extras. She asked Clio if she would like a massage. Clio said that perhaps they could do it another time, when it was not so hot, and she went to ask Judy what Devi had meant by extras.

"Oh, you know," Judy said, making a pitcher of margaritas. "Stuff to relax you. Depending, of course, on whether you're a gal or a guy. Extras." She turned on the bar blender.

Clio looked at her hands. "Like a manicure?" she shouted over the noise of the blender.

"Not exactly," yelled Judy.

Unlike Clio, Tommy's friends did not spend much time thinking about ambiguities of speech or gesture. They had no prejudices, and few preferences. Clio had spent most of her life as a guest, both in her father's house and later at Emma's, and she had accustomed herself to the sensitive, somewhat dubious position of the guest. It was soothing for Clio to be in a house where the interpretation of behavior or language was so irrelevant as to be a kind of bad manners. Clio had staggered through childhood under the weight of puzzlement and it was a lovely surprise to discover that things in Tommy's house were quite what they seemed.

Tommy's friends were nice. Clio liked them. They often spoke roughly to each other in a teasing way, but they did not really have strong opinions about things. They were not interested in books or science or art or even in other countries, and they were not interested in politics except for local issues, like the banning of cigars in the Sports Arena or the shooting of coyotes from helicopters. They sometimes talked about clothes and food. They always talked about movies.

There were friends who had followed Tommy to Hollywood from the small mill town in western Massachusetts where they'd grown up, surly and restless teenagers, setting fire to railroad ties and throwing cats into quarries. There were friends from Tommy's early days at Disneyland, where they'd performed skits about traffic signals. There were black friends from his Saturday basketball game in the Valley. There were small-time pimps; men who got girls or drugs or laid bets for the friends too famous or too busy, or not famous enough, to make the calls themselves. There were rich kids who made dinner reservations at three or four restaurants every night, just in case. There were friends he worked with in films—directors and underwater camera operators and good-looking stunt men. There were people he had met on location—an Indian woman from South Dakota and a destitute English art dealer who hoped Tommy would someday commission him to buy some real paintings. There were many, many friends.

Clio grew accustomed to their presence in the house. She was often awakened in the morning by a smooth, thin man named Yuseef, who would open the door of the bedroom and whisper, "Hey, Tommy, a little one-on-one, man?" Clio realized she'd never hear Yuseef coming, no matter how hard she listened for him each morning, because the blue wall-to-wall carpeting that Tommy had put on every floor surface of the house, including the garage, muffled the sound of the bouncing basketball and Yuseef's expensive sneakers. She missed Yuseef those mornings when he didn't come to her bedroom.

Clio was not treated much differently than the crew except that she was allowed to stay through the night. She tried very hard to do her part. She was willing to give Tommy whatever he needed. She was fond of him. The irony was that although he did what he was supposed to do—pull her into the current—he didn't seem to want very much in return. He seemed relieved just to have her around. She was no trouble, as he had known she would not be.

She sometimes wondered if Tommy, like her step-mother, Burta, mistook her stillness for a lack of will. Some women, she knew, would have been grateful to be left alone, and she wondered why she minded. It was not as if she were used to adoration, or even attention. She had assumed that when two hearts really did become one, a certain alteration, a rearranging and even forfeiting, was demanded—out of fondness as well as necessity. She was surprised to have her hours and her days, and even herself, returned to her so quickly.

Clio had entered a period in her sexual life in which ca-resses, kisses, and embraces, all the delights and torments of a preliminary nature, were dispensed with in favor of immediate resolution. Puna Silva had liked to make love every day, snapping off his black rubber wet suit to fall happily on top of her. There had not been much erotic contemplation with Puna Silva. Although he had been graceful and passionate, he had not been very curious. Clio was not too surprised by Tommy Haywood's lack of exploratory interest, but he was neither passionate nor curious.

Although Tommy believed that sexual intercourse was good for one's mental and physical regimen, he was not a sensualist. Clio realized that he would not be able to make love to a woman who he didn't think was physically perfect. He said "Good muscle tone" when he looked at Clio's legs, and "You must be a great swimmer" when she lifted her arms to braid her hair for sleep. It would have been a reflection of himself that would have made him very un-comfortable, and even anxious, had he discovered too late that a woman to whom he was making love was ten pounds overweight.

He was quick at his lovemaking, his head buried in her

neck, his small hands gripping her shoulders. He jumped up as soon as he regained his breath, and went to the mirror. He tilted his head boyishly so that he looked up at himself, and ran his hands through his thick black hair. He smiled at himself. Then he took a long shower.

He sometimes bathed three times a day. He would not take a bath if she had used the bathtub unless the tub was scrubbed down with cleansing powder. She had made the mistake of admitting, reluctantly, that she sometimes urinated in the bath water. It was very like Clio to tell the truth, and he made her feel guilty about it. She had read of a prime minister in India who drank a glass of his own urine every day as a tonic and she told him this. He was shocked.

"I just feel better if the tub is clean, that's all," he said. "It makes me feel good. I'm the Number Four Box-Office Star in America. I like to feel clean. I don't give a shit what some Arab does."

In the rare instance when she was alone with him, when he sent away his friends and bodyguards and trainers, and rarer still, when there was a kind of tenderness and intimacy between them, she asked him questions. She could see that he became interesting to himself in a new way during those unaccustomed moments when she prodded him and pulled from him a spontaneous truth. Those occasional hours were, she realized, the only times he ever interested her. He, too, but in an unclear way, because he wouldn't have known how to make it clear, must have realized intuitively that Clio was leading him to his best self, even if it were against his will.

It was very difficult for him to talk about his childhood. Clio, who was overwhelmed by her sense of the past, had married a man who had no past. She knew that it could not be coincidental. He refused to admit to having any feelings about his family—he almost refused to admit that he had a family—except to say that his father had played more with the family dog than with him. He claimed never to have masturbated, even as a boy.

One night, in the back of a limousine coming home from Santa Barbara, where Tommy had accepted an award from the Theatre Owners' Association, he said, "Remember when you asked me about the first time I had sex? Well, you got me thinking about it. It was in the Vermont woods the summer I was fifteen. I couldn't really even see her, it was so dark. I didn't even take off my jeans. When I got back to the cabin where my friends were, I looked down to make sure my fly was closed and I saw my jeans had blood all over them. I thought, Fuck, I hurt myself, I hurt my dick. But then I checked and saw I was all right. I thought I must of hurt the girl. For a minute, I even thought maybe I killed her. I didn't know what to do. I went down to this pond and took off my jeans and sunk them in the water and rubbed them with stones until my hands were so fucking cold I was shaking. Then I put them back on and snuck into the cabin, dripping water everywhere, still wearing my jeans. I don't know why I put them back on. In the morning I could hardly move my legs, I was that stiff. But the blood was gone."

She stared at him, his handsome face illuminated now and then by the headlights of passing cars.

"Did you ever figure it out?" To her surprise, she was aroused by his story. She took his hand in the dark of the car and put it under her skirt.

"What?"

"The blood. That she was menstruating. Or perhaps that she was a virgin."

"Not a virgin. Shit, it was her idea, the whole fucking thing." He paused. "Yeah, course I figured it out."

Perhaps the nearer we are to Los Angeles, she thought,

the less he is his true self. She knew she'd have to work fast to take advantage of the time left to her. She pushed his fingers against her. "It might have been her first time, even if she did think of it."

"Hey, you weren't even *there*, babe. I forget what happened." He pulled away his hand. "Want to stop at Jemima's? I'm hungry." He rolled down the window and looked away from her, his face vacant in the neon lights of Malibu.

One day, Clio found a naked redheaded woman choking to death by the pool. To Clio's astonishment, Judy calmly read a script while the woman gagged soundlessly. Clio rushed over and knocked her to the AstroTurf.

The woman sat up, furious. "Christ!" she screamed.

Clio stared at her in that interested way one has when another person is beautiful, but unlike one's self. Clio was slim and long. The woman screaming at her was small and sturdy. Her skin was the color of butterscotch. Her nipples were very dark, her breasts small. Clio was accustomed to naked guests. Tommy and his friends often did not wear clothes around the house, and she had noticed that it was easier for a woman to remove her clothes if her breasts were small. Clio thought that her own breasts were too big for her to lie nude by the pool with Tommy and his friends, and she kept on her bathing suit.

"Mimi the Great," Judy said, not looking up from the script. "This is Clio. Say howdy."

Clio knew about Mimi. Mimi had been Tommy's girlfriend when he first came to Hollywood from Disneyland. She had been in a police series with him. He had told Clio that Mimi was the first person he ever knew who bothered to make coffee in a pot rather than just using instant.

"Haven't you ever seen anyone do chin exercises? You could of killed me! Fuck!" She rubbed her jaw.

"I'm sorry," Clio said, staring at her.

Mimi leaned forward to look at her closely. "You could probably start doing some of these stretches yourself. It's never too soon, girl."

Clio nodded. She had expected disdain, not advice. She was absolutely ready to begin chin exercises. She ran her hand over her throat.

"Mimi is very hedonistic," Judy said with a sigh.

"Like you even know what the word means," Mimi said, smiling at Clio for the first time.

"You spend all your money on body treatments and clothes. How can you spend your money on seaweed body facials? on clothes? You know what a dress is worth two minutes after you leave the store?" Clio was surprised to see Judy so indignant.

"I think that buying clothes is the very definition of luxury." Mimi lay back on a rubber mat. "All that money on something so beautiful and so worthless." She closed her green eyes and shuddered with delight. "It wouldn't mean as much otherwise."

"It's like drinking expensive wine," Judy said, looking up for the first time. "It's just gone when you're finished. You might as well eat a hundred-dollar bill."

Mimi licked her lips. "But a hundred-dollar bill has no taste," she said. "Or has it?"

Judy shook her head in disapproval.

Clio laughed. She had never thought of luxury in quite that way.

"Clio understands," Mimi said, opening one eye to look at her. "Don't you, baby?"

"I think I do," Clio said as she basked in the ease, the swiftness, of her corruption.

. . .

On the days that Mimi and Clio did not sit in the shallow end of the pool listening to Doug Sahm records and drinking margaritas, Mimi drove Clio into Beverly Hills. Clio was not allowed to use the beautiful Bentley that Tommy had given to her in Honolulu because Tommy, who had worked in parking lots when he first arrived in Los Angeles, disapproved of the way that attendants handled the cars. She was happy to have Mimi drive her. She admired Mimi's expediency, and her even, generous temper. She liked that Mimi did not envy her.

Mimi introduced Clio to her manicurist and to the maître d'hôtel at La Dora and to the salesgirls at Carole Lee. She took Clio to her electrolysis technician. Mimi had had every hair on her legs and arms removed—a process that had taken twelve years. She was having her pubic hair plucked into the shape of a heart.

She took Clio to luncheons at her girlfriends' big, clean houses. The women were full of gaiety and affection. Even though the lunch party might be in celebration of a new husband or a new part in a movie, the women often brought presents for each other, very expensive presents—pink leather jackets and Georgian silver place settings. They drank champagne, and then, suffused with confidence, spread out through the little streets between Wilshire Boulevard and Santa Monica Boulevard to spend money. The women bought things for their children, their maids, their mothers and husbands and sisters, perhaps because there was little more, no matter how tirelessly and imaginatively they tried, to buy for themselves.

Like Tommy, Mimi lived in the present, at least as far as hangovers and due bills were concerned. Her credit card statements were divided, not always evenly, and mailed to the business managers of several of her boyfriends. Bad headaches at five in the afternoon were averted by drinking straight through the day. "It is only if you stop," she said to Clio, "that you feel bad." It was a theory, Clio thought, that could be applied to most things.

One chilly afternoon, Mimi took Clio to a baby shower at the house of her friend Deirdre Michael. Clio wore flannel trousers and a sweater, not knowing better, but the women, taking advantage of the cool weather, wore kid gloves and tight suits with peplums, and suede boots to the thigh. They sat on their knees on a thin Aubusson carpet, their skirts hiked to their panties. The walls of the room were covered in pale green moiré silk. When one woman stood to make a telephone call, her high heel caught in the carpet. The woman righted herself gracefully and smiled at Clio.

"But what if you are in love with him?" asked a woman in a cocktail hat with a veil. She was smoking a cigarette through the veil.

"If you fall in love, you've only yourself to blame."

"Listen to Maya," Deirdre Michael said sweetly to Clio as she handed her a glass of champagne. "She's the Scheherazade of Holmby Hills."

Maya lifted an eyebrow, unsure if this were a compliment. "Sherry who?"

"Maya was married to Mort," Mimi whispered to Clio as if she would understand. "Second wife."

"I always keep a garter belt or just one black stocking, in my purse," Maya said. "I pretend I'm looking for my compact and I pull out the garter belt as if by mistake and I say, 'Oh, jeez, what can this be doing here?' " She smiled. "It helps if you can blush a little. It makes him anxious. Which is just how you want him. Anxious all the time. It's what keeps him hot."

"It works for Maya, but it never works for me," Deirdre Michael said quietly to Clio.

"Too bad for you," Mimi said under her breath.

"What, Mimi?" Deirdre asked. "Did you get some champagne?"

"I wouldn't be very good at it, either," Clio said to Deirdre. "I'm the one who is anxious."

Mimi took a silver cigarette box from a table and looked at it closely. " 'To one son-of-a-bitch from the rest of the son-of-a-bitches,' " Mimi said, reading the inscription on the box. "Is that grammatically correct?" she asked Clio. She made Clio nervous.

"I love your shoes, Mimi," Deirdre said.

A maid announced that luncheon was served.

"I'm dying to see the dining room," a woman said, pulling down her skirt. She straightened her legs and there was the sliding sound of silk as her stockings rubbed together.

"Oh, me too," Deirdre said happily as she rose to lead the way.

Mimi turned to make a face at Clio, mouthing the words, " 'Me too'?" as they followed the chattering, lovely women into lunch.

Mimi often came back to Malibu after the day's adventure. She and Clio sat on the brown suede sofas, surrounded by shopping bags and European fashion magazines, and drank tequila while they waited for Tommy to come home from the studio.

They were too lazy to turn on the lamps, and the room slowly darkened around them. They were like sleepy animals lying in a cave, eyes glazed, flanks outstretched—high and a little bored, but not unhappy. There was a fragrance of Russian olive and casuarina from the hills, and the fields behind the house were red with the light of the setting sun.

"Was it a terrible shock when you found out that you were a girl?" Clio asked Mimi one warm evening.

"Excuse me?"

"When you first understood that the rules aren't quite the same for us as they are for boys."

Mimi leaned forward to pour more tequila into their glasses. "You mean, when they wouldn't let me shag balls in the outfield unless I paid them?"

"Yes."

"Not a shock, exactly."

"I'm afraid to ask what they wanted in payment."

"Something only I could give them."

"Yes, that's what I thought."

Mimi lay her head back against the arm of the sofa and exercised her ankles. "To tell you the truth, I was absolutely thrilled I had something boys wanted," she said gravely. "I still am."

"I've thought about this quite a bit," Clio said. "Trying to understand. It was a tremendous thing for me, discovering that being a girl was going to be held against me."

"Well, Clio, honey, it depends."

"I make a special case of myself, and I *don't* make it, if you see, but there was something in the way that I grew up—in the country, in the ocean—that made me take the news particularly hard. I also had the news rather late. In the city or the suburbs there are sports—organized games and teams like Little League—but for an island girl there is just nature. Nature doesn't pick teams. I could swim and climb trees and jump off the big rock as well as any boy. There was nothing a boy could do that I couldn't do, except piss standing up, of course, and I was happy to give him that. It was only when I went to school that I discovered that I was not going to be treated the same, not be allowed to play by their rules." She paused. "The funny thing is that I was embarrassed. For them. For all of us."

"You are very upset about this," Mimi said in amusement.

"Oh, I know being a tomboy at least gave me a kind of physical confidence and courage, and I'm grateful, but it isn't enough. It's only a slight advantage, not being frightened of mice."

"You make a very good girl, Clio. Much better than I do."

"Do I?" Clio asked, thinking about it. "That's the irony. That is just what it means to be an island girl, oddly enough. Resourceful, courageous, uncomplaining. But the very fact of one's competence is what makes it so difficult when you discover that competence, if you're a girl, only counts on the lacrosse team."

"I'd rather fuck the lacrosse team than be on it."

"Well, of course you would. But I'm not talking about now."

"Then, too."

"Well," Clio said, "I suppose the ideal would be to play on the lacrosse team *and* fuck them."

"I don't need to play," Mimi said. "I leave that to you, island girl."

"I used to wonder why the women in my family didn't prepare me for this discovery. Of course, the women in my family *were* men. They ran ranches and sugar plantations and built schools."

"Funny you should say so. The women in my family, too," Mimi said, sitting up in excitement. "My grandmother was a butcher."

"Gosh," said Clio, very impressed.

"I mean a real butcher. Sausages and lamb chops."

"Oh," said Clio, a little disappointed.

The front door opened and Tommy came in with his driver and exercise trainer and his friends, and the boys turned on all of the lights and the big-screen television and noisily lifted the shopping bags over the backs of the sofas and dropped them onto the Mexican tile floor. Talking and laughing, they slapped the dust from their boots, and Clio smiled drowsily. She felt as if she'd been awakened by the sudden arrival of a gang of friendly cowboys.

One of the few things that her mother Kitty had taught Clio was the importance of being ready for your man when he came in from work. Clio knew that in Kitty's case, work would have meant exercising a polo pony or grafting an orchid, but Clio held on to this advice as the only intimacy she'd ever had from her mother. She always rose happily to greet Tommy when he came home.

She kissed him on the cheek and went to the kitchen to get him a beer and a lime. She knew that there had been someone to give him a kiss and a drink for some time, ever since he played Wild Bill Hickok in his first hit movie, and she knew that he didn't really care who met him at the door, so long as she didn't want something.

She'd once started to tell him about an outbreak of wood fungus in the sauna, but he had interrupted her to say, "Not now, babe." There was not much of anything that he wanted to hear, but out of some hopefulness, and some foolish tribute to her mother, whom men adored, she still jumped up when she heard him come in the door.

One night Mimi and Clio sat with Tommy during the halftime of a basketball game on television. He had an early call the next morning and his friends had been sent home after a big Sunday night dinner of tuna tamales and whole-wheat enchiladas. Now and then the wind blew hard against the chain-link fence and it sounded to Clio like music played on a saw.

Mimi, who was wearing a beauty mask she'd made from

egg whites and some aloe vera that grew at the bottom of the driveway, idly asked Tommy the name of the last book he'd read. She was wearing one of her favorite costumes, a khaki girl-scout uniform she'd found in a thrift shop. It was very short and very tight. She wore it with brown oxfords and short white socks. It was what she put on, she told Clio, when she had to seduce someone. She was having cocktails later that evening with the director Billy Michael.

Clio certainly knew, and perhaps Judy, who was working late, knew, that it was an ironic question, but Tommy, without glancing away from the halftime entertainment, a free-shooting contest with Viet Nam veterans in wheelchairs, asked, "All the way through? Easy. *Sacajawea, Bird Woman*. Tenth grade."

"Tommy, you bullshitter." Mimi tried to speak without moving her mouth.

"On my mother's grave," he said, surprised.

"Your mother's not dead," Judy said, making a stack of eight-by-ten photographs of Tommy on a palomino. She was answering fan mail.

"Okay. But it's still true about the book."

Clio had asked him on the plane from Honolulu what his parents would think about their sudden marriage and he had said, turning the pages of the airline magazine, "To all intensive purposes, I don't have family." So Clio was very curious about this mother, dead or alive. Far more curious about her, in fact, than the possibility that Tommy had not read a book since he was sixteen years old.

"I never knew you even had a mother," she said. Despite herself, she had begun to watch the men in wheelchairs spinning around the basketball court.

"Everyone has a mother," Tommy said in mock amazement.

"Where is she?" Clio asked, turning reluctantly from the television to look at him. "I'm interested in mothers."

"What?" he asked.

Judy looked up, a pair of scissors in her hand. The conversation, with its possibility of intimacy, was beginning to make her nervous.

"Your mother," Clio said.

"Did I say I had a mother? Did anyone hear me say I had a mother?" He slid his eyes from the big screen to look around slowly, daring them to claim that he had said he had a mother.

"My mother died when I was born," Mimi said. "In Puerto Rico."

"I was in Puerto Rico for *Jupiter's Run*," Tommy said, gazing at her absently.

"What about your father?" Clio asked.

Mimi started to laugh and quickly put her hands to her face as pieces of the mask fell into her lap. Clio blushed.

"My dad's never been out of the United States," Tommy said. "Maybe once to Canada. He sort of doesn't believe in it." He turned back to the television.

"He must be one of those people they make those commercials for, the ones about American goods. I always wondered." Mimi pretended to be relieved to have figured it out at last.

"Wondered what?" Tommy asked.

Mimi collected pieces of dried egg white from her lap and held them carefully in one hand. "Who those commercials were made for."

"You don't care about those things? You like to see America sold down the fucking river?"

Clio jumped up and stood on the sofa, moving her arms in slow circles. "Look! Sacajawea!"

Judy laughed and flicked one of Tommy's photographs at her. Clio tried to catch it.

"Can I have that?" Mimi asked as Clio dropped into a corner of the sofa to look at the photograph.

"*May* I have it, you mean," Clio said, holding it out of reach.

"No," Tommy said.

They turned to stare at him.

"You can't have it," he said.

"Maybe you could buy it from him," Clio said to Mimi. She was behaving a bit recklessly and it excited her.

"Forty-eight cents," Judy said. "At cost."

Tommy grabbed the remote-control box and held down the button until the sound was very loud.

"Who's winning the game?" Judy asked Tommy. Tommy made her nervous when he was in a bad mood. Clio had told Mimi that it would be very hard for her to be frightened of someone for whom she had to buy a box of Tucks sanitary wipes every day, but that was Clio's carelessness.

"All I wanted to do was watch the basketball game in fucking peace," he said sorrowfully. "Just a quiet evening at home. Not too much to ask."

"I wanted to know about your mother," Clio said. "I was interested."

He looked at her.

"You know, the Bird Woman," Mimi said.

He slammed the remote-control box down on a table.

Judy, sitting on the floor cross-legged, jumped in place, like a cat.

"I hope you're satisfied," he shouted as he pushed past Clio and went up the stairs to the bedroom.

"I knew it," Judy said with melancholy superiority.

"Now we can watch 'Star Search,'" Mimi said as she picked up the remote-control box with her toes.

"What about his mother?" Clio asked, but Judy was busy signing Tommy's name and greeting ("Yo, pardner") on the photographs.

"This time you guys really went too far," she said.

"I could have gone further. How about you?" Clio asked Mimi.

"Well, a little further, I think."

Clio sighed and looked at the ceiling. She knew that she would have to go upstairs in a few minutes to make sure that he was all right.

"You guys," Judy sighed, shaking her head. "You're going to get in trouble. Really."

Tommy invited Clio to visit him on the set. She sat in the director's chair, sateen crew jacket over her shoulders, and watched the filming. Tommy introduced her to the director, Billy Michael, and to his makeup woman and his double, and Clio had lunch with him in his trailer drawn onto the sound stage like an unhitched wagon before a campfire. She didn't expect or require Tommy to amuse her, but she could see that he was distracted and ill at ease, and she did not visit him again.

One afternoon by the pool, Mimi told Clio that she thought Clio should go to the set more often. Mimi was naked except for a USC baseball cap and a pair of ankle weights. It was very hot and the sky, cloudless and bright, looked like blue Mexican glass.

"He hasn't invited me again."

"Well, I just think it's time to make another appearance, that's all. Some of those bims don't know he's married and I just think they should get a look at you." She lay on her back and moved one leg in a circle, counting to herself.

Clio noticed that Mimi's pretty breasts did not fall to the side when she lay on her back, as did her own. "I don't think he likes my being on the set," she said.

"Oh, God, Clio, what do you care? Just come with me. I'll take you."

"Not if he doesn't want me there. You go and you tell them he's married."

"There was a little trouble last week, if you must know. Apparently, Tommy wouldn't come out of his trailer when he was called for the scene and Billy got really, really mad."

"And?" Clio looked up at the sky and closed her eyes.

Mimi sat up impatiently, forcefully tucking her red hair under the cap. "For someone nearly thirty years old, you can be pretty fucking dumb, Clio. Where have you been all these years?

"Where *have* I been all these years?"

"Tommy said he'd be right there, that he was watching the last minutes of a play-off game, you know how he is about sports, but Billy got furious and stormed into the trailer. There was a girl with Tommy, supposedly, and Billy just picked up the television, he's really strong, and threw it out the trailer window. There was a big explosion when it landed."

"How do you know this?"

"Billy told me."

"Billy Michael?"

"I've been going out with him. Secretly."

"There was a girl?"

"That's Billy's wife."

"I mean in the trailer."

"Oh. Yeah. That's what I heard. She had her head in his lap or something." Mimi sat up and poured coconut oil into her hand and rubbed it on her stomach and breasts.

The smell of the oil suddenly reminded Clio of Emma. Emma had taught her to make her own infusions in Mason jars, the transparent *pikake* petals floating in the heavy oil.

"You mean she was going down on him," Clio said.

"Maybe. Maybe not. Probably not. Could you do my back?" She handed Clio the bottle of oil and turned her back to her. "Is everything okay? I mean, between you guys?"

"That is the word I would use. Okay."

"Do you, you know, still make love?"

"I'm not sure that Tommy's so interested in that. Perhaps he just isn't interested in me."

"You probably need to take him to Dr. Snowie again."

"Dr. Snowie?"

"You know. The gynecologist. I took him once. Oh, a long time ago. You know, when we were going out. He wanted to. He bugged me about it for months. I kept saying yeah, okay, it's a definite maybe, but he kept nagging me. I thought he was jealous of Dr. Snowie, but he wasn't. He just wanted to see what it looked like."

"What what looked like?"

"You know. It. I asked Dr. Snowie and he saw no reason why Tommy shouldn't, so he came in with me and I got up on the table and Snowie turned on the klieg lights and I shouted 'Action!' and he pointed things out to Tommy." She looked around at Clio. "Clio, could you do the oil, please?"

"Tommy didn't know?"

"Of course he knew! He just wanted to really see it."

"To help with his acting, do you think?"

"It certainly didn't help with much else, did it?" She laughed wistfully. "Oil, Clio."

Clio rubbed the oil on Mimi's back and shoulders.

Mimi stretched out on her stomach on a towel. She held her feet a few inches above the AstroTurf and moved her ankles in little circles.

"But why would you do it?" Clio asked after a few minutes.

"Do what?" Mimi's eyes were closed.

"You could have given him one of those children's books that make it look like an apple cut in half."

"I couldn't actually see him or Dr. Snowie, you know, with the sheet over my legs, just hear them. Snowie said, 'Now this is the this, and this is the that,' and Tommy said, 'Uh-huh, uh-huh.' "

"It's so actorish. All of you performing."

"I don't think so," Mimi said. She was offended. "I wouldn't have told you at all if I thought you'd get mad."

"I'm not mad," Clio said, astonished.

Mimi opened her eyes. "I won't tell you anything anymore if you make it mean something."

Clio's conversation with Mimi did not convince her to take Tommy to the gynecologist and, if anything, it filled her with resolve not to go again to the set. Perhaps unwisely, she did ask Tommy if it were true that Billy Michael had thrown a television through his trailer window while he watched a play-off game and a girl held his penis in her mouth.

"Who told you that?" he shouted.

She was startled when he began to yell so suddenly, not even bothering to explain himself.

"That fucking Mimi! What a fucking troublemaker! She always was a liar."

"What does it matter who told me?"

"Well, it's not true, that's what matters, and I want you on the set to see for yourself. Tomorrow."

"Why would my coming to the set mean it wasn't true?" she asked stubbornly.

"Be there, that's all. I'm not interested in your fucking logic."

Clio sat alone in Tommy's trailer, looking out a window that had no glass in it. Mimi had told her that the actress in the movie, Tracy Bond, refused to use the foot pump to flush the toilet in her trailer. Every day after lunch, the teamster who drove and maintained the trailer would quit. Another teamster would be sent over by the union. He would last a few days until, infuriated by the humiliation of having to flush Miss Bond's toilet, he, too, would quit. There had been twelve drivers in two weeks.

Clio watched the new driver. He sat in an aluminum beach chair just outside the circle of lights and read a newspaper.

Tommy jumped up the stairs and came inside the trailer. There was a new television on the kitchenette counter.

A man put his head through the open door. "Want anything, kid?"

"Want anything?" Tommy asked Clio.

She hesitated.

"He has anything you want. Soda, chewing gum, Hershey bars, rubbers."

When she smiled, Tommy said, "That's his job, babe."

As she turned to thank the man, her hand slid between a seat cushion and the back of the couch. She gasped as she cut her finger on a thin piece of glass that had fallen behind the cushion.

"You sure? I have to go back to work in a sec," Tommy said, studying a page of dialogue. "Come and watch this time."

For a long time after, Clio wondered why she had not held out her hand, the second finger bleeding, instead of hiding it behind her back as if she were the one who should be ashamed.

She left during the next take.

She had gone down to the kitchen for a bottle of spring water, and when his voice came out of the darkness, she jumped in surprise. He walked slowly into the dining room. It was as if he'd been waiting for her.

"You held up the fucking shot."

"I cut my finger."

"Good reason. Real good. My own wife holds up the shot."

There was an album cover lying on the dining table. She picked it up and skimmed it gracefully across the room at him. It hit him in the face.

"I couldn't have done that if I'd tried," she said.

He came quickly around the table, holding his forehead. "Don't you ever do that again," he said, jerking her arm into the air. "Do you hear me?" He was flushed and his breath came in small gasps.

He held her wrist tightly and the sleeve of her kimono slipped over her shoulder. Her wrist burned and her hand grew numb, but she gave no sign that he was hurting her. She wanted him to release her, but she feared that if she let him see that, he would only hold her more tightly. She might have asked politely, but she was wary. The years of guerrilla training she had undergone in her struggle with Burta had left her mistrustful of the possibility of fair treatment.

Her stillness infuriated and aroused him. He bent her wrist awkwardly behind her neck and brought her face to him. He pressed his teeth into her mouth, biting her lip. When she would not open her mouth, even in pain, he reached up and ripped the kimono from her shoulders.

She tried to turn away, to hide her face in her shoulder, but he held her tightly by the chin and forced her to look at him. He put her finger, the one that had been cut, into his mouth.

He moved her wet finger across her bare stomach, following its path with his mouth. Her blood mixed with his saliva, until his mouth was at last on her own lost fingers, pushed inside of her, and she was moaning with fury.

Clio knew better after that night than to ask again whether Billy Michael had thrown a television set through the window of Tommy's trailer. She knew the answer. That she had cut her finger on a piece of glass that had fallen from a broken window was not in itself proof that Tommy was lying, but she knew that the story about the girl was true.

She sat on the suede sofa and looked around at the stucco walls of Tommy's house, at the paintings of cowboys and metal sculptures of sea gulls, and was at last surprised that she was there, surprised that her heedless flight had led her to Tommy Haywood and his house in the Malibu hills. I am no longer swimming out of the current, she thought. I am in it now. But, like my grandfather who drowned one winter evening of rapture of the deep, I am swimming in the wrong direction.

She jumped up to find Judy, to ask her to take a walk with her. Judy did not think a climb through dry fields was a very good way to spend her time and Clio could see that she did not want to go with her. "I'm doing this for you, Clio," she said. She brought along her steno pad and pen.

As they walked up the steep macadam driveway, Judy said, "Lou Gordon's new Rottweiler puppy got killed last week by coyotes. It just disappeared. He called to see if we'd seen any around the pool, looking for water."

"How did he know coyotes killed the dog?"

Judy shrugged. "He was mad because the dog was so expensive. He said if he'd known that coyotes were going to eat a thousand-dollar dog, he'd have just gone to the pound." She stopped to write something in her notebook and Clio waited patiently. When she finished, they turned onto a side road that led to a grove of pepper trees. There was a small camp of mobile homes near the trees. The trailers looked as if they'd been there for years, dried leaves and branches banked against the scalloped metal borders of each small plot. If they took the side road, they'd reach the pepper trees without having to go through the camp.

"Are there ever girls here when I'm away?" Clio asked. She looked at the flat ocean far below them, embarrassed by her question. There was a smell of salt, and wild mustard.

"Girls?"

"When I'm with Mimi. When I'm not here."

"Sometimes there are girls here," Judy said hesitantly, "but you know them—Jumbo's girlfriend comes with him, and C.Z.'s wife."

"Did you ever go out with Tommy?" Clio pulled a long stalk of mustard flowers through her fingers, and her hand was suddenly full of tiny yellow petals. "You know, like Mimi." She ate some of the flowers. "You seem to know his ways. Much better than I do, I think."

"He's my brother," Judy said.

Clio stopped in the road to gaze at the petals as thin as wet rice paper in her hand. The air smelled like hot tar. Waves of heat rose in oily streams around them. She tried to shake the petals from her palm.

"I never knew whether he told you or not."

Clio's palms were moist and the petals stuck to her skin. "Why do you do it?" she asked.

"He likes me to be nearby."

"No. I don't mean that."

"If I'd stayed at home, I'd be working in a submarine shop."

"Submarine shop?"

"Making those long sandwiches. At least here I get to meet people. It's never cold. I get to go swimming in a pool whenever I want."

"That is why people live in California."

"It's better than what they had."

"Why is it a secret?"

"A secret?"

"Yes."

"It isn't a secret, really. He just doesn't think about it. It doesn't mean anything to him." She hesitated. "Maybe you better not let on you know, if he didn't tell you. Maybe he doesn't want you to know. He might be mad."

"I think that is called a secret."

Judy pulled the top from the pen and ran it along the metal spiral of the steno pad. It made a bright clicking sound and the insects singing in the field suddenly fell silent.

"Do you think he'd fire me?"

"Oh," Clio said, furious, "I don't know." She began to walk.

"I was surprised when he married you," Judy said, catching up with her. "He never tells me these sort of things, but he said you were quiet. You knew how to behave. He's not used to that. And it was time for him to get married. For his career, I mean. Everyone thought it was a good idea. You had class, he said. And you weren't after him because of who he was. You were the first one who wasn't. He didn't know anyone like you before." She was out of breath.

"I wasn't after him," Clio said, stopping to look at her. "I was trying to get away."

"Away? Away from what?"

Clio saw the sudden glint of a satellite dish in the trailer camp and it was blinding for a moment. She put her hands to her eyes. "From home. Like you." She turned and started down the mountain.

"Are you mad at me?" Judy asked, following her. "I don't know anyone like you, either."

"I think you should find another job. We both should."

"You do?"

"No more Tucks boxes."

"You know, I used to be embarrassed to buy them. In case the checkout girl thought they were for me! Can you imagine! I know it's silly, but I was. And now she just pulls a box off the shelf every morning and puts it on the counter. I'm not embarrassed anymore. I've learned something in this job. I could ask for anything now."

Clio told Tommy that she wanted to move into town.

"You must be joking, hon. What's wrong with here?"

"I mean by myself."

He exhaled in exasperation and rested a barbell heavily across his chest. He was lying on the blue carpet, a towel around his waist, working with a new set of weights. Clio noticed for the first time that the carpet was the same color as his eyes. She wondered if he had picked the carpet to match his eyes.

He grunted as he lifted the barbell from his chest. "This isn't like you, babe."

"I wish you wouldn't call me that."

"Call you what?" He did ten quick sit-ups.

"It wouldn't make any difference to you whether I were here or not."

"Come here." He gestured to her to come to him.

"I don't mind not making a difference," she said. "I just don't want to not make a difference with you."

"You been smoking dope again with Mimi?"

"No."

"Come here." He pulled off the towel and threw it onto the bed. He was naked, his legs bent at the knee. He took his penis in his hand.

"How long have we been married?" he asked. "Look, I'm insulated enough as it is. It's one of the drawbacks of this business, but it's a trade I'm happy to make. I can't leave the fucking house. I get mobbed. My home is everything to me."

"Don't you mean isolated?"

He frowned.

"Not insulated. Walls are insulated," she said.

"This an English class?"

"I am trying to understand exactly what you mean." She looked away, ashamed by her lie. She realized for the first time that she was afraid of him.

"Look, I like having you with me. I actually can be around you. I knew it the first time we were together and I don't know things very often."

She smiled.

"I haven't been around women too much," he said, encouraged by her smile. He moved his penis idly in his hand. "You're like a buddy, except not."

"Perhaps I'll go away for a little while," she said quietly. "Not to Los Angeles. Would you mind that?"

He sighed loudly. "You don't get it, do you? You're coming with me to Morocco. It's all arranged." He put his arms over his head and stretched, showing her his erection.

"A deal is a deal." He winked at her. "By the way, we've been married six months, babe."

"Or, as you would say, a deal is sort of a deal." She walked to the door.

"Whatever." He stretched again and reached for the barbell.

For a moment, she wondered if he were going to lift it with his penis. She imagined the bar falling across him, falling against his throat and killing him. She was ashamed of her cowardice—not the cowardice of wishing his death, but the inability to say what it was that she meant, what it was that she wanted.

Mimi was very jealous. She had hoped to go on location, too, but Billy Michael had promised his wife a trip to Africa. "It isn't even Africa," Mimi said bitterly to Clio. "She thinks she's going to see elephants and stuff. Lions. She's not going to be very fucking happy when she realizes it's not Africa."

They were sitting by the pool. There had been brush fires in the hills and the air was heavy with smoke. Clio was reading a guidebook to Morocco and she held it up so that Mimi could see the continent on the cover.

"I mean not Africa-Africa!" Mimi said irritably. She was eating a taco. "You've never been, so you don't know! Location is this really sexy summer camp, except there are no rules. You're treated like a king. Sorry," she said, "like kings and queens. It's better than that other thing. You know, Nirvana."

It was not only unlikely that new friends would continue to see each other once the movie was finished, Mimi explained, or that lovers would continue their luxuriant deceptions when they returned home, it was unappealing. Being on location was thrilling just because it was temporary. It was a return to an imagined adolescence, except that you had money. There were no parents. Often, if you were lucky, there were no wives or husbands.

"Don't tell Tommy that I've been seeing Billy Michael. Promise not to tell. On Tommy's mother's grave."

Mimi had asked Tommy to take her to Morocco as his assistant and he had refused, so she especially did not want him to know about Billy. "Of course, he's so fucking dim, he still wouldn't figure it out," she said to Clio. "He thinks I actually wanted to work for him."

"This isn't like you," Clio said. "To care what Tommy thinks." She sneezed.

"Well, it's to protect you, so don't complain." Pieces of cheese and lettuce fell from the taco onto Mimi's knees and she brushed the food onto the AstroTurf.

Clio was distracted for a moment by the beauty of color, the bright orange cheese on the plastic grass, and the pale green of a piece of lettuce lying across Mimi's big toe, the nail painted fire-engine red. "Me? Well, thank you very much."

"Haven't you ever noticed what happens when your man discovers that your best girlfriend has a lover? He freaks. If you knew that Billy Michael was sleeping with someone, you wouldn't assume that Tommy was going to rush out and find someone to fuck, right? But Tommy would start suspecting you if he knew that I was fucking Billy."

"That makes sense."

Mimi put down the taco. "How can you be so dumb? This is why they get nervous when women have lunch together." She lowered her voice. "They're convinced we're talking about their dicks. They *wish* we were talking about their dicks."

She put her legs in the pool. "See, I'm like Tommy. No family, thank you very much. Oh, I have a sister somewhere. Alaska, I think. My father was one of those merchant-seaman Communists. He was in Malaysia or some fucking place and he was walking down this deserted beach and he heard someone calling from way up on a bluff. It was a man's voice. 'Do you speak English?' the voice shouted and my father shouted back yes. Then the voice yelled, 'Do you play bridge?' My father stayed eight years. Meanwhile, I was sleeping on a pullout couch at my bad aunt's in Detroit."

"Do *you* play bridge?" Clio asked. "I've been looking for a fourth. Actually, for a second and third as well."

Mimi kicked water at her. "You look like the type who would play bridge. How many times do I have to tell you? You have to be tough with men. My father had no one to boss him. You have to give them rules. You know, 'Home by eleven.' 'Don't desert your kids.' It's actually kind of amazing when you think of it, but ball-breaking works."

"My brother, Dix, says that rules are meant to be broken. That's why they're called rules."

"You sure he doesn't mean balls? Look, you don't know how to handle a man, Clio. I've been meaning to talk to you about this." Mimi wiggled her fingers in the direction of her margarita and Clio handed it to her. "You don't even try to do it and that's a big mistake."

"Do what?"

"Look, I say to Billy when we're in bed that he can only touch my legs. My legs and my ass and that's it. And then I just lie there naked with my back to him and it drives him completely nuts."

"Of course it would."

"Clio! He likes it."

Clio shook her head. "We have to deduce a general principle from Billy Michael's behavior?"

"You ask Tommy. I give you permission. Only don't say it's me," she quickly added. "Pretend you have this friend who told you. You'll see."

"I don't want to ask Tommy."

"You're wrong, Clio. I know about these things. This is not your area." She turned toward the house and yelled, "Is Tommy home?" She looked back at Clio. "They wrapped early today." She called again. "Tommy!"

Tommy came out of the house. He was wearing a bathing suit and running shoes and wristbands. He had oil on his back and chest, and the definition of muscle on his chest and stomach made Clio think of the ridges in a steak platter. He looked very handsome and it made her smile.

"Hi, babe," he said to her. "I was sort of looking for you. Do you think we can play tennis with this smoke?" He put out his palm as if testing for rain.

"We were talking about someone you know," Mimi said quickly. "Remember that girl who was a friend of Judy's?" she asked, turning to Clio.

Clio frowned, hoping to stop her.

Tommy flipped his racket restlessly from hand to hand. He was not very interested. A small towel was tucked into the waist of his bathing suit.

"Clio and I were just talking about her," Mimi went on. "She has this boyfriend and she's really strict with him, right? She'll only let him touch her in certain places. On certain days. And she means it. Like Mondays he can only screw her from behind, or sometimes she'll only let him use his mouth. She changes the rules all the time, but she's strict. Sometimes she won't let him kiss her, but he can do anything else. Anything."

Tommy had the sheepish expression of a boy who is pleased but hopes not to show it. To Clio's surprise, it made him interesting for a moment. She had an unexpected glimpse of his sexuality, a sexuality that Mimi would claim was predictable and a little too easily sated because he was a man. "Just remember," Mimi had said many times to

Clio, "his orgasm means it's over. Your orgasm means it's beginning."

"So, what do you think?" Mimi asked Tommy. She stood in the shallow end of the pool with her hands on her hips and looked at Clio triumphantly. "What would you do?"

He didn't know what to say.

"Come on, Tommy, commit yourself for once," Mimi said provocatively.

It was no pleasure for Clio to see him embarrassed. Mimi was trying to humiliate him, and to show Clio that she knew nothing about men. He looked at Clio with an expression that she had never seen before. She realized that it was beseechment.

"He's going to play tennis with me," she said. "But he is only permitted to use his left arm. And he has to take off one shoe. Actually, I'm going to remove it with my nose and put it in my underpants."

She heard him release his breath.

"Sounds sort of great," he said, spinning his racket again. "You want to watch?" he asked Mimi. Clio had given him the time that he needed and he was grateful. She glanced at him, unexpectedly shy. He winked at her.

"Maybe another day," Mimi said, angrily taking off the top of her bikini and throwing it onto the deck.

"Oh, I almost forgot." Tommy grinned and reached out to pat Mimi on the head with his racket. "Billy will be at your apartment after rushes. Have the daiquiris made and the Jacuzzi on, he said."

"Fuck you," Mimi said, lowering herself into the water. She swam underwater across the pool.

"What'd I do?" he asked Clio.

Clio shook her head, unable to explain. "I'll get my racket."

"I liked that story about the girl," he said.

I n the Casablanca airport, the passengers on the plane from Los Angeles were detained by soldiers and taken to a small room. They were left to sit for hours. Clio was surprised that the soldiers did not care that Tommy was a famous American movie star, and Tommy was more surprised than anyone when the soldiers laughed at his demand to speak to the president of the country. They waited in the humid, stinking room and Tommy and Billy Michael worked on a few scenes that Tommy had always thought were underwritten. At the last minute, upon discovering that there would be no elephants, Mrs. Michael had decided not to go with them.

Clio paced back and forth, watching a man who sat both languidly and primly on top of a trunk. He was using the time to make sketches in a large notebook and he caught her glancing over his shoulder. He introduced himself. His name was Alecko Santos and he was a painter. He had a small, worn, delicate face. She was not sure, but she thought that he wore kohl around his eyes. She admired his deftness of application.

Mr. Santos invited Clio to call on him at his house in the Old City in Marrakech. Tommy came up to her as Mr. Santos was writing his name and address on a piece of dark blue paper (Majorelle blue, he later instructed her, after the French painter who'd lived in Marrakech), and Tommy frowned when she took the paper and put it carefully in her pocket. He pulled her away, cutting her off as she began to introduce Mr. Santos. "Who's the guy in the mascara?" he asked loudly.

She went to see Alecko Santos in Marrakech. He lived with a young man named Abdullah, who he said was his nephew "à la Jean Cocteau." They taught her the history of the city and took her to the good shops in the medina, and Santos introduced her to writers and painters and some of the royal family who were staying at the old palace of the Glaoui. Abdullah patiently spent hours with her in the Medersa and the Bahia.

There is not that much to see in Marrakech, Clio wrote to Emma: "It is the last big oasis before the Sahara. A mysterious, rosy city, not Mediterranean and shabbily dissolute like Tangier or oriental and aristocratic like Fès. It is African, the last Berber outpost before the Atlas Mountains fall away into the hard, dangerous south." As always, I have paid attention to my lessons, Clio thought as she read over her letter. What a good girl am I.

Santos took her to a *thé dansant* given by the minister of commerce. The minister had brought the Gipsy Kings from Marbella for the day. The Yugoslav ambassador was there, and some people from Yemen, all seemingly related. The Yemeni gentlemen were in beautiful English suits and striped dress shirts with white collars a little too pointed, a little too stiff. The women were so burdened with the weight of their afternoon jewels, and dresses encrusted with sequinned and beaded embroidery, that they had little strength to dance. One of the women, a sheika, sat next to Clio on a narrow sofa. She had just come from Paris and she was astonished when Clio admitted that she'd never been to Paris.

The reception rooms of the minister's palace were decorated in gold and white. "In the style of Versailles," the minister whispered to Clio, as if it were a confidence. When the music began, His Excellency danced in turn with each of the women. On one of his graceful passes, he asked over the head of his partner if Clio had any plans to go on to Fès, where his mother lived. His mother would be happy, he said; honored, in fact, to welcome an American film star so famous as herself.

"But I am not a film star, Your Excellency," Clio said in surprise when he stopped before her and lowered his exhausted partner into a small gilt armchair. Clio worried that the woman would not fit into the small chair. When the woman sat down, some of the sequins on her dress broke away and rolled across the marble floor.

The minister smiled at Clio knowingly. "My dear." He rocked on his feet, his hands in his white cashmere jacket. "You are from Hollywood, no?"

The sheika smiled at him, and nodded her beautiful head.

"It's my husband who is the movie star. Tommy Haywood." Clio did not know if the minister were flirting with her by pretending not to believe her or whether he really did think that she was a movie star.

"You should have told me," the sheika said to him with a pout. She turned to Clio. "Do you know Dirk Bogarde? I promise you, he is a very old friend of mine."

Clio saw Alecko Santos across the room, sitting on a tabouret, his slender legs stretched before him. He was talking to a pretty woman in a pink chiffon sari. Clio wondered if she could sit with them.

"Has he ever told you that delicious story about his dog?" the minister asked Clio. "A sheep dog, I believe."

"Who?"

"Dirk Bogarde."

"But I don't know him."

"I promise you he is in Switzerland," the sheika said. "Charming villa. It used to belong to the Begum. The first Begum." She was beginning to be a little bored with Clio. Clio had not been to Paris and she did not know her old friend.

"It is the most amusing story, really. You should get him to tell it to you. There are missing fingers and lost sheep—marvelous!" the minister said, shuddering in delight.

"Would you like more tea?" Clio asked the sheika. The tea service had been put down on a small lapis lazuli table next to Clio. She lifted the heavy silver pot and a servant wearing a little curved knife at his waist appeared as if by magic, as if she had summoned him. He took the teapot from her with a frown. The sheika pursed her lips and gave a scarcely discernible shake of her head and the genie disappeared as swiftly as he had come.

Clio was very relieved when one of the young princes, a student at Brown, asked her to dance to "My Way." Clio knew it was just the sort of thing the minister himself might say, but she did think the Gipsy Kings did the best of anyone with a bad song. The prince held her rather close and said that he was eager to take her some afternoon to his brother's stud farm, but she never heard from him again.

In the late afternoon, Clio would sit alone on the terrace of the Café de Paris, on the second floor, overlooking the

Djemma el Fna, and try for the tenth time to read the chapter "Harems and Ceremonies" in Edith Wharton's book on Morocco.

There were thousands of people in the square. The bells of the water sellers in their hats jiggling with red pom-poms, the fast beat of the drums of the snake charmers, and the raucous cries of the women selling oranges rose to her at the small metal table where she watched and listened. She thought that the harsh, bleating horn of the storytellers might have been the outriders of Idris I summoning the martyrs to paradise.

The sky slowly grew dark around her. Fires were lit in greasy charcoal braziers, and heavy blue smoke, smelling of fat and ash, bloomed haphazardly across the square. She left reluctantly just before nightfall, taking pleasure in each step of what had become her own ceremony— the payment of the small bill; the exchange of farewells with the waiter, once dismissive, now kindly; the melancholy pleas of the boys who waited in the damp tiled stairwell to beg for the Coca-Cola bottles she'd left on the table.

It was during that month in Marrakech that Clio discovered that it was possible for her to be alone. It was a tremendous thing to discover, she knew, after all those years. She had never been on her own before. She realized that she could take care of herself, even in an essentially masculine and unsympathetic culture, and this gave her courage, and happiness.

Although it was extremely hot there at the edge of the desert, Tommy liked to play tennis when he was not needed on the set. He would play with Clio on the red clay court in the hotel garden for an hour or two in the late afternoon when the day had grown a little cooler. It was one of the few times that they were alone, but play was so strenuous that they did not really have the time or the strength for much talk.

One evening after their game, they walked through the garden to the bar. Clio was out of breath. She wondered what he was thinking about; perhaps the joy of beating her. He did not like to lose, especially to wives. That she played with her old wood racket irritated him. He saw it as part of a general stubbornness in her, an adherence to things that he considered old-fashioned, like wearing white on the court, another of her habits that irked him. Although he behaved as if she were the only person left in the world who played tennis in white clothes, she understood how her habits could be irritating. She had, of course, learned to play with a wood racket, dressed in white, from Emma. Tommy liked to play in his bathing suit to keep up his tan, and although she had never objected to his costume, she had been pleased to find a card in their room requesting that guests dress in white while playing tennis at the hotel.

"I would like to live on my own when we return to Los Angeles," she said, trying to catch up with him on the narrow path. She could suddenly smell oleander.

"You need to talk to Jerry." He spoke straight ahead as he walked and Clio had trouble hearing him. "We've had this conversation before."

"Jerry?" she asked loudly. "That therapist who plays pool at the house? The one who wears an ankh?"

"What's an ankh?"

"It is a kind of torture for me, Tommy! I can't imagine, I don't imagine, that you would really mind my not being with you. It is just this idea that you have, that someone put in your head, of how you are supposed to live." For a moment, for an instant, she asked herself why it should matter so much if he did mind. It seemed very odd, even to her, that she was asking his permission to leave.

"Look, babe," he said, pausing at the steps to the bar. "I don't know what the fuck's the matter with you. Talk to Jerry or to someone else, Mimi or Judy. Jerry's an imminent psychologist." He balanced on the balls of his feet and bounced up and down. "What do you want to fuck things up for?"

"I would like to work."

He laughed. "Work?" He banged his racket on the back of a metal chair, and millions of insects jumped in the beam of the yellow terrace light. "When have you ever worked in your whole life? What would you do? What *do* you do? You write things down and you record things about dead people and you read. Big deal. You want to talk about books? You want to write down Hollywood family trees? That would be real interesting. Extinct birds? Hula dances? Look, you wouldn't be able to travel with me, like to here, if you had a job. Jobs are for people who need them, babe. I have a real job at six o'clock tomorrow morning and you want to talk about torture." He shook his head in disgust and walked into the bar. "Howdy, Hussein," she heard him say to the bartender.

She sat on the steps. There was a light breeze from the mountains, bearing the fragrance of eucalyptus. She shivered as she began to cool beneath her damp shirt. She was always exhausted after playing tennis with him, although she refused to show it. He tired her because he played as if she were another big man out there in a Speedo bathing suit. She was too stubborn to give up, even when she was so exhausted that she could barely return the ball.

She wondered if she could play him for her freedom. She wiped her face with the hem of her white shirt. Not until I've had some lessons, she thought.

. . .

Alecko Santos urged her to make the trip, two hours by car, to Essaouira, an old town on the coast. Abdullah was unable to take her, but Tommy's driver was free. She did not know him very well. He was called Mohammed, although Tommy had shortened his name to Mo. Tommy had told Mo that when the movie was finished he would take him back to Los Angeles as his driver, and Mo had believed him.

It was a fast drive through groves of olive and pine. Mohammed stopped the car so that she could buy a bottle of warm beer at a roadside stand, and she noticed that the leaves of the small trees curled into themselves with the dust and the dryness.

Outside the white walls of Essaouira, a sixteenth-century Portuguese fort rose straight from the sea. Once besieged by Barbary pirates, now besieged by lonely Atlantic gales, the fortress was abandoned. Mohammed had borrowed Tommy's Walkman and he listened to it in the car, singing loudly to Willie Nelson as Clio walked among the ruined batteries. The cannon bore the arms of Aragon and Castile. Along the esplanade were palms, tattered by the winds, and bleached mimosa.

When Clio came back to the car, she said that she would like to swim, but Mohammed shook his head.

"What do you mean?" she asked, opening the back door of the car. She shook the sand from the cuffs of her trousers.

He shrugged and said, "It's too rough. I'm in charge, anyway. Mr. Tommy told me to take care of you."

It was very cold inside the car, the air conditioning too high. She caught his handsome eyes in the rearview mirror as he pulled the Walkman headphone back onto his neck. She was tired from the heat and the journey, and angry that she had been taken in charge.

"Why aren't you in the movie?" he asked as he drove slowly through the lanes of the town.

"I'm just not," she said. "Do you mind, Mohammed, making it less cold?" She put on a sweater that she had left in the car.

"It is always cold in the desert at night. Haven't you heard that?" He leaned forward to turn down the air conditioning. "I will go to school in California," he said. "To study pharmacy."

When she did not answer, he said, "I have an uncle in San Jose."

She nodded, knowing that he was watching her in the mirror.

"I will work for Mr. Tommy and go to school at night. I will work for you, too." He looked over his shoulder to grin at her. She gazed out the window. She did not wish to encourage him.

Scattered in the fields beyond the town were big rocks, the color of new rust. They looked as if they'd fallen from Mars. Clio leaned out the window to look back at Essaouira. The old city was the color of blood in the light of the falling sun. She wondered whether she would ever return, thinking with melancholy that she would not. Warm air blew into her face. It grew dark in an instant and the fort was suddenly silhouetted behind them, now the color of black grapes. Her mouth and nose were dry with dust and salt. She slowly rolled up the window.

They reached a crossroad and Mohammed stopped the car. Inside one of the small mud houses, a man held a child. It seemed to Clio that the night revealed rather than concealed. A candle had allowed her to see, for a moment, the domestic life of a stranger, and it made her happy again.

He passed back an orange to her and she peeled it and ate it. The smell of it was strong and fresh in the closed car. They rode in silence. Perhaps Mohammed was tired, too. He'd told her that he'd never been to Essaouira.

She felt the car begin to slow. Mohammed stopped at a shuttered tourist stand and lifted himself stiffly from the car. He stood with one leg in the road, and looked up and down, his hands on his head.

"We're lost?" she asked, leaning over the front seat.

"Not certainly," he said cheerfully, jumping back into the car. As he moved the car in a tight circle, the steering wheel made a thumping sound.

"I should have been straight at the village," he said. His eyes found her in the mirror. "*Je suis désolé*. Now we shall be late for the celebration party."

She had forgotten about the party. Or perhaps not forgotten, as she had picked that very day to make her journey to Essaouira.

There had been a young film student, Rob, assigned to the picture as a favor to his father, the head of the studio. Tommy and Billy Michael had not known what to do with Rob until, on the plane to Marrakech, Billy had said to the boy, "Listen, pal, you're the only one who can do this, so don't let us down: you're going to have to be the mensch who finds the donkey who screws the girl."

Clio had seen Rob two or three times as he rushed down the narrow dirt alleys of the *souk*. She wondered if she should tell him the truth, that the job of finding the donkey was only a trick to keep him from the set, and she did stop him once, in the lemon market. She had to pull his sleeve to get his attention, so feverishly was he questioning an old woman. "I'm working on it!" he had said quickly. "I'm almost there. Wednesday night," and he had rushed off, a band of street boys running after him.

And he had done it. It wasn't a joke, after all. Clio had never really thought that he would be able to arrange such a thing, not because such entertainments were not available, or because she disapproved, but because he did not seem sufficiently competent. The crew was really up for it, Tommy told her; even if it had started as a joke.

As the car moved swiftly through the dark countryside, she wondered if bestiality had been a favorite entertainment of the Castilian mercenaries who once defended the Portuguese fort. Perhaps the winding streets of Essaouira had echoed with the raucous shouts of lonely soldiers, far from home, as the animals and slave women were brought into the courtyard. She smiled in the dark: *"Je m'amuse."*

"I did not know that we would be returning so late," she said to Mohammed.

"It is the end of the wonderful movie, the time to say good-bye and thank you to many new and wonderful friends. It is my fault for being lost."

She hesitated. "I'm not sure that I want to see the entertainment that has been arranged."

"But I know the man who has made this celebration! He is my mother's cousin's husband. He is famous for the fireworks. It will be *un spectacle*! I am sorry to miss it. You are sorry to miss it, I may assure you." He leaned forward and looked through the windshield as if hoping to see Catherine wheels spinning over the Atlas Mountains.

"I thought there was something else. Not fireworks." She paused. "A donkey."

"Perhaps. I don't know. I don't think so." He shrugged and increased their speed, anxious then to get back.

It was midnight before they drove through the arched red-burnt gates of Marrakech. She stepped from the car in front of the hotel. He jumped out and they shook hands and she apologized for causing them to miss the celebration. He, too, apologized and she assured him truthfully that it was not his fault.

She ordered mint tea and asked that it be brought to her in the garden. She did not want to see her husband. Every night before bed, he sat at the art deco dressing table and read the next day's lines into the mirror. He asked her to read the part of Nancy Drover, the beautiful Red Cross nurse played by Tracy Bond. He then liked to make love, as he believed that sexual intercourse made him look refreshed for the camera.

She sat deep in the empty garden beneath the trees laid out four hundred years earlier by the Saadian kings and listened to the thousands of swallows who lived in the bougainvillea rustle irritably in crowded sleep. The air was cool; full of the scent of roses and the honeysuckle that climbed the desiccated pink mud walls of the Old City.

A waiter in a white tunic brought the tea to her on a silver tray. The teapot was silver, too, and the tray and the teapot and the boy's buttons all shone brightly in the darkness. She watched him come across the garden, shining as he found his way among the trees.

In the hotel, men and women prepared for sleep, their sudden thin shadows slanting on the walls of the lighted rooms. The figures leaned on the balconies, smoking peacefully, and looked out into the dark garden, turning now and then to speak softly to someone in the room behind them. Two men rested against one another, their elbows on the parapet, and kissed.

There were voices in the garden, American voices. A man and a woman. People from the movie, Clio thought; returning from the party. The voices were soft. It was nice to hear her language spoken without effort.

Clio recognized the voice of the costume designer. "They got the donkey! But they did it all wrong!" Clio heard her say. "They did it all wrong!" The woman sounded as if she were weeping. A man and woman came into view at the end of a path. The man took the woman's elbow and they went hurriedly up the marble steps into the hotel.

Clio sat in the garden all night.

C lio wrote to Emma from Marrakech that they were going on to the south, to Taroudant and Ouarzazate. Clio thought that they would be in Honolulu in April for a short visit. She sent Emma a silver necklace, a hundred years old, in the shape of a snake. It was an open circle without a clasp. Emma would have to force it on like the Bedouin women who wore it before her, fitting her neck between the snake's silver tongue and its smooth tapering tail.

Emma was wearing the Berber necklace the evening she came across the lawn at Hale Moku, frowning as she tried to make out the face of a woman sitting on the lanai with Mabel and Tadashi.

As the woman rose awkwardly to greet Emma, she swayed against the bamboo orchids. "It's a funny story, really," Clio said quickly. She reached down to still the trembling orchids, clutching them as if they could, in their frail impartiality, steady her. "I mean odd, not amusing."

Emma stared at her. Clio's eyes were swollen and flooded with blood. A suture across her cheek looked as if it would break open if she smiled. Flakes of red pepper seemed to float in the hair at her temple, and Emma realized with a shock that it was not pepper, but dried blood. She leaned

over to kiss Clio, but stopped herself, afraid that she might
hurt her. She quickly brushed the side of Clio's head with
her mouth, unable to keep from wincing.

"Has the *Lurline* docked yet from San Francisco?" Mabel
asked impatiently. She held a *pikake* lei in her lap. As
always, Mabel was expecting her college friend from Mills,
Miss Melanie L. Simpson. Mabel had not seen her since
1921, when Miss Simpson attended Mabel at her wedding.
Clio often wondered if Miss Simpson were still alive. The
Lurline, she knew, had not sailed in many years.

"It has not arrived, Grandmother," Clio said. Although
I have only been home a few hours, she thought, I am
again caught in the efficacious lies of the past. She looked
at Tadashi in acknowledgement of their old complicity,
but Tadashi, used to such things, had turned away with a
handful of dried leaves she'd plucked from Mabel's hairnet.

"What a pity," Mabel said sadly to Clio. She was very
disappointed. "What will we do with Miss Simpson's lei?"
Mabel seemed not to remember that Clio had been away.
"Clio, child, you wear it." She shook the garland of ivory-
colored jasmine buds in Clio's direction. "*Pikake* is Melanie
Simpson's favorite flower," she said. "She claims she can
dream the smell of it. Just dream it up!"

Clio took the lei from her grandmother but did not put
it around her neck.

"Thank you, girl," Mabel said quietly. She held out a
hand to touch Clio's face. She quickly stepped aside, and
Mabel's hand glanced across Clio's neck.

"We're going to the seawall, Mother. Will you excuse
us?" Emma asked. "The sun is going down."

"I know that!" Mabel said furiously. "Mr. Kageshiro is
coming to feed the orchids!"

My grandmother is that very interesting thing, Clio
thought. An unreliable narrator. She tells lies.

"Do you hear?" Mabel shouted. "He is on his way!"

But Clio and Emma had already started across the lawn and could pretend that they had not heard her.

They sat with their legs hanging over the side of the seawall. Clio lay the *pikake* on the grass. The waves splashed over their bare feet. Clio had pulled her skirt around her waist so that she could sit, and swing her legs, and the white triangle between her thighs reminded her suddenly of girlhood. I have not worn white cotton underpants in some time, she thought. Not since Stant's.

"This is an evening for the moon goddess, Hina," Emma said, looking across the ocean. "Her shadow is on the water. She is hunting her favorite delicacy, the *kala* fish. I myself have seen it."

Their legs were soon wet in the breaking waves and the spray. Clio watched the green reef disappear in the rising tide. The ocean lay unbroken to the horizon. Rain fell far at sea, moving quickly to the west in faint gray sheets, like ghosts fleeing the light.

"What happened to you, Clio?"

"I think salt water will help. Healing, I mean. To swim in. Not to drink. Not yet." She put her hands to her face. "It really does hurt to laugh. I always thought it was just an expression."

Tadashi came across the lawn with a tray. She tilted forward precariously, as if she were about to fall over onto the grass.

"I used to wonder if Japanese women walked that way out of custom," Clio said as she watched her. "The toes, turned inward, suggest a bashful obsequiousness, don't you think? They may have taken it, as they took many things, from the Chinese; the walk of women with suppurating feet. Ritual bridles. Ritual brides. Or perhaps, less romantically, their kimonos make it difficult to walk." Clio realized that she was trembling.

Tadashi gave her a glass of iced tea, made with fresh guava juice, and mint from her sister's garden in Manoa Valley. Clio drank down the tea without pause. Tadashi placed a bowl of lichees on the grass, then sat back on her heels and smoothed her kimono over her knees.

"Do you remember when Grandmother was first blind?" Clio asked, laying her empty glass on its side. Her hands were shaking. Tadashi leaned forward to pick up the glass and set it on the tray. "She insisted on doing all the things she'd done before, like gardening or walking on the reef at low tide, only she couldn't see. She really couldn't see at all. So she would cut off all the orchid buds by mistake and walk on the reef with her eyes wide open, arms outstretched, until she would step into a hole in the coral and disappear. I would think, There she goes again, and I would swim out to get her. She was on her way to Tahiti."

"She also believes that it is June of 1888," said Emma. "And why not."

Clio thought about it, as if Emma really were asking why her old and incontinent mother should believe in the present.

"I was frightened of her with her cloudy white eyes, but I couldn't let her drown on the reef just because she believed that she could see." Clio could feel herself becoming a little hysterical. "That is what I did, too, when I married and went away. I convinced myself that I could see."

"My mother," Emma said, trying to calm her, "believes that she was fishing and gossiping with her Great-Aunt Estelle yesterday. You remember, Estelle claimed she'd been the mistress of Robert Louis Stevenson. In fact, my mother thinks that Mr. Stevenson is coming to lunch today.

She has even asked Tadashi to make the sweet rice balls with fish that Mr. Stevenson is said to have liked so much. You've come just in time, Clio."

Behind them, Tadashi rose, unsteady with age, and tiptoed across the lawn to the cottage. Clio watched as she struggled with the salt-swollen door of the cottage and went inside. She reappeared a few minutes later, dragging the *lau hala* floor mats after her. She went back inside. Menus from the old dining room at the Royal Hawaiian Hotel in Waikiki suddenly flew out the cottage door.

Tadashi stood in the doorway and recklessly skimmed wooden bowls and palm fans onto the lawn as if she'd been waiting for just such an excuse to loot the cottage. Clio smiled. Tadashi hadn't much reverence for the things that Emma had spent her life trying to save.

"How did this happen to you, Clio? Who did this?" Emma asked again.

The garden was clamorous with birds and insects. "I'm not sure it's possible for me to live this way. Like a ghost," Clio said as she picked up the lei of jasmine flowers and put it around her neck. "Do you think this is what Grandmother has done, in her way? Escaped through make-believe? My mother, too. Mother often spoke about the cane fields of Hale Moku and the cattle rides with the *paniolos*, but the minute, the very second, she was able to get away, she left it all."

"Your mother was really not like any of us," Emma said. "She had skills. Of a sort. All she needed, really."

"Is that what you call it? Skills?"

"Perhaps I am being harsh. I don't think your mother ever liked Hale Moku very much." She hesitated. "To tell you the truth, I couldn't abide her."

Clio smiled. "I know."

"I suppose you do," Emma said.

The storm at sea had moved to the west (or to the East,

as Clio used to insist when she was a child), toward Japan. She rose, groaning with the stiffness of her knees, and pulled down her skirt. As she leaned over to kiss Emma, the lei fell across her face. The scent of the *pikake* was very strong and her head throbbed with the closer fragrance of it.

"You're safe here with me," Emma said. "You know that."

Clio walked onto the lawn, holding her side. The birds, light-boned and nervous, spun around her in the last light, diving for insects. "I was very frightened," she said into the trees. "Not an island girl."

Clio was happy living with the three women in the big house by the ocean. Emma brought her poultices of *limu* to heal the wounds on her face. She did not question her again, and Clio was grateful. Her broken rib began to mend on its own, as they do, and she was not in so much pain. The bruises on her face were less violently colored, but bright blood still floated in her eyes and there was a pink line along her cheekbone where the stitches had begun to dissolve. The salt and the *limu* and the sun healed her.

Clio sat with Mabel on the lanai, Mabel's wheelchair turned so that she could better feel the warm wind from Kona, blowing from the southeast. Clio ate Japanese candy, putting the paper wrappings in her pocket, and listened to the orchids scratching in their shallow pots.

Clio knew that her father and stepmother would learn that she was at Hale Moku, even though she had not ventured very far from her grandmother's garden. She wondered if she should call on them. They would not torment her, they no longer could do that, but she was not eager to see them. She knew that should the fragile and artificial civility that made their occasional meetings just bearable ever be lost, the terror of her childhood and the fury that she felt because of that casual terror would overwhelm her.

"Have you recovered?" Mabel asked.

Clio was surprised. Mabel had never spoken of Clio's injury.

"I myself have not been well," Mabel said confidingly, not waiting for Clio's answer. "As perhaps you are aware, I suffer from *kadami no yoru*, an inconvenient attachment to my daughter Emma. Inconvenient because it hinders my path to perfection. It is a Buddhist belief, this 'darkness of the heart,' and it pains me, Clio." She arranged the hem of her muumuu over her bare feet.

"I'm not sure we could bear it if you were any more perfect," Clio said, relieved that Mabel had so quickly lost interest in her.

"Don't mock me," Mabel said quickly. "You don't yet know what it means to be attached to this earth. Don't make the mistake of imagining that experience is something available to everyone. Experience is a luxury." She turned toward the ocean and blinked her white eyes. "We used to swim the horses here," she said, leaning to smell the salt in the air. "Have we any horses left?" Mabel was one of the last old people to speak Pidgin with an antiquated accent, passed down from the Yankee missionaries and Irish cabin boys who were her ancestors.

Before Clio could answer, she said in irritation, "Of course we have no horses! You know nothing, Clio!" Her contorted hand fished impatiently in a quart jar on her lap, searching for sour cherries, as she urinated through the webbing of her chair. *"Anata no atama wo watashi no, mata ni shikkari hasami,"* she said.

Clio recognized the poem. It was in one of the anthologies of *waka* that she often read to Mabel: *I hold your head tight between my thighs and press.*

Clio didn't feel as if she did know very much, and she wondered if perhaps her grandmother were correct; perhaps she knew nothing. It was a self-pitying, even sentimental idea, Clio knew, and she went to fill a watering can to rinse off the lanai.

John Lynott and his wife, Burta Yamada, lived in Nuʻuanu Valley in a large stone house that Clio's mother had inherited from her first husband, Kimo Danforth. Clio's mother had never lived in the house, preferring the hot days and nights of the coastal plain. Queen Emma had built her summer palace in cool Nuʻuanu, and at the cliffs of the Pali, Kamehameha I had pushed his last opponents into the ravine to finally unite the islands under one king. Clio's ancestors used to move to Nu'uanu in the summer just to sleep through the night, lulled by the rain and the mist pluming off the mountains.

There was a waterfall in the back of the garden. Clio could tell how heavily it had rained in the night by the sound of the stream each morning. She had fished from its muddy sides for crayfish, using the spines of tree ferns. For many years after she left Nuʻuanu, it had been hard for Clio to sleep without the sound of the stream, without the thrumming of rain on the tin roof and on the swaying stalks of ginger and furled red hibiscus. She had missed the sound of rainwater sliding plumply, reluctantly, into the folds of the gardenia. She had missed the low song of the mourning doves in their gray habits, moving along the dark-leaved paths like nuns. She had missed the smell of vegetable decay and wet black wood.

As a child, Clio had understood that her mother, Kitty, and her father had little interest in her. But she also believed, mistakenly, in the child's confusion of act and will, that it was she who had somehow caused the people in whose care she lay to turn away from her.

She had found refuge in the rain forest. Only there did she have form and substance. On the damp, aromatic banks, under the dripping vines, sitting among the trees at night, she became visible to herself. She had arms and legs; she could feel them. Hands. She became invisible the moment that she left the forest. Until the day that she left Nu'uanu, the bottoms of her feet, wrinkled and white from the dampness of the forest paths, were proof, had she known it, that she did exist, after all.

Her proud, bewildered refusal to explain to Burta just how she'd lost her new pen made Clio seem sullen and stupid. She knew that her inability to defend herself allowed Burta to treat her with more contempt than she would have shown a child who could defend herself, who could justify a melancholy but harmless existence, but Clio could not help herself. Because Clio found it almost impossible to speak in the presence of her stepmother and father, Burta Yamada was able to convince Clio's father that there was something wrong, something backward and perhaps even damaged, about Clio. And because Clio was powerless to prove Burta wrong, her father really did lose sight of her.

John Lynott never once heard Clio whistle through her front teeth so piercingly loud that she could be heard a quarter of a mile away. He never saw her take apart the engine of a car and put it together again. He did not know that she could string a large hunting bow, and he would not have believed it had he been told. Clio really could do these things. She had learned them in hope of being admitted to the Squids, a club formed one summer by her brother, Dix, and his rough, handsome friends. She had learned these things in the hope of becoming a boy.

The Squids had understood that while it would be unfair

to forbid Clio membership, they could set her tasks so difficult to accomplish, one after another, that they would all be old before she fulfilled her membership requirements. They were as untiring in their creation of tasks as Clio was in the execution of them. Once she'd finally finished assembling the ham radio they needed for the clubhouse, they gave her the task of mending the big net that had washed up at the point. When she had repaired the net, having learned from an old-time fisherman how to weave the difficult knots, they told her she would have to throw the giant boomerang.

She wanted to be in the club because it would give her companionship during the long summer days; even though the Squids' motto, To Poke Squid Forever, was a local expression that referred to the female body and what they hoped to do to it. She had learned how to whistle like a longshoreman in the hope of loitering around the clubhouse with Dix and his friends, smoking Kools and eating Fritos, and she had felt lucky even to be considered for membership.

She was on the waiting list for eight years and she didn't regret one minute of it, even though she never was inducted into the Squids, even though the boys had never intended to let her into the club, she later realized, despite the fact, or perhaps because of it, that when she eventually mastered the boomerang, she could throw it farther than any of them.

Clio stood in the sunlight in the center of the lawn, the lawn where she and Dix used to hold Love Contests, and looked at the forest with pleasure and sadness, to greet it and to thank it for remaining, despite time and the world, as she'd remembered. The smell of it made her smile with relief. She pulled a guava from a tree and bit into it. As she stood there, and plucked a worm from the center of the fruit, she had the feeling for a moment that the things that Emma had sought and that she herself had been taught to seek—the spirits of trees and springs and winds—were complicitous, more availing and more sacred than she had ever wished to admit.

Clio looked at the birdhouses nailed to the sides of the poinciana tree. There were birdhouses on the *mamane* and *plumeria* tree. The thick-waisted monkeypod tree, with its feathery seeds, had two birdhouses, one on each side. There were delicate birchbark houses made by Ojibway Indians, conical Zulu huts with thatched roofs, chalets that looked like clocks, and half-timbered Tudor-style bird manors. Burta had turned the garden into a miniature golf course. In a large blue mosaic birdbath in the shape of a pagoda, two cardinals flailed loudly as if they were fighting rather than bathing.

Burta called from the edge of the lawn. She had had an operation to make her eyes rounder and it had left her with an expression of constant surprise. Her thin black hair was pulled tightly into a ponytail, which did not lessen the effect of startlement. She held a glass of vodka, the bottom half of the glass in a knitted holder, like a tiny sock, that she called her snuggy. It kept her fingers from getting cold, or wet with condensation.

Burta had been a legal secretary in John Lynott's office. She was the widow of a fireman who had been killed on duty, not in a fire but in a firehouse accident in Eugene, Oregon, and she had wisely used her insurance and pension benefits to move to Honolulu and to put herself through business school. One Saturday evening after a round of golf, John had introduced her to Dix and Clio. Clio had stepped forward shyly, and held out her hand. Mrs. Yamada took Clio's hand in her fingertips as if to mock Clio's

politeness, and stared at her with such shrewd malevolence
that Clio understood that not only had her measure been
taken but that Burta had seen, in a matter of seconds, that
Clio would be no trouble at all. Clio could tell by the cool,
careful look that Burta gave Dix that Burta suspected Dix
might be another matter altogether. But Dix did not have
any more of a chance than Clio, even with the advantage
of his charm. Burta did not intend to be the least incon-
venienced by them. They would not get in her way, any
more than the rare trees she planned to cut down in the
garden. She could snap them in two, like *kiawe* saplings.

"Mrs. Yamada and I are going away for a few weeks,
and when we return we will be married," Lynott said,
winking at the children as he handed Burta a martini.

"Will Mrs. Yamada be living with us?" Clio asked,
confused by the wink.

Lynott had laughed, but Burta had not been amused.
She turned to him and asked, "Is she for real?"

It was, unfortunately for Clio, a reasonable question. She
wondered how Burta had discovered her secret so quickly.
Clio looked at Dix. He was winding his yo-yo so tightly
that she was sure the string would break.

"Are you for real?" Burta asked again.

"May I be excused?" Clio whispered to her father.

Burta tapped Clio's chin with her finger. "I asked you
a question, missy. Are you for real?"

"Where do you think you're going?" Lynott called as
Clio began to run. "I don't believe you've been excused,"
he shouted.

Clio did not need to glance at Burta to know that Burta
would not help her.

"What?" Lynott asked. "I can't hear you, Clio."

"May I be excused, please?" She was trembling. "And
Dix, too?"

"Dix can speak for himself," Lynott said, making himself another drink. "You didn't answer Mrs. Yamada's question."

Clio looked across at Dix, who was doing a rather good walk-the-dog. "No," she said carefully. "I don't think that I'm real." And because she believed it, she turned away from them and walked into a plate glass door.

It was Dix who picked her up, holding her under her arms, his fingers entwined with string.

"Your yo-yo," she said, reaching for it. "It stopped." She clasped the yo-yo in her hand, and fainted.

Although Clio knew that Burta could no longer harm her, the very sight of her in her plaid shorts and her red shoes, her bowlegs pale and scabbed, conjured up such memories that Clio caught her breath. She had always thought, perhaps unwisely, that it was in a practical and even in an abstract way very difficult to hate someone in person. But as she watched her stepmother standing there, she was suddenly full of doubt.

"Did the old *kamani* die?" Clio asked, coming across the lawn. The *kamani* was one of the few plants brought to Hawai'i by the mysterious Polynesians and it was thought to be very good luck to have one. She realized too late that it was an awkward greeting. It would be useless to start anew; Burta did not allow amends.

"It was fifty feet tall and filthy dirty," Burta said. "I keep cutting it and it keeps growing back."

"It would, wouldn't it," Clio said vaguely.

"Your father's not home yet. He's working on some case where two Hawaiian men got in some lighthouse and wouldn't come out. Hawaiian activists, they call themselves. As if there's anything to activate. They claim it is on sacred burial ground or something. So what? So stupid."

"Father? Or the boys?"

Burta squinted at Clio over the top of her glass. The ice slid noisily to the bottom of the glass as she slowly lowered her hand. Pre-Burta, as Dix used to say, dividing their lives into two shogunates, Clio had believed that the Japanese race was in possession of all the refinement and elegance in the world. As a girl, she had read *The Tale of Genji* as a primer of aesthetics. Clio would have learned sooner or later that there were all kinds of Japanese, but Burta had hastened her loss of innocence.

"Where are you staying?" Burta asked, taking something from under a fingernail.

"With my grandmother."

"You can stay here with us," Burta said smoothly, full of conventional propriety.

For a moment, Clio rashly considered jumping the chasm of falsehood that separated them, that had always separated them, but she stopped herself. She wished to remain separate from Burta, but she was infuriated by the vast distance between what she understood and what she could say.

"Where's Tommy?" Burta was an admirer of Clio's husband.

"I don't know," Clio said.

"You don't know? Ha! I wouldn't let that guy out of my sight."

Burta had been surprised, as she constantly said to everyone, that a movie star as famous as Tommy Haywood would be interested in her stepdaughter.

"I think he is in Morocco."

"I read about it in *Parade*. You *think* he's in Morocco?"

"Yes. I think he's in Morocco."

People who did not know Burta well, people she and Lynott met in the Peninsula bar in Hong Kong or the Athens Hilton, thought that Burta was wonderful. She was so boisterous, especially for a Japanese. She could go on all night and start again at lunch the next day, they said in admiration. Clio knew that it was only bullying—whether of tired restaurant musicians who just wanted to take their tips and go home to bed, or of her husband, who just wanted to win enough flamboyant cases to run for the Senate, or of her son and stepchildren, who only wished to be left alone. Dix and Clio had spent much of their childhood slinking noiselessly on bare feet from shadow to shadow to avoid arousing Burta's attention. And if she spotted them, flattened against a wall in an attempt to pass unseen, she would scream, "What are you doing, you little sneaks, always creeping behind my back!" Of course they were.

Despite Burta's appearance, she was nervous. Her nervousness did not come from any sensitivity or delicacy of response, but from impatience. She was jumpy because she was waiting, and she did not like to wait. Because she was impervious to the needs of anyone else, she eventually got what she wanted. It is possible that, at least unconsciously, she would have preferred that Dix and Clio had perished in childhood, but since she had not been capable of actually seeing to their deaths, she had done the next most effective thing: she had behaved as if they did not exist.

That is one of the reasons why they were always hungry as children. Until Burta's son, Steamy, was born, when Clio was eight and Dix was seven, there had been no food in the house that could be considered edible by a child. There were bottled green olives, vodka and sherry, hot peppers, anchovies, pickled herring, rye *brot* from Sweden, chutneys, flat tins of kippers, many kinds of mustard and marmalade, capers, boudin, and tongue. This was deliberate on Burta's part. She boasted, rather illogically, that she liked to eat as if she were in Denmark, one of her favorite cold countries.

Fortunately, Burta was not interested in the fruit in her garden. Had she known that Dix and Clio were eating the lichee and strawberry guavas and mangoes, she would have sawed down the old trees herself. Once Dix had a rash around his mouth from eating green mangoes and he told Burta that it was impetigo he'd caught at school from one of the scholarship kids. Clio was shocked at the lie, not because of the implied prejudice but because she was sure that Burta would know that he was lying. But Burta believed him, or pretended that she did, and as punishment for getting the rash, Dix had to quit the baseball team. The scholarship students, with all their supposed contagions, tended to be good at sports.

"What's wrong with your eyes?"

"My eyes?" Clio asked, lifting a hand to her forehead.

Burta laughed. "You've become quite the actress. Must rub off when you live in Hollywood."

The gardener, an old Japanese man with white hair, was trying to pick mangoes with a homemade pole. A net bag had been tied to a metal clothes hanger wound around the top of a wooden pole. The man was so old and his eyesight so frail that it was difficult for him to hold the pole. The birds waited querulously for a mango to fall from the tree. They flew to the fallen fruit, shrieking with excitement.

Burta smiled coyly. "Well, what happened? You look bad. It takes two to tangle. Mr. Hama!" Burta yelled. When the old man did not answer, she yelled again in Japanese, and he began to whimper.

Clio threw her half-eaten guava into the bright English border. Behind her, she heard a mango fall noisily through leaves. The sound of the mango hitting the earth and splitting open was soothing in its sudden finality. "Two to tango," she said, walking to the house.

Her mother's house. Her house. On the walls of the

lanai were tableaux painted in the 1930s of natives beating *kapa*, hauling in nets of fish, planting *taro*. The men had strong jaws and powerful arms and thighs and feet. The long-haired women, wrapped in red and yellow *pareus*, pulled bananas from trees with thick, lovely arms. The eyes of the men and women were slightly bulbous and the tips of their fingers were broad and flat. In their pale and faded stillness, the figures in the murals were like ancestors moving quietly along the walls. Clio used to talk to them when she was a child. They had been good companions to her and she nodded to them.

Burta came toward the house. Mr. Hama, stiff with age, waved his arms awkwardly to frighten the birds away from the mangoes. He looked as if he were dancing in the Bon festival.

"You want a drink?" Burta shouted from the bar. The bar had beer on tap and pub signs that Burta had collected in England. She came onto the lanai and sat down, taking a puzzle book from a basket of magazines next to her chair. She opened a cloth-covered pencil box she'd made from a pattern in *Woman's Day* and chose a pen.

"Your father was going to pick up cold cuts. If you want to stay for dinner."

Emma used to say teasingly that there were certain words that island people did not use. "Cold cuts" was not an island expression. "Debutante," "cardigan," and "pasta" were mainland words. It was not that these words did not apply—nonapplicable words was another category, with entries like "basement" and "galoshes."

Burta enjoyed games of a competitive nature. She could zip right through a puzzle book. Dix and Clio used to sit in Clio's room and listen to their father and Burta argue violently over a badly played bridge hand, and Clio once

saw Lynott shove Burta for suggesting that he had sur-
reptitiously turned a backgammon cube.

Happily, Burta was adamant about working on her puz-
zles unassisted. Clio watched her. As it grew dark, the
figures on the walls disappeared. Clio whispered good night
to them.

"Steamy's been in his studio all day," Burta said. "I'm
not allowed in, of course. He's taking pictures. For some
museum."

Burta had given her son, Steamy, the rooms where Dix
and Clio had once lived, and Steamy had turned them into
a darkroom and a photography studio. He was taking
photographs of the volcano, Kilauea, in eruption, in the
hope of publishing a book. He also took pictures of Oriental
girls. Although Steamy's nude photographs were used on
calendars in Japan and Korea and Hong Kong, Burta did
not know about his lucrative sideline. Clio could not imagine any objection that Burta might have, but Steamy wished
to keep it a secret. Burta thought Steamy spent all his
time locked in his studio shooting stuffed Hawaiian honeycreepers in artificial flight. Steamy had told Clio that he
hoped to get into live filming soon. Live honeycreepers.

Burta reached to turn on a lamp. "Emma Fitzroy let
that old house of hers downtown get that way just to show
she was better than anyone else, didn't she? But, of course,
you lived there with her. I guess you thought you were
better, too."

"Better?" Clio felt a little cold. She wondered if it were
about to rain. The wind often rose before the coming of
rain, fluttering in a show of its own importance.

"She could of fixed up that old house, but she wouldn't.
No. She refused to move. She could of made a fortune
selling it. Where she gets her arrogance, I don't know. The
nerve of her. Who does she think she is? No one cares

about that old Hawaiian stuff! Who your ancestors are. Who the hell cares? It hasn't done them any good that I can see. She and your nutty grandmother used to give that luau every New Year. People talk, talk, talked about it for weeks. They used to kill a pig. Do they still have it?" Burta looked up from the puzzle book. "Everyone says she's broke, but I don't believe it. And now it's too late to sell. That house should have burned down years ago. When your grandmother ran off with the yardman."

"I'll say hello to Steamy before I go," Clio said, turning away.

"He won't see you," Burta said as she bent over to fill in the letters of a word. "He's got turtles in there."

As Clio thought he might be, Steamy was arranging a very pretty naked girl against an enlarged backdrop of Chang-kyungwon Park in Seoul. She held a branch of plastic cherry blossoms and a stone lantern.

Steamy was very happy to see Clio. He jumped up to kiss her. "This is great! This is really, really 'ono! Here, hold this!" He took the heavy lantern from the girl and handed it to Clio. "It makes her perspire and then her body gets all shiny and I have to do it again, because she can't reach certain spots and, well, it's a nightmare." He fussed around the girl.

Clio said hello, but the girl took no notice of her. Steamy blotted the backs of her knees with a tiny powder puff.

"You might invest in better supplies," Clio said, looking around.

"I'm free-lance, you know." He sounded hurt. "Here, you do it." He put the puff in Clio's hand and stopped to look at her. "I've missed you, Clio."

Clio put down the lantern and smoothed the girl's back with the greasy powder puff. "Did you steal this from

Burta's handbag?" The girl turned obediently. Clio felt as if she were basting her.

"Where's Tommy?" Steamy asked, winding film into a camera. "I thought you'd be gone for months. Years."

"You sound like your mother," Clio said.

"Thank you very much. Could you get her down on her knees, no, sitting on the back of her heels, there, legs a little apart. Just a hint. There's sweat just pouring between her bosoms."

"Breasts."

"What?"

"Not bosoms."

The girl helpfully held apart her breasts. She understands English, Clio thought.

"Oh, sorry," Steamy said. "I forget these distinctions when you're not around to remind me. You leave town for six months and I say 'bosoms' again. You see how I need you? Breasts. This is Tae Jing, Clio. These are her breasts. Her American name is Tammy." He looked again at Clio. "What's wrong with your face?"

"Car accident." She stood back to study the girl. "There. It's the best I can do."

Tammy kneeled in front of the backdrop. She was already wet with perspiration.

"Let's go swimming," Clio said.

Steamy looked up from his camera.

"If Burta asks about Tammy, you can say that she came to pick up the turtles."

He frowned, not understanding.

"The turtles that Burta thinks you're photographing."

He had forgotten his own lie.

Steamy, who grew up doing almost anything that Clio wanted him to do, short of setting Burta on fire, a request Clio always denied making, handed Tammy a towel. She looked worried. She, too, was free-lance. "That's it?" she asked angrily, speaking for the first time. "If I do swimming, I get paid extra." To their astonishment, she did a very competent backflip.

"I'm going to the forest," Clio said with a smile.

It had been no consolation to Clio that her stepmother's lack of maternal feeling had extended to her own son. Steamy was so glum and so eager to please that Clio had allowed him, little by little, to follow her into the forest. If Clio was not gratified by Burta's coldness to her own child, she was interested that her stepmother, who so clearly hated her, would entrust her son to her. But perhaps Burta did not even notice that Steamy spent his days at Clio's side.

When they climbed a slippery green hill, the air suddenly cool in a clearing of *'ōhi'a* trees, his new eyeglasses would become opaque with condensation and he would not be able to see. Clio gave him the name Steamy. By the time he began school, his friends called him Steamy, too, and he no longer minded wearing glasses.

The forest was full of the tall tree fern *hapu'u*. At the base of the stem grew a fine wool called *pulu*. When Steamy tripped one afternoon on a coralberry root and cut his forehead, Clio bandaged the cut in strands of *pulu* and they continued on their way, proud of their work.

That night, Burta screamed when she saw Steamy. There was dried blood on his T-shirt and filaments of *pulu* dangled around his face like tendons. Steamy had to put his hand to his head to remind himself of just what had happened, so effective was Clio's dressing.

Burta hit Clio with a ruler.

Steamy, suddenly terrified that he was going to die, allowed Burta to comfort him.

His shame lasted a long time, far longer than the small

white scar on his forehead. Clio explained to him that Burta would have blamed her regardless of any explanation he might have given, but since he believed himself, even early on, to be already in Clio's debt, he regretted not having had the courage to return a small portion of what he felt he owed her. He did not owe her anything, of course, because she loved him, but he always believed that he had betrayed her for one of Burta's awkward embraces.

He sneaked into Clio's room that night and sat in a corner with his back against the stone wall. There were centipedes in Nu'uanu, some of them six inches long, and he kept a constant watch for them. As Clio tried to read *The Wilder Shores of Love*, a book she'd borrowed at the school librarian's urging, Steamy scanned the floor and asked questions: But why did your own mother leave? Where did she go? Why didn't she take you? What did she look like? Is my blood different from your blood? Your blood is better, isn't it? How many women has my father married?

Clio would have been happy to answer his questions. Her hesitance to answer was not lack of interest or resentment, but ignorance. She, too, was eager to learn about the world and that smaller, more worrisome thing, the family, but she was as confused as he was about these things. That she didn't know the answers to his questions was more reassuring to Steamy than if she had been able to tell him what he wanted to know. It confirmed that they were in the same mess. When she knew, she'd tell him, and he believed her.

Years later, she would suddenly say, "Because she didn't want us, and Rory Armacost wasn't strong enough to insist." Then Steamy would have to guess which question, after all those years, Clio was finally able to answer. If they were not alone, he was not able to shout out the old question in triumph, but his expression told Clio that he, too, now understood, both the question and the answer, and she would nod in dignified alliance.

Clio could smell the resin of the turpentine trees. The sky seemed always to be just ahead of her, the color of a wet abalone shell. She had often noticed that at the moment of nightfall the wind held itself back, a considerate wind, reluctant to disturb the trees. She heard Steamy behind her on the path and she walked faster, dropping down the path to the swimming hole.

Clio took off her linen dress and lay it across the branch of a *pua kenikeni* tree. With the scent of the small white flowers, she thought of Emma.

Emma proudly claimed that she did not swim in still water because the water did not want her. She believed that the ocean was a water god that, given the slightest chance, would seize her and drag her back to her rightful place. "We come from the ocean and it has never forgiven us for escaping. It has claimed my father and my brother, McCully. When I swim, I feel the water god trying to take me, reminding me that I have forsaken him, pulling me back to him. That is why the ocean is so dangerous." Clio understood, but she liked swimming in still water for the very reason that she was not ready to be reclaimed. The ocean was implacable, but the pond bore no grudge.

She gasped as she eased herself into the cold water.

"You might have waited," Steamy said. "You always get to go first." He took off his jeans and shirt, but left on his underclothes.

He jumped noisily into the water. Tall stalks of wild ginger grew around the pond. The stalks swayed with the sudden movement of the water, and their fragrance was stronger for a moment.

He swam to her and put his hands on top of her head, trying to hold her underwater.

Trying to drown me, she thought. She pulled away from him and floated on her back and her long braid streamed behind her like a water snake.

"I haven't been here since the last time I came with you," he said, splashing her.

"I'm ashamed of you."

He stopped splashing water at her. "You've always been ashamed of me."

"Well, maybe when you feel sorry for yourself."

"It's easy for you, Clio. You somehow find a way to disappear when you don't like something. You left Nu'uanu. You left Emma." He paused. "You left me."

She turned over in the dark water, moving her legs beneath her to keep warm. She did not answer him, her mouth in the water.

"You look like a crocodile," he said. "Your eyes are so big."

"And my teeth."

"Coming to eat me."

"That is your idea of easy?"

"Coming to eat me?"

"You think that I disappear when I don't like something?"

"You're not here, are you?"

"I think it's about time that *you* left."

"Where would I go?"

She blew bubbles in the water with her nose. "It doesn't matter. It's the going."

"It's different for you, Clio. You're a woman."

"This is going to be an interesting argument, I can tell."

He spun around in the water. "Stop confusing me, Clio. What I mean is that you know things. You aren't half of anything, the way I am. Half-Japanese. Half-brother."

She watched him twirl in the water, around and around, making himself dizzy. "What is it that you are trying to say?"

He stopped. "No one ever told the truth. Or even knew the truth. Except maybe you. Maybe you knew. And you went away. I was left with Burta and our father. I find it hard to call him 'our father,' don't you? It's as if we were praying."

She laughed.

"You fell out of a mango tree when you were ten and I sneaked inside and called for help because Burta wouldn't take you to the hospital. I asked Burta about it once, why she wouldn't take you, and she had no memory of it. She said I made it up."

"As Mabel would say, you mustn't make the mistake of thinking that memory is fact."

"You're agreeing with Burta? You're actually saying to me, Steamy, your brother, your *half*-brother, that you didn't come crashing down out of the tree because you'd put a hundred mangoes in your pockets?" He was furious.

"Of course I fell out of the tree. And you saved me. You called the fire department." She smiled at him, her mouth underwater.

"She never knew that it was me who called. So I can't take too much credit for it."

"Yes, you can."

He reached for her braid. She moved away, but he caught her by the leg and pulled her to him, embracing her, his hands finding her in the cold water. He put his hands on her hips. Her skin looked very white in the water.

"Steamy!" she said, kicking him. She swam to the side and lifted herself onto a rock. She twisted her braid like a dishrag and water ran down her arms. The light was almost gone and the pond looked like a hole in the middle of the forest. She climbed over the rocks, arms outstretched to balance herself.

It was not until she was in the grove of Norfolk pine that she felt crisp again, light in the cool air, not sad, not rushing. She liked the feel of chilled skin on bone. She shivered, and remembered that when they were children they had called a shiver a cheap thrill.

Behind her, she could hear Steamy kicking and splashing furiously in the cold pond that didn't want him, that didn't want any of them.

lthough Clio had been at Hale Moku for a month, she still had not seen her father. She'd called several times, and she had been relieved when he'd said that he was too busy preparing for the trial of the Kilohana brothers to take her to lunch. The Kilohanas had trespassed on government property, claiming the land was given to their grandfather in the Great Mahele, the nineteenth-century proclamation that granted homesteads to native Hawaiians. To Clio's surprise, her father was prosecuting the Kilohana brothers, not defending them. Emma was not surprised, however. "Your father is the most practical man I've ever known. He always has been," she said. "In some shrewd way, he's figured out what will do him the most good. He's always been at the front of the backlash." She had laughed at her joke, but she was furious.

Clio finally made an appointment to see him at his office downtown. She was early, and the secretary told her that she would have to wait until Mr. Lynott was free. She was too restless to sit in one of the chairs in the big reception room. She stood at the window. She could just distinguish Wisteria House, nearly hidden by the buildings surrounding it. She thought of Lester, dead then, and the evening he had made her listen, over and over, first to Willie Smith, then to Wes Montgomery, so that she could tell them apart in her sleep, and she wondered if it were true that traces of life disappear quickly. The house far below had not yet vanished, but she knew that it would not be long before it did, lost in its dusty, dry repose. She was startled when the secretary, a pretty blond girl, called her name. Mr. Lynott was able to see her. Clio realized that her father had not told the secretary that she was his daughter.

He looked up when Clio came into the room. They shook hands and then, conscious of their awkwardness, leaned stiffly over his big table to kiss on the cheek. He was not tall, but he was full-chested, like a mating bird. His gray hair had a natural disposition to curl and it stood out from the back of his head like a ruff. She looked at his beautiful English suit and smiled. She had never minded his smaller vanities, although she'd been embarrassed as a child whenever he wore his straw planter's hat.

She sat on the stiff *koa* settee that her mother had left behind with her children and a few other burdensome things when she moved to Australia. The only thing that Clio remembered her mother taking—Clio had silently watched Kitty pack the whole fast week before she went away—was a silk negligé with her new initials embroidered on the bodice in tiny pearls that looked like grains of rice. Clio wondered what else Kitty must have liked enough to take with her, but she could never remember anything other than the pale green nightgown sewn with Biwa pearls.

"I thought you were in Morocco, Clio," he said, looking down at a paper on the Philippine refectory table that he used as a desk.

She was uncomfortable on the horsehair sofa in the big glass room, Honolulu floating soundlessly all around them. The flat gray ocean reminded her of one of Steamy's backdrops. When she did not answer, he reluctantly raised his head to look at her. She saw that his eyes were as gray as the sea around them, and as unreflective, and she wondered if she were afraid of him, if he still had the means, and the will, to harm her.

"When do you go to trial?" she asked.

"Those Kilohana boys are making a lot of trouble for themselves. And for everyone else. Even if the land does turn out to belong to them. There's a lot of this useless agitation in the air. This grass-roots shit. It's got to be stopped before they all get big heads. Hawaiian rights! It'll scare off the Japanese. You know, it's one thing to go up against the Hawaiian Land Trust, but to take on the Feds, you have to be pretty stupid. Or full-blooded Hawaiian." His laugh was like a short, sharp shout.

"It is one of the things I've always regretted not being," Clio said.

"I would hardly regret not being stupid."

She hesitated. "Yes. That's it. I have really regretted not being stupid."

He winked at her. "I'd hate to ask what else you regretted."

Clio smiled in embarrassment, not for herself, but for him, and looked through the glass at Diamond Head, moving out to sea like a big brown ship. The ocean was still; it did not seem to move from so great a height. "There aren't many things that I regret," she said.

"I shouldn't think so, married to a movie star."

His gaze fell again to the papers on his desk. He forgot for a moment that she was sitting there, and when he looked up and saw her, he blinked. "Well," he said, slapping the tops of his thighs. "What can I do you for? You know where to find me if you need me."

She turned her gaze from the band of gray sea that seemed to encircle and confine them. "Why would I need you?"

"Don't tell me you're upset about this Kilohana business. Has Emma Fitzroy got you all riled up? Just think about

it a minute before you get on your high horse, Clio. These
two local guys, one of them not even wearing a shirt or
shoes, for Christ's sake, hole themselves up in a deserted
lighthouse. They don't even use lighthouses anymore. Did
you know that? It's all computerized." He stopped for a
moment, distracted by Progress. "So there they are, two
Hawaiian kids with a few fishing knives and some fer-
menting poi in a plastic bag, claiming that the lighthouse
land is theirs. It was sad, Clio. If it weren't so embarrassing
for the Hawaiians, I'd be tempted to feel sorry for these
boys." He shook his head. "Maybe they thought they could
light the lighthouse with luau torches."

She wondered, as she had before, why the arguments of
the ignorant had a greater clarity and seeming truth than
the more complicated, more subtle, arguments of the wise.
Her sense of powerlessness made it difficult to know what
to say to him. She might as well try to explain, at last, how
Dix had broken the Chinese lamp with his Frisbee.

"Perhaps," she said, "the Kilohanas are aware of the
hopelessness of their act. Perhaps they can no longer bear
the difference between expectation and reality. Perhaps that
is unbearable for them."

"Oh, Clio," he said, shaking his head. "You haven't
changed, all these years. I thought Hollywood would have
made a difference. Thought you might have grown up.
What was that again? The difference between 'reality and
unreality'?"

She realized that he was laughing at her, unaware of
her curiosity, and the subdued interest she had always
possessed, and the wish, still vivid after all, that he would
love her and that she, more importantly, would love him.
She had given him the means to patronize her. She was
angry with herself.

"Come on, Clio, I thought you had the usual upper-class
disdain for sentimentality."

Her anger made her slow to understand his meaning. She suddenly felt her profound, abiding dislike of him. She saw in her quick way that she knew too much about him. She was so ashamed for him that she could not look at him. As she rose from the sofa, she understood for the first time why Kitty had not taken it with her, and she wondered idly if she and Dix had been as unaccommodating as the sofa.

"Sounds like you have that end-of-century thing, Clio. You know, *mal de siècle* or whatever it's called. Pull yourself together, honey. Your grandmother probably collects the rent on that lighthouse. You're a vested interest."

She walked out of the room.

They lay on silk cushions in the library, their arms on ebony armrests. Tadashi opened the *shoji* door on her knees and slid a tray of tea across the mats to them. She, too, complied with Mabel's wish to live, at least in one room, in another century, in another country. Clio sometimes thought that Tadashi didn't know the difference. Mabel was mad, but Tadashi really didn't know, or care, whether it was the Tokugawa shogunate or the Edo period.

There was a call for Clio, Tadashi said. She carefully emptied the *tansu*, piece by piece, until she found the telephone and brought it to Clio in two hands.

"Do you wish to speak in private?" Emma asked, and Clio shook her head, gesturing to her to stay.

"Hello?" Clio said.

"I'm not too happy about this," he said. "I've been back in Malibu for two weeks and I've been looking for you. Your mom told me where you were. The two man-haters are together again at last, is what she said exactly. What the fuck does she mean?"

The simplicity of Burta's suggestion that women who lived together without the company of men by nature hated men had a puerile logic that Burta must have known would appeal to Tommy.

"As usual, Burta has it wrong. There are not two man-haters here, there are four of us. Or is it man-eaters? I haven't been so happy in a long time. Eating men, that is."

That Mabel had endured a longing for a man who had been dead for thirty years, a longing that had eventually driven her crazy, was something Clio would never tell Tommy. She preferred that he believe Burta rather than know the truth. The truth would do him no good. He still would not understand.

"So. You coming home, babe?"

"Never."

"Isn't that the wrong tact?"

She considered for a moment whether to correct him.

"Everyone says you've flipped out. Even your cousin."

"My cousin?"

"Here, she wants to say howdy."

"Hi, Cliome," said a woman's voice. She spoke with a slight accent.

"Who is this?"

"I can't believe you're not here, Clio."

"Is this Claire?" Despite herself, Clio began to smile.

"What are you doing? You're supposed to be here! That's why I stopped in Los Angeles. To see my cousin. Imagine how pissed I was to find you gone. Although Tommy has been unbelievably nice. Some Japanese went to buy the plantation and the right-of-way to the beach in the hope of building a hotel, turn the palm grove into a water park. I'm on my way home."

There was not much cash, Clio knew, not much loose cash to fight off Japanese speculators. Mrs. Clarke had recently, reluctantly entered negotiations with the Japanese. Clio was sure that Claire was on her way home to sell anything she could to the gentlemen from Osaka.

"When are you coming home?" Clio asked.

"More important, when are you?"

"That's not home. And I'm not coming."

"Don't be stupid, Clio. Could be a *gigante* mistake." Clio could tell from the way that Claire spoke that Tommy was in the room with her.

"Don't think so."

"He really misses you." Claire laughed loudly and dropped the receiver. "He just made me a margarita," she said when she came back on the line.

"Tommy made it?"

"Well, you know, that cute guy who cooks for him. I'm having such a great time, I've changed my ticket about eight thousand times. I left Nando at his horrible mother's in Sintra and he's furious because he thought I was going straight home to see Mamie and Mother, but being in Honolulu, not to mention Waimea, is not exactly my definition of fun, no? Is anyone there?"

"Where?" Clio was confused.

"In Honolulu, Clio," Claire said with exaggerated patience. "Don't be mean. Just 'cause you're stuck there. Is Steamy there? I promised I'd pose for him. You know, like that naked Spanish queen on the soap."

"May I speak to Tommy?"

"I wouldn't stay away too long if I were you."

"Hi, babe," said Tommy. "She's great. She wants to do something in films."

"I'm not coming back, Tommy. I just wanted to tell you that. I don't imagine that I'll ever see you again. Even in the movies. Especially in the movies."

He paused. "You're not going to do something you'll regret, are you? Or something I'll regret."

"If you ever," Clio said, "try to speak to me again, I'll file a complaint and you'll go to jail."

He laughed in relief. "A Moroccan jail? I don't think so, babe. They totally love me there. Besides, you need proof. There's no proof. I checked it out."

She put down the phone. Her hands were shaking. She looked around, but she was alone in the library. She tried to put the telephone back into the *tansu*, but she couldn't do it. She wouldn't do it. Mabel would be agitated if she knew the telephone were sitting on a twelfth-century ink-stone box, but Clio could not help it. She took the receiver off the hook and covered it with one of her grandmother's silk pillows.

Clio read the newspaper while she waited for Dix. He was late. She had looked around the club for him, but he was not on the volleyball court or in the water. The men in the bar played cards and watched a golf tournament on television. There were women with naked children on the little beach.

"Up to no good, I see," Clio heard someone say, a man, on the other side of her newspaper.

She rose and held the paper crushed against her chest. It was her father.

"Do you mind?" he asked, pulling out a chair and gesturing to a waiter at the same time. "I've only got a minute." He laid his seersucker jacket across his lap.

Clio folded the newspaper and put it under a leg of her chair so it would not blow away. "I'm meeting Dix for lunch," she said as she sat down again.

"Dix?"

"My brother. Your son."

He looked around the terrace, his gaze held for a moment by a woman in a bikini at the next table. "Hello," he said with a smile, nodding his head at the woman. He turned back to Clio. "Hope you're paying. What a bum."

"He's looking for a job."

"Sure." He ordered a vodka martini, straight up, from the waiter. "What about you?"

"A job or a drink?"

He gave a loud cry of laughter. "Marriage must suit you after all, Clio. Is that what you call irony?"

"I don't think so." She looked out at the ocean. There was no surf and it was hot.

"You were always a wild little Indian. Didn't see you for days on end," he said, looking again at the woman at the next table.

"Where was I?"

"When?"

"When you didn't see me for days on end."

"Playing. In the forest. You were never around." He winked at Clio. "I don't remember, to tell you the truth. I wasn't a very good father, I suppose. Too busy. Too involved with things. Although it doesn't seem to have done you any harm. You've done all right, Clio."

"You were a very bad father."

He nodded, not paying attention. "We're having a dinner for Claire Clarke. She's a duchess now, you know." He tapped his front tooth with his fingernail. "Your mother, Burta, is very excited about this. She's even been down to the Historical Society to check the precedence of seating. You're coming, of course, although Burta is undecided about Emma, even if she does have royal blood."

"Who has royal blood? Claire? This is wonderful news for the family. Portuguese royal blood? Just what we've been missing."

"She's arriving on the tenth," he said, ignoring her. "Burta wants Claire afforded all the honors."

"How nice. Burta's giving her a medal."

"Relax, honey. I told you, you're invited. And Emma, too. Maybe."

"Emma won't go."

"Don't be so sure."

She looked at the big white hotels streaming along the beach. "I'm very sure," she said.

"Just be sure you're there. I think Mother has put you next to the Philippine consul. Nice little man. Gets things done, even if he is the president's cousin."

"I hope Claire remembers to come."

"I'm told Claire has changed." He spoke as if it were Clio who had a reputation for irresponsibility. "She's coming home to see if she can do anything about that dreadful situation with her sister, Mamie, and their gardener. Apparently, the mother has no objections and is not putting her foot down. Your cousin is actually living with the Japanese gardener. Must run in the family."

"I thought Claire was coming home to sell the plantation," Clio said. "Claire isn't interested in sex, she's interested in money."

He looked at her shrewdly, interested for the first time. "What do you know about that?"

"Why are you prosecuting those Hawaiian men?" She bent down to pick up the newspaper. There was a story about the Kilohanas on the front page. "Natives' rights? Women's rights? Dolphins' rights?"

He looked at the woman at the next table and grinned, afraid that she had overheard Clio.

She held the paper out to him, but he did not take it. "The men who occupied the lighthouse. The Kilohanas. They're not dangerous. This isn't the Gaza Strip, Father."

"Oh, Clio," he said wearily. "The press is good. The publicity. The challenge of impossible cases. How do you take the deposition of a whale? Or attach the assets of a fire goddess?" He waved away the paper. "I've seen today's news, thank you. I get awfully tired, you know, doing the day-to-day crap. I get very, very bored. I always have." He smoothed down his hair. "It's formal, you know. No Hawaiian wear."

"Hawaiian wear?" Clio was still thinking about the surprising connection between boredom and justice.

"For the duchess," he said, waving to Judge Chang, who had just arrived. "I'll be right there!" he called to the judge. "I think you'll find it interesting," he said to Clio. "We can put on a show here as good as anything in your Hollywood. This isn't the sticks, you know." He winked at her.

"I'm sure you can put on a show, Father," she said. "I've never doubted it."

"Good," he said and went to have a drink with the judge.

Clio had been too far ahead of Claire at school to have seen much of her, but later, at the Outrigger and at parties at the old Walder estate, after the shopping-cart millionaires from Kansas City bought it with cash they carried in suitcases, Clio had seen more of her. Claire had worked hard to become Clio's friend, perhaps because of Clio's attachment to her older sister, Mamie, or perhaps because Clio was just the right age to introduce Claire to a more prosperous group of men than the college boys Claire tormented so successfully. Clio had not seen her in two years, not since Claire went to Portugal.

Claire telephoned when she arrived in Honolulu, a few days before Burta's party, to ask if she could stay at Hale Moku. A certain good nature always accompanied Claire's opportunism, so she was not particularly disappointed when Clio explained that their grandmother did not want any more guests in the house. Claire did point out that she was more a relation than a guest. "Grandmother never liked me," she said mildly.

She came to call the next afternoon and managed, even before confusing Tadashi by asking for a Rob Roy, to behave rudely to Mabel. The women were on the lanai, listening to a Gabby Pahinui record of slack-key guitar. Mabel put out her contorted gray hand, as ugly as a bird's talons, at the sound of Claire's footstep and said, "Welcome home, my dear."

Claire did not bother to take the root-hand held in her direction, but leaned stiffly toward Mabel, as if she were loathe to touch her, and kissed her quickly on the top of her head.

"Hi, Grans," she said. "You're looking well." She made a face at Clio, but Clio refused to acknowledge it. "Has the lesbian fad that's racing through Europe reached Hawai'i yet?"

Before they could answer, even in their astonishment (Clio thought at first that she'd said thespian fad), Claire said dismissively, "Probably not. Not here." She sighed and stretched out on a *hikie'e*.

"Lesbian fad?" Clio asked, unwilling to let it go.

"I've never understood about orchids," Claire said, gazing at the descendants of Mr. Kageshiro's flowers. "Sometimes they don't even smell. Yes, Clio, lesbian fad. It's a big deal. Someone said it was postmodern, whatever that means. It's become really cool to pretend you're a dyke. You don't even have to do anything. You don't even have to look like one. In fact, it's cooler if you don't. It's incredibly fun to be at some ball, all dressed up, and ask another woman to slow dance. Everyone is freaked out and excited at the same time."

"Decadent Europe," Emma said.

"Have you been there, Aunt Emma?" Claire asked in surprise.

Emma did not answer.

Tadashi, with more than her usual tentativeness, tiptoed onto the lanai with Claire's drink. There were many cherries rolling around the bottom of the glass.

"Now this is delicious, Tadashi!" Claire said, taking a big drink. "They don't make very good ones in Portugal, I can tell you. Too sweet."

Tadashi shakily stood three bottles of beer on the table next to Emma, who nodded to let her know that she had done everything perfectly.

"Does Claire remember how to play 'Net of the Moon'?" Mabel asked loudly as Tadashi placed a plate of sushi on her lap.

"Your husband makes a very good cocktail," Claire said to Clio, smiling slyly.

"You already told me."

"Did I? I don't remember. Nando always scolds me because I lose track of things. Nando's my husband. It's short for Fernando," she added, turning helpfully to Emma. "I have no memory," she said. "None whatsoever. Nando does his exercises, well, sit-ups really, he calls them exercises, every day naked in front of this big gold mirror, and he makes me sit there and count while he grunts and sweats. Before I even get to twenty, he stops and rests and I forget where I am and he gets really, really mad. He wants to start over again, but I say no, just begin at fifty." She sighed. "He's old."

Emma handed Clio a beer.

"He's no Tommy Haywood," Claire said. "Maybe we could trade."

Something in Claire's tone—guilt and defiance and self-delight—made Clio look at her closely. "Maybe," Clio said. "But then I'd get Nando."

"Well, after you said you were never ever coming back, I thought it was all right to stay with Tommy at Malibu. What a cool house! I mean it was all right, anyway, but

after you said that, it was really all right. He was pretty
pissed at you. Something you said about seeing him in the
movies."

"Did you help with his exercises?"

"Cliome," Claire said primly. "He doesn't need to exercise."

Clio took a drink and looked at Claire. "Really?"

Claire gasped suddenly. "Have you heard about Mamie?" She shuddered. "I certainly have no *problemas* in
this area. My first boyfriend was Orval Nalag, who lived
in the workers' camp. Do you remember him, Clio? God,
he was handsome. There wasn't anyone who could tongue-
kiss like Orval. Mamie used to say, 'Here he comes, walking
the camp walk.' "

"I remember him," Clio said.

"I wouldn't give up those nights in the banyan tree for
any duke in the world—well, maybe I would—but it's
one thing to sleep with them and another to actually make
it your life. Mamie's going to turn into Mother. A nice
version of Mother without Mother's famous gardens. But
with the gardener." She laughed and looked around at
them. "That was funny! Mamie and Frank Harimoto. He's
the gardener," she said helpfully to Emma. "They're teach-
ing Hawaiian kids all the things they should already know,
like how to spearfish. It's weird, isn't it?"

"I don't think so," Emma said. She was furious.

The women sat silently, waiting for the unacknowledged
antagonism that had suddenly risen among them to stretch
and yawn and creep back to its usual hiding place in Claire's
pocket.

Clio was relieved to see that Mabel had fallen asleep.
My grandmother's life, she thought, was ruined by cowardice and prejudice, but my cousin Mamie is able to live,
as Mabel had not been free or brave enough to do, with a
Japanese man. It does not do my grandmother much good.

"You know, there's one thing I've learned, if you can believe it," Claire said abruptly, wrapping her hair around her finger. "You do pay a price for everything. The big thing is to figure out whether it's worth it. For example, it takes about two hours for me to go down on Nando. It's difficult for him. It takes him a long time. But then I think: two hours for a Chanel bag. Is it worth it?"

Clio saw Emma look at Claire's bag. It was a quilted leather satchel with gold chains.

"You can't keep the high-wire act going forever," Claire said, shaking her head. "Even if you wanted to."

"Now you tell us," Emma said.

"None of us can. Women, I mean. By the way, I don't know what you're doing, Clio. You don't do it at all, which I personally think is a big mistake. How could you let Tommy go? He said something about your getting incredibly mad in Morocco over a sex act and then you disappeared. I mean, Cliome! He was really worried. He said you were scared or something, that's why you left Morocco."

"Scared?" Emma asked angrily. "Clio, scared?"

"There is a little more to the story than that," Clio said calmly.

"Well, that's what he said. He said you were afraid."

"Why would you believe Tommy rather than Clio?" Emma asked.

Claire shrugged, not interested.

Clio wondered if Claire had really meant it when she'd boasted that she had no memory. "Do you remember," Clio asked, "the time we went fluming and Lily Shields broke her wrist for the second time and we were afraid to tell her father because he'd warned her to be careful until it healed? We made a cast in the garage out of wet newspapers and paste and she went in to lunch and vomited on the table."

"You and Mamie made the cast, not me. I had nothing to do with it. Dr. Shields couldn't get it off." Claire yawned with a little yelp. "I didn't have anything to do with it. I only watched you guys make it."

"I don't think anyone is accusing you, Claire, twenty years later. Dr. Shields scolded us because we didn't come for help, not because of the cast. I tried to tell him the truth, that it was because we were afraid. He said fear is never a good excuse."

"I kind of remember. Why?"

"It is one of the things I most remember. I wasn't afraid in Morocco, but I should have been. I think Lily's father was wrong. I think fear is a very good excuse."

"Well, you've always been obsessed by courage, hasn't she, Aunt Emma?" Claire gave Emma a big smile, as if she had just noticed Emma's coldness. "At least you used to be, Clio. I haven't seen you in a while." It was difficult for Claire to take responsibility for anything, even an opinion.

She suddenly looked at her watch. "I'm supposed to pick up my new bracelet in Kaimuki at four-thirty. Shit." Like Emma and Clio, she wore a gold bracelet engraved with her Hawaiian name. "I get a lot of questions about it in Europe. People always want to know what my Hawaiian name means. My real name means beach plover, but I lie and say it means beautiful-flower-of-heaven. I'm getting a bigger bracelet. As thick as yours, Emma. The biggest one they have, even if I'm paying for it myself. Well," she said, sitting up, "even if Nando is paying for it. You know, he thought Hawai'i was west of South America. He was surprised I was white. Of course, I told him we didn't have running water or lights." She picked up her costly bag and finished her drink.

"It is west of South America," Clio said, working it out.

"What is?"

"Is that why your husband remained in Portugal?" Emma asked. "He thinks we live without electricity?"

Claire smiled. "I certainly didn't want him in Waimea. He thinks we're rich. Nando sees the lovely allowance he gives me as a kind of investment against future returns. Christ, could you imagine Nando in Waimea?"

"No," said Emma.

Claire stood and stretched her pretty arms above her head. "Ciao, angel. Ciao, Emma. Don't get up."

But Emma was already standing. She was so eager for Claire to leave that Clio was sure that Claire would be offended, but Claire didn't seem to notice.

As if she were fearful that Claire might change her mind and stay, Emma waited in the driveway until Claire's black Cadillac limousine disappeared down the road. She walked back to the lanai and took a long drink of beer.

"Do you think if Señor Nando were able to achieve orgasm a little faster," Clio asked, "Claire would have to give up Chanel? Really, she's wrong to complain." She frowned as she pretended to solve it mathematically. "If Claire were clever, she could save the plantation. An acre for every twelve acts of fellatio."

"I don't think it works that way," Emma said as she finished her beer. "Not for Claire. She likes things she can hold in her hand."

Clio agreed to meet her brother, Dix, for drinks on the terrace at the Outrigger with the understanding that he pay the check. He had been in Thailand for three weeks working on possible imports—or was it exports? He always confused the two. There was an extremely high restaurant and bar bill on Clio's account, dating back many months. Someone had been using her membership number.

Dix denied it.

"I was in Phuket," he said.

"Before that."

"Bali."

"You're lying, Dix. You use my charge and you lie. You used to tell me the truth."

"I never told you the truth," he said, looking around to see who was on the terrace.

Now and then a wave broke with a loud crack against the coral seawall, spraying them with water. The sun was falling and the people on the terrace and the swimmers coming in from the beach were stained the color of amber. The canoes were out, training for the races, and the paddlers were silhouetted against the sky. Beyond the big hotels, stretching out to sea, was the long black flank of mountain called Waianae.

"I have some great ideas," Dix said. His arms fell loosely over the sides of his chair. He put his feet on the edge of the wall, and his clean, strong toes curled over the edge. He was wearing a silk aloha shirt that Emma had given him. Clio noticed that the hair on his arms was bleached white by the sun and the salt. He watched a catamaran coming into the beach. "But I need to talk to Tommy."

"Well, call him," Clio said.

"You wouldn't mind?"

She hesitated. "I mind, but you'd do it, anyway."

"Making up for lost time," he said, patting her arm. "You know, there are people in Bangkok who will kill someone for ten dollars. You can buy a whole family for twelve dollars. A whole family! For the night, that is."

"Who would want a whole family, Dix?"

"Not me. I don't want anything to do with families, mine or theirs." He waved to Ching See for another beer. A man wearing swimming goggles came out of the water and Dix excused himself and went out onto the beach to talk to him.

He came back to the table. "I owe him money," he said, and Clio stopped admiring him.

"I've written this really great screenplay. That's why I need to talk to Tommy. He could get it set up. That's all I need. Someone to fucking read it. I need an in." He became excited just thinking about it. He asked Ching See for a double order of meat sticks and some sashimi.

"Tommy's bad," she said.

"Clio. Bad is better. Haven't you figured that out? I know he's a shit sometimes. But bad gets things done. Look at Dad. I really need this to work, you know? There was a bit of business I could've picked up in Bangkok, but it was risky, a little too vague, a little dangerous. I could've made millions, but I said no, I'll go home and I'll talk to Clio. She'll know what to do." He waved to a friend. "All Tommy needs to do is read it."

"Well, that's just it." She did not like his presumption, or his implication that he'd given up a fortune running guns or drugs or children in order to consult her about his future. It was cynical and it was dishonest.

"Okay, have someone else read it then! Do you think I give a shit whether he really reads it or not? Just so he makes it happen." He took some chopsticks from a paper wrapper and rubbed them together.

A pretty girl stopped at their table. "Hi, Dix," she said. There were comb lines in her wet hair. She smelled like sandalwood. Clio knew she was from the mainland because she wore low mules. Local girls went barefoot or wore cheap rubber slippers they bought at the supermarket. Clio smiled at her and moved her chair to make room at the table.

"Jana's father works for the Marines at Kaneohe," Dix said.

Clio had known girls at school whose fathers were officers in the service. The girls were flirtatious and bossy, accustomed to being around men conveniently designated their inferior. They were almost always blond, Clio remembered. They wore Dr. Scholl's sandals to school, but that wasn't why they were never quite accepted. It was island snobbery, Clio had realized with surprise. The disdain of the clerisy.

"I'd ask you to sit down," Dix said, grinning, "but my sister's making me pick up the check."

"That's okay, Dix," the girl said sweetly. She wandered away, flicking water from the ends of her hair.

"You're inspiring," Clio said in admiration. "Do you always get away with it?"

"Away with what?" He looked at the girl's legs as she sat down at another table. "Listen, I may be cute, but you're the hotshot."

Clio stared at him.

"You were the one who always stood up to Burta and Dad while I was under the house trying to blow up her dogs with cherry bombs." Ching See brought the food and Dix ate hungrily. He remembered, a little late, to offer some to Clio, but she did not want any. "Remember how starved we always were?" he asked. It was the first time in the conversation, Clio realized, that he had spoken straightforwardly to her.

"One of the delights of Wisteria House was the food," she said. "It was there that I developed my extreme fondness for canned Le Sueur peas."

Their mother, Kitty, had insisted on reviewing the week's menu with the cook because she believed it was the way a woman of refinement ran her household, but she had had no interest in food. It was the Filipino cook who had determined what the children would eat, and Dix and Clio had eaten rice at every meal, including breakfast. Their idea of dessert was sour pickled fruit or egg sushi. They ate rice every day at school, too, often with a big slice of Spam. They had no complaint, they loved rice, but it was not until Clio went to Wisteria House that she had what she called her first white food. Her first *haole* food. Food like artichokes and wiener schnitzel.

Dix and Clio had been brought up like plants, although not very rare ones. They'd been given water and food and sunlight, but not much else. When Burta married their father, she dismissed the Filipino cook, who was fond of the children, and brought in servants of her own who only spoke Japanese. There was certainly enough money for food, but Burta announced cheerfully that the old days were over for good: there were going to be economies. She replaced the fresh milk with powdered milk, the rice with Rice-A-Roni, the fresh pineapple with canned pineapple chunks. The children were allowed a glass of powdered milk full of undissolved lumps of soybean at each meal. They were made sick by the smell and the texture of the milk. Clio could not drink it without gagging. Because they were no longer allowed pocket money, they could not buy food. Burta confiscated their lunch cards, telling them to find a way to pay for their lunches at school. Since she had no money to buy lunch, Clio just stopped eating, but Dix convinced the school dietician to give him a job scrubbing pots in the cafeteria, a chore customarily available only to those students who had scholarships. Clio would sit with her girlfriends at lunch, proudly refusing their offers of food, pretending that she was not hungry. Sometimes she would catch a glimpse of Dix at the food line, dragging away a stainless steel cauldron to wash, and she would admire him.

Fresh orange juice was kept in the refrigerator—Dix said it was for Burta's hangovers—and the children were forbidden to drink it. It was very tempting, just the idea of it sitting there in the cold and the dark. One very hot day, Clio could not resist sneaking into the kitchen to take a long drink of juice straight from the pitcher. She was reading Greek myths at the time and it seemed to her that she had just tasted nectar. She went back once or twice more. On her last visit, she was shocked to find that the pitcher was almost empty. She had not taken that much: someone else was drinking nectar, too.

The children had dinner in the playroom every evening at six o'clock. If they were late, the housekeeper, following Burta's orders, took bits of food from their plates for each minute that they were late. Sometimes they were late on purpose, but their very hunger kept them prompt. That evening, Clio looked closely at Dix and Steamy for any sign of complicity—flecks of orange on their lips, a smell of citrus—but there was nothing.

Lynott came into the playroom, a martini in his hand.

"There is a thief in this room," he said. He sounded excited and Clio wondered for a moment if he were drunk.

Dix looked at him boldly.

"Someone has drunk Burta's orange juice," Lynott said, coming to the table. "Was it you, Dix?"

Clio noticed that Dix's hairline was damp with sweat. "Dix didn't do it," she said.

But it was too late. Lynott took Dix into the next room and beat him with his belt. At the end, Lynott was grunting with the effort, but Dix did not make a sound.

Dix came back to the table. He did not look at Clio or Steamy. Clio felt light-headed. She wanted to touch him, but she knew that he would not allow it.

"I'm sorry," she said.

"Don't be," he said.

"I'll eat your Velveeta." They bartered their food every night, trading ruthlessly with each other. She knew that he hated Velveeta. She hated it, too.

"Okay," he had said reasonably, giving her the chance to forgive herself and getting rid of the cheese at the same time.

She watched Dix eat the sashimi. "It's not Velveeta, is it?"
He looked up at her. "It's not what?"
"Velveeta."
He didn't know what she was talking about. He ate the last piece of tuna and wiped his hands. She saw that he was worried. His expression had changed. It is because we've been talking about Burta and our father, Clio thought. She suddenly felt sorry for Dix, and sorry for herself. She wanted to comfort him as she had wanted to do when they were children together in the damp, dangerous house, when he used to explain that Burta and their father were evil. Clio had insisted that evil required intention. It had been impossible for her to admit that their father's cruelty was merely carelessness. She was making a useless distinction, Dix said. The effect of evil was the same. "I could even argue," he'd said, "that careless evil is worse."

"Do you really think I can send the screenplay to Tommy?" he asked, anxiously tapping a chopstick on the side of his plate.
"Yes, I do."
He jumped up, relieved and happy. "I'll be right back."
Clio watched the lights go on in the big hotels curving along Waikiki Beach. The green and red lights of the channel markers moved with the tide, and there were lights in the houses built on the hills behind the city. When she was a girl, sitting on the same terrace, trying to talk Ching See into giving her a cocktail, there had not been many lights back in the hills. It was not until she noticed people getting up to go into the dining room and the waiters

lighting the torches on the beach that she realized that Dix
had left her to pay the bill.

Clio was late to Burta's dinner party for Claire. Honolulu,
even so far into the twentieth century, was a very provincial
place. You were asked for dinner at seven o'clock, and you
were expected promptly at seven.

Clio moved along the edge of the lanai, nodding dis-
creetly to the figures painted on the wall. She saw Burta
on the lawn in one of the silk mandarin coats she had
made in Hong Kong. She was talking to Dix. The Duchess
de Corilhã was nowhere in sight.

Patsy Yasunabe, the senator, was talking to Johnny
Klein, who owned a hotel on the windward side of Oʻahu
that was so unsuccessful he gave weekend rates to the rice
farmers and construction workers who lived nearby. The
hotel was full from Friday to Sunday with local families
who brought hibachis and cooked on the stained cement
balconies. Senator Yasunabe had made sure that Mr. Klein
was awarded the contract for the new sports center.

Desiree Humphreys, who kept kangaroos and other unhappy animals at her house at Niu, waved gaily to Clio.
She was with Buzz Chun, the movie critic and gossip
columnist who had so much influence through his weekly
column, "What's Happenin', Brah," that no movie director
or beauty-contest winner left town without taking Mr.
Chun to his favorite Algerian restaurant in the Kahala
Mall. Buzz spun around to see who had attracted Desiree's
attention. He blew Clio a kiss as he turned deftly to Mrs.
Yung, the Taiwanese secretary of trade. The minister mys-
teriously held up her plump forearm for him to smell.

Steamy was on the lawn. Behind him, a grove of silver-
leaved *kukui* trees glittered amidst the dark *koa* trees, and
Clio thought of the Hawaiian proverb "The gum sticks to

the *kukui* tree." It referred to a child clinging to its mother. It is not a proverb that applies to me, she thought as she crossed the lawn to him.

"I've something to tell you," Steamy said as she kissed him.

"I'm just going to drink tonight," she said. "That way, when it all falls apart, I won't remember any of it."

A waiter came out to them with a plate of deviled eggs. Steamy took two and put one in his pocket. The head of Asian Studies at the university, a scholarly gentleman who was said to be one of Chiang Kai-shek's illegitimate children, smiled and bowed his head at them.

"It's already begun," Steamy said, nodding back at Mr. Chiang. "Dix wasn't invited, but Claire brought him because it's her party and she thought she could have anyone she wanted. Like the song. But she never asked Mom and she forgot to tell her. Mom told him he had to leave."

Clio turned to look for Dix. He was walking angrily away from the house. Burta stood on her toes, smiling, making sure that he did not stay.

"It's rather like a dream, isn't it?" Clio said. "It always has been, here."

Steamy nodded. "Nightmare, you mean."

Clio saw her father moving among his guests in a ritual of introduction and recollection. He was good at it. No sooner would he start one little fire of conversation than he would be off with his gold flint to spark another.

"It is going to rain," she said, looking back at the forest.

"I didn't know Claire knew Tommy," Steamy said.

Clio was thinking about her father, and did not answer.

"Clio? Have you disappeared already?"

Clio turned back to him. "She doesn't know him. She stayed with him for a few days in California." Clio nodded to a woman who owned a hotel on Maui where guests were taken to their rooms in hay wagons. "Claire's late, after all," Clio said, watching Burta gesture impatiently to her guests to come inside.

A woman in a muumuu and a necklace of polished *kukui* nuts stopped Clio as she stepped onto the lanai. "How is your auntie, my dear?" the woman asked. "I am only in town for a few days. Will you call me? Come to tea. Or cocktails, even better. I am staying at Diamond Head with Chimpy. I was hoping to see Emma tonight." Mrs. Alexander and Emma had been in the same class at Punahou. She lived on the Big Island, and was not often in Honolulu.

"Emma would never come here," Clio said. "I'm surprised that *I* am here."

"I am often amazed that we all still speak to each other in this desolate place."

Clio laughed. "Desolate?"

Steamy was at the door of the dining room, waving at Clio, trying to get her attention.

"Am I related to Claire Clarke?" Mrs. Alexander asked. "Her great-cousin, perhaps? Please don't make me work it out."

"I wouldn't dream of it," Clio said. "In fact, I beg you not to."

"And how is your grandmother?"

"She is very well, especially since Mark Twain came to lunch yesterday."

Mrs. Alexander nodded. "Alone?"

"The queen may have been with him."

"How nice." She paused. "What did they have to eat?"

"Very traditional. *Haupia*, poi, *lomi*. Quite a bit of rum."

"I'm sorry not to have been asked. Lots of gossip?"

"I should think. Grandmother has been smiling to herself all day."

"Well, she would be accustomed to it," Mrs. Alexander said, not unkindly.

"Accustomed to it?"

"To gossip, my dear. Talk."

They stopped at the door of the dining room. Steamy had disappeared. "Was there much talk about them?" Clio asked. "I've always thought there must have been."

"Your grandmother was fearless. I don't know if you know that. So was Emma."

Clio hesitated. "I've sometimes thought they were too fearless."

Mrs. Alexander looked at her in surprise.

"They should have given up," Clio said. "Their interest in saving the past, or repudiating the past, whatever it is that they have both tried to do with it, has cost them so much."

"Oh, my dear," Mrs. Alexander said, her voice full of disappointment—not in Clio's aunt and grandmother, Clio realized, but in Clio herself. "They had no choice."

Suddenly Steamy was next to Clio, pulling her aside. She turned back to Mrs. Alexander, but she was gone. Clio looked round for her. She wanted to tell her that she had meant no criticism of Emma and Mabel, but her hand was caught tightly in Steamy's hand.

"What a nice date you are," she said with a sigh.

"You'd never go out with me."

"Steamy, I'm your sister."

"Half-sister. We wouldn't have to have children."

"Oh, in that case."

"There's something I've been trying to tell you all night, but you won't let me."

"I can't imagine what it could be. You've been doing quite well."

"It seemed like they were, you know, old friends." Steamy made the local gesture for sexual intercourse.

"Who?"

"Claire and Tommy. Your husband. Your husband, the movie star," he said. "Remember him? You could have married me instead, you know. But then you might not have remembered me, either."

"My husband?" Clio was struck by the expression on Steamy's face. What she had mistaken for nervousness, she suddenly realized, was shame. She grabbed his arm. "He's here?" She was shocked. "Tommy is here? Tonight?"

"It was Burta's surprise." He looked down, embarrassed. "That's why she's so excited. Mom can't stand the idea of losing Tommy. That the family is losing him, I mean. She wants you to get back together. He just arrived this afternoon." He forced himself to look at her. "I only found out an hour ago when his bodyguard borrowed my hair dryer."

If she strained to listen, she could hear the stream. The smell of leaf mold and wild ginger was suddenly stronger than the smell of the women's perfume and the candles. The purple flowers of the *kukui* trees were almost within reach.

As she picked up her skirt in readiness to run, Tommy came into the dining room. Claire was behind him, her hands around his waist.

"Look who I have!" Claire yelled. "Toot! Toot! Here we come!"

Hundreds of white moths had folded their wings and settled tremulously on Claire's head. Clio was distracted by the loveliness of it until she realized that Claire was wearing a *haku* lei around her head. The slender wands at the center of the white ginger blossoms quivered like the antennae of insects.

"Hi, babe," he said.

Clio dropped the hem of her skirt.

"Isn't he great?" Burta asked loudly, looking around.

He wore a black suit and a gray linen shirt buttoned at the neck, and black cowboy boots. He shook his head at Clio in mock exasperation. As Clio saw the envious, pleased faces of the guests, she realized that she was the only one in the room who did not admire him. She saw that he saw it, too, and that it infuriated him.

Burta tapped a knife against a glass. "I want to make a toast," she shouted. "Sit down, everyone!"

"People! People! *Keikis*! Time for *kaukau*!" Lynott called to those guests still on the lanai. "Clio, find your seat!" Clio saw that he, too, was very pleased.

"Surprised?" Tommy whispered to her. "You don't look too happy."

"Don't touch me," Clio whispered. It was all she could say.

"I knew he was coming all along!" Claire sang gaily. "I'm not stupid. And I get to sit next to him. And Steamy's on my other side." She patted Steamy on the shoulder as an afterthought.

"You knew?" Clio asked Claire in astonishment.

"I said I want to make a toast!" Burta shouted.

"You look great, babe," he said, relieved that she had finally spoken. "Been working out? Judy and Mimi and everyone, all the guys, say hi. They miss you. I missed you, too."

"I asked the waiter to hide two bottles of wine under my chair," Claire said to him. "To get us through dinner. Clio, aren't you thrilled? Isn't this great? We put you between Senator Yasunabe's husband, he does something at the electric company, and Robert Siento's boyfriend. He's the new Samoan dancer at the Hawaiian Village."

"That was thoughtful," Clio said.

Buzz Chun sidled up behind Tommy. "What's happenin', brah?" He held out the palm of his hand.

"Yo, Floyd!" Tommy shouted as he slapped Buzz's

palm. Buzz had done an interview with Tommy for *Aloha* magazine.

"Buzz," Buzz said, but Tommy had turned away.

A woman, her hand held flat against her stomach, wiggled between Tommy and Clio. She smiled and squeezed Clio's arm as if they shared a secret.

John Lynott stood in the doorway, arms outstretched, red in the face from vodka and a good afternoon of marlin fishing. "Sit down, everyone!"

"You don't seem very glad to see me," Tommy said to Clio, bending his head close to her. "I even brought something for you." He patted his jacket pocket.

"I picked it out," Claire said, leaning around him. "You don't deserve it!" She stuck out her tongue at Clio, pretending to be jealous. Or not pretending, Clio thought.

"Claire—Duchess, I mean! You're over here," Burta shouted across the room. "Tommy?" She pointed to the chair next to her own.

Clio listened to the room begin to quiet as the men and women at last found their places. Some of the men stood behind their chairs, waiting for the women to be seated. The Filipino waiters watched patiently from the pantry, small hands clasped behind their backs.

A woman brought her cocktail glass to the table and placed it beside her wineglass, and Burta leaned over the woman's shoulder and whisked away the glass, handing it to a waiter. The woman looked around in astonishment.

Claire threw a piece of bread at Tommy. Steamy, forgetting himself for a moment, tried to catch the bread in his mouth. It fell onto the table. Burta frowned at him and he quickly picked up the bread and put it in his pocket. Next to the egg, Clio thought.

"You're just surprised, babe, that's all. You know you're crazy about me." Tommy shook his head as if Clio were a naughty, amusing child. He had forgiven her.

It is a dream, Clio thought. I was right. And as if in a dream, she slowly turned away from him. Away from Burta plucking at his sleeve, away from the waiters carrying in the Portuguese bean soup in honor of Claire, away from her mother's pretty dining room. Away from all of them.

There was a man walking toward the house. She thought it might be Senator Yasunabe's driver or one of the waiters. He stopped in the driveway when he saw her.

"Who are you?" Although she had not hurried, she was out of breath.

"I'm going to the pond," he said. He spoke quietly. She could tell from his voice that he was Hawaiian. He did not speak Pidgin English, but it was not quite English, either. He cut off his words tensely, as if it did not matter to him whether or not she understood him.

She could not see his face. He was wearing a dark T-shirt and jeans and rubber slippers. His hair was long.

"I used to swim here when I was a kid," he said.

"You must be one of those boys my stepmother wanted to have arrested for trespassing."

Behind them, the stream moved swiftly under a small bridge. Only the loud rush of water was steady; the other sounds rose and fell without rhythm.

"When did you used to swim in the pond?"

He didn't answer.

"I ask because I must know you," she said.

He looked at the big lighted house in its ornamental garden. The incessant cries of small animals grew louder in the silence and there were other sounds, too, of conversation, and knives and forks on china and the thin clang of pot lids.

"I don't think so," he said.

She moved closer. She could smell him and the swollen

leaves all around them. Someone opened the back door to throw a bag of garbage onto the kitchen steps, and he reached out and took her by the arm to pull her deeper into shadow, as if they were waiting there to murder Burta and her guests.

The rain Clio had been awaiting all evening still had not come. The air was heavy with moisture. The trees, like Clio, paused in expectation, eager for the mountain winds to chasten the vapor into rain.

"Come with me," she said.

She led him along the house, across Burta's stepping stones, and into the forest. She heard him moving quietly behind her.

It did not take long to get to the pond. He sat on the bank. She undressed quickly, without talking, without looking at him, although she knew that he watched her. She took off her underclothes. There was light trapped in the netted vines, and her pale skin looked gray.

She threw herself out over the black surface and dropped deep into the pond. The shock of the cold water made her gasp and she burst out of the water with a cry. She kicked her legs, turning the water to milk.

It began to rain. The plump drops shuddered on the surface of the pond. A bat from the banyan tree dropped low over the water, chasing insects. The rain was warmer than the pond water. She lifted herself onto a rock. The scant light reflected on her wet skin, and the bones running down her back looked like a knotted silk rope.

"I never saw you here," he said. "When I came to swim."

She climbed over the wet rocks. "I was here every day," she said.

"No," he said. "I'd remember you."

She realized then that he was younger than she, that he had come to swim in the pond after she went to live with Emma, one of the boys who had infuriated Burta by walking through her garden. Burta had refused to understand that the pond and the forest had been used, since the beginning, by all who came there. Landowners did not enforce trespassing laws, especially against those whose land it once might have been.

He stepped onto the rock that jutted over the pool and put his hand in the water. He looked like one of the figures in the mural, pulling *taro* or handing in a heavy netful of fish. One of the figures has come to life, she thought.

It was raining harder. She gathered her clothes, holding them in a bundle against her chest, and went up the path into the grove of Norfolk pine. The pine needles were dry under her feet. She heard him behind her on the path, but she could not hear him once he came into the grove. She sat on the pine needles and leaned back against the trunk of a tree. The bark was rough against her bare skin and she sat up straight, away from the tree, her white voile dress in her lap.

He sat down next to her.

"I grew up here," she said.

"I know."

His leg brushed against her, and, to her surprise, she felt herself shudder. Cheap thrill, she thought. He lay back on the pine needles and leaves.

The moon had risen, pillowed by clouds. The rain rattled through the forest, slapping onto leaves and rocks, jinking down the stalks of ginger. Now and then, rain found its way through the laced branches of pine to fall on them. He lay beside her, his fingers entwined beneath his head.

Her skin was wet, but she was not cold. She listened to the *ḳahuli*, the land shells, scratching in the trees, celebrating the rain, and she listened to the birds rocking deep into their ground nests, birds so innocent they did not know to build their nests in trees. For a moment, she thought that she heard the whine of the brindled spirit dog, Pa‘e, who guarded Kapena Falls deep in the valley.

She put on her clothes. He did not look away. She lay back again and the white dress opened around her like a flower.

"Do you know Prince Lunalilo's poem to the princess?" She could feel the cloth of her dress drawing the wetness from her skin.

"No," he said.

When she was silent, he said, "Are you going to tell me?"

"I'm not sure that I remember it all."

"I'm going to Moloka‘i in the morning," he said. "We have until then."

She smiled in the darkness. She realized that he could not see that she was smiling. "I'm smiling," she whispered as she rose onto her knees under the wet pine branches and settled herself again on the dry ground, as if the poem had been written for her.

They listened to the night birds and the restless blundering insects, and sometime in the night she recited the poem to him:

> For this body, beloved, brims with my love.
> At the thought of your mouth my heart leaps
> with love remembered in a magic pool.
> At brink of Ka-pena Pool no magic now
> in this cool watershed of upland Nu‘u-anu.

C
lio was awakened by a rattling at the screen door, as if someone were trying not just to waken her, but to force his way into the cottage. She put on a summer *yukata* and went cautiously into the front room. She was not cautious out of habit. Anyone who knew the cottage and had reason to be there, even at six o'clock in the morning, would have known to come inside, even if she were still in bed. So whoever was troubling the door was a stranger who did not know that the cottage door was never locked, only warped from rain and salt.

She thought at first that he had feathers in his hair. The branches of the palm trees seemed to spring from the top of his head. His hands curled around his eyes as he tried to peer through the screen. She went to the door and opened it with a hitch, holding her robe tightly across her chest.

"You didn't say goodbye last night, babe." He rubbed his hands up and down his chest. He was wearing an orange and white University of Texas sweat suit, and running shoes.

Clio held herself flat against the door as he brushed past her. She knotted the sash of her kimono tightly around her waist. She went into the kitchen and got a bottle of mineral water from the refrigerator, and glasses, and put them on a table.

"I don't remember ever saying hello," she said.

He rolled the bottle of water across his flushed forehead.

She sat cross-legged on a *hikie'e* and pulled the pillows into her lap, making a little battlement on which to rest her hands. As she unfolded a quilt across her legs and feet, she realized that she did not want him to see any part of her.

"You certainly made a scene, babe." He took off his cap and skimmed it across the room, trying to hook it onto a pair of antlers, the antlers of a deer she had killed when she was sixteen, but the cap fell to the floor.

"Did I?"

"Claire and Steamboat took me to Lombo's Club Polynesia after dinner. It was sort of great. Lots of fags in drag. Hawaiian fags! And Japanese. It was weird. I didn't know there were Hawaiian fags."

She leaned forward to pour water into a glass.

"So why did you do that?" he asked. "Walk out like that." He stood before her, restlessly swinging an arm.

She looked at him.

"Were you sick or something? Giving you the benefit of the doubt." He bent his leg at the knee and grabbed his foot with his hand, stretching his thigh muscles. He could not stand still.

"No, I wasn't sick."

He hesitated. "Well, what's your excuse then?" He stretched the other leg. "You're always making these crises and the rest of us worry. I'm not sure you deserve the present I got you." He let his foot drop to the floor. He was angry, but trying not to show it. "Claire says you used to leave parties all the time." He moved his head in a circle, loosening his neck.

"No, I used to give parties all the time."

"She thinks you're her best friend. She really likes you. She likes you better than her sister."

"She would."

"What do you mean?" He went into the kitchen and came back with a bag of banana chips. "It's a compliment."

"No, it's not."

"What's not?"

"It's not true that she likes me, and it's not a compliment."

"You don't understand her," he said, eating the chips noisily.

Clio looked out at the garden.

"You make it hard for people," he said. "You're too proud."

She realized then that he had been talking to someone about her. She didn't think that she was too proud. Perhaps she was wrong, but she couldn't imagine that he thought she was proud, either. He had never thought about her at all.

"You have this idea that wanting something entitles you to something in return," she said. "Love, for instance. It's a sentimental idea, Tommy. I'm afraid it doesn't work that way."

He sat on the edge of the *hiki'e*, his legs extended stiffly over the side. "Look," he said, "I know you haven't had such a great time. They told me about your mother running off and taking all the money and all about your stepmother, who Claire says was always real nice to her, but supposedly not too great to you."

"Claire has certainly been a help to you. Local history, I mean."

"I didn't think she was that bad, personally."

"Who?"

"Your mother."

"My stepmother."

"Whatever."

"No."

"What?"

"Not whatever."

"Look, babe, this isn't what I came by for."

"I'm not very interested in your impartiality. I like subjectivity. And conviction. I admire people who take sides. I sometimes even like intolerance. That's why you can't say 'Whatever.' Oh, I know that you can say anything that you want, you, Tommy, but I don't have to like it."

He looked confused. Confusion, especially his own, made him petulant. "I came to take you back, not to piss you off." He jumped up and walked over to pick up his cap.

"Take me back?"

"I'm not leaving without you." He smiled and looked at his watch, tucking the cap into his waistband.

Clio rose, knocking the pillows to the floor.

"I don't mean now," he said hastily. "Christ, babe." He took three guavas from an old ceramic bowl and began to juggle them. "I have a television interview this afternoon. Meet me at the Outrigger later." He raised his eyebrows in invitation and tossed the guavas, one by one, back into the delicate bowl. Clio winced involuntarily as each guava landed heavily in the dish. "Just us. No one else. Margaritas and teriyaki-burgers. We'll talk. It will be like old times. I'll make the crew sit at another table."

"We don't have old times."

"What?"

"I'm not meeting you."

He wiped his palms on the back of his sweat pants. He looked around for the first time. "Nice place," he said, nodding his head as if the room needed assurance. He walked across the room and opened the door to her bedroom.

"Do I get to meet the crazy grandmother?"

"Not at six-thirty in the morning."

He was eager for some sign from her, some gesture of affection, so when she darted under his arm and stood blocking the way to the bedroom, close to him for a moment, he thought that she was pleased with him.

Clio did not want him to go into her room. She did not want him ever again to see how she lived—the lingerie on the chair, the strewn bed linen, the tapes and books and damp bath towels and tubes of sun block, the blue box of tampons, the pot of cold tea on the floor. She so did not want him in her room that she allowed him to touch her, an intimacy that should have been more upsetting, she suddenly thought, than his seeing her unmade bed. Clio did not want him to see her bed because she did not want him to desire her.

"Show me where you sleep," he whispered.

As Clio looked at him, she realized that she had forgotten that he was Tommy Haywood, the movie star. There was a small pimple on the side of his nose. His eyelids were pink. It seemed impossible that she had ever slept with him, and impossible that she ever would again. This is the materialist view of love, she thought; the Marxist view of romance. If towns prospered because of good rivers, and fine weather that ensured rich grain harvests, not because of the actions of statesmen or kings, then it might be possible to say that my husband's visit is not going well because of a pimple. He needs to wash his face.

He put his arm around her waist and drew her to him. "You miss me? Come on, babe," he said into her neck. "It's me."

"That's just it."

He glanced over her shoulder into the bedroom. She slept in a carved opium bed that Mabel had bought in 1975 from a Vietnamese general passing through town on his way to Cannes. A smell of old incense came from the brocade bed hangings. He tried to back her into the room, pushing her with his legs.

She was astonished by her own perversity. She would never live with him again, she knew, but it was stubborn, and even dangerous, to provoke him by refusing to let him into her room. She was determined that he should not know one more thing about her—whether she was menstruating, what books she was reading, what kind of tea she drank.

He grabbed her by the arm. "There's someone in there, right? There's a guy in there, right?"

"Yes, that's it," she said, relieved. "There's a man in there. Naked. In the closet." She laughed. "Actually, he's under the bed. With an enormous erection. That's why he can't come out. He's stuck. Because if he could, he would!"

He shoved her against the door and went into the room, arms held away from his sides in readiness, and arousal. He reached down to lift the bed skirt to look under the bed. She came after him, close to him, daring him to humiliate himself further, and he was confused by her presence.

He slowly straightened, dusting his hands, and looked at the closed bathroom door. He looked at Clio, then again at the door. He hesitated for a moment, then pushed past her and walked out of the room, calmly and deliberately kicking the teapot across the floor. It broke in two and cold tea splashed over her bare feet.

She walked slowly into the front room, the hem of her robe stained with tea, and watched him struggle angrily with the swollen door. It was he who felt misused.

She opened the door with a brisk jerk, the knob rattling in her hand. She was trembling.

He put a hand on her shoulder and she jumped onto the wet grass like a grasshopper.

"So. We'll sit on the Hau Terrace and wait for the green flash when the sun goes down. You can swim before dinner. Steamy told me you're really only happy in the water, anyway. You should have let me know. I could have drowned you!" He grinned and put on his dark glasses. They were fastened with a fluorescent elastic band around the back of his head.

There was the loud click of a gecko and he looked around, startled by the sound. He winked at her in embarrassment as he put on his cap, working it down over his brow with two hands, the bill in back. "You won't be sorry, babe. Trust me. Was there anyone more devoted?"

He trotted across the garden. His limousine was waiting at the end of the driveway. "No one more devoted," he shouted over his shoulder, but Clio did not hear him. She was already inside, packing her bag.

When Clio asked Emma if she would mind if she went that afternoon to the island of Moloka'i, Emma took her into her bedroom and pulled a small silk bag from under the *koa* bed and emptied the bag onto the quilt. Black pearls, Emma's jade hairpins, three jagged teeth, and three small emeralds tumbled onto the bed. Clio had to spread her arms to keep them from rolling off the bed.

Emma picked up one of the pearls. "Take this and go to Hoon tomorrow."

Clio stared at her. "Is this what you've been doing? Taking things to Mr. Hoon?"

Emma put the pearl in her hand. "You must see Auntie Rowe when you're on Moloka'i."

"Why don't you come with me?"

Emma shook her head.

"Tommy was here this morning," Clio said.

"I saw you on the lawn."

"He is going to make it very hard. I don't understand why, but he is going to make it hard."

"You will need to understand. Otherwise, he is too dangerous."

"Women do want the things that men have simply because they are men," Clio said. "Anatomy is fate. Or is it faith? I suppose it is possible that women really do want an actual penis, but, Emma, here is what I think is so very interesting: men want penises, too. I mean that, like women, they don't have them."

"What a funny thing you are," Emma said, smiling at her. "You always have been, you know. Do you remember the day you came to Wisteria House? All cut up by the branches at the gate, and so ungainly. I know that I was meant to be the teacher, but I have thought all along that I was the pupil. I have learned so much from you."

"Have you ever held a man in your hand, perhaps after making love, when he is no longer aroused, and thought what a difficult thing it must be to be a man? The penis, like a bird in a nest, so fragile and delicate."

"You make me think of Johnny Fitzroy," Emma said. "The most beautiful women in the world are the Tahitians."

"Is that why you didn't go with him? You thought that you weren't beautiful enough?" Clio was surprised. "Surely not," she said, outraged.

Emma waved her arm, taking in the treasure, and the room, and the house itself. "It was all of this. I believed that without our work, without our belief in the past, all of this would disappear."

"It will disappear whether we believe in the past or not."

Emma nodded her head. "Some people turn away from the future because they fear they cannot master it. They fear they have no place in it. But that is not why I have been a ghost. I have always felt that the past is a mirror that persuades us, that compels us, to behave well. That is why I studied it and why I taught you, so that we would know how to live." She suddenly looked tired. She rose from the bed with a sigh.

"I distrust history," Clio said. "I always have."

Emma took Clio's chin in her hand. "The bruises are almost gone." She lightly touched the pale scar that ran down Clio's cheek. "What happened to you, Clio? I haven't wanted to ask. I suppose I haven't wanted to know."

"You have never asked questions, Emma. Even when I was a child. The day that I arrived at Wisteria House, so ungainly as you say, you never even asked why I'd come." Clio smiled. "And you didn't ask why I left."

"I was moved by your reticence. I used to look at you and think: 'onipa'a. Be steadfast. I was so moved by you. You needn't tell me anything, even now."

Clio took a breath, and nodded slowly, as if she knew that she did not have to explain herself to Emma. She looked at the pearl in her hand, as luminous and mysterious as a moon, and she began to speak.

"They wouldn't take me to a hospital because they were afraid the work permits would be taken away. A doctor came to the hotel. There was a boy guarding me, the boy from the movie crew, Rob, the same boy who'd spent all those weeks looking for the donkey. He sat at the door. Can you imagine?" She looked up at Emma. "First the donkey, then me. He'll think he has a career." She smiled.

"I said that I would jump off the balcony if they allowed Tommy into the room. He sent bouquets of roses, Marrakech roses, every day and the room was so full of the smell of them that I could not stop sneezing. I told the boy that I was afraid I would break open my stitches, and when he carried the flowers to the porter's room, I ran away. You know how good I am at that. I had hidden a bag under the bed, waiting for my chance.

"One of my cuts opened again when I hit my head on the door of the taxi. I was in pain, holding my forehead, frightened because I was sure they would come after me. They had to stop filming for a few days because Tommy had broken his hand and they were very worried about scandal. But I was calm as the soldiers at the airport went through my lingerie, most of it soiled. I hadn't been allowed to send my things to the laundry, lest a maid run straight to the king with my bloodstained clothes. And then the soldier who was going through my suitcase pulled a pair of handcuffs from beneath my clothes." Clio laughed nervously, and she saw that Emma was startled.

"I'd told Tommy that my life with him was a kind of torture. He said that he'd rather be unhappy with me than unhappy without me, and as a joke, he called it a joke, he gave me the handcuffs in Morocco. He got them from the propman. They were in the bottom of my suitcase, where I'd put them to keep from seeing them, and I had forgotten about them until the soldier found them."

Clio looked down at the pearl in her hand. It shone with the dampness of her wet palm.

"You might wonder why I hadn't just thrown them away," she said. "We never used them, although I would sometimes get excited thinking about them. But even if I had understood it better, just why the thought of them was exciting, it wouldn't have done me any good, because I couldn't have done it for him."

She looked at Emma to see if she understood. To her relief, Emma did understand and she nodded to tell her so.

"The soldier held the handcuffs on the end of his machine gun and called over another man, and they passed the handcuffs back and forth, holding them with the tips of their fingers, as if the handcuffs might bite them. And they might have. I offered to let the soldiers keep them. It sounded flippant and the first soldier looked at the cuts on my face and asked to see my papers again and I said suddenly in French, 'The handcuffs are a gift from my husband,' which was the truth, and which in some awful, astonishing way worked. Although it is hard to imagine a Muslim woman wearing handcuffs under her burnous, and unnerving to realize that one had been naive enough to think that the pleasure of binding a woman was a delight limited to the West, the soldiers nodded in understanding and even sympathy with my husband and dropped the handcuffs, which I didn't want and had never wanted, into my suitcase and let me go."

Clio lowered her head. "When I told him that I was leaving, it was so easy for him to hurt me, he was so without guilt or shame, that I thought I must have been very bad or he could not have felt so justified. It was only when I pretended to lose consciousness that he stopped. No more fun. It was wrong, and careless, not to have been afraid of him. My mother would have known how to handle him. And 'handle' is the word she'd have used. You see, I thought that if I made a pact with the devil, the devil was at least bound to hold up his end. But the devil doesn't have to pay. He's the devil." She held out her open hands.

"I don't know where to begin," Emma said slowly. "Many people marry without love, child, but they are not beaten for it. Nor do they deserve to be."

"I've thought for the longest time that it was my fault. Even before Morocco."

"None of it has been your fault. We might start with that. Surely you know that." She took Clio's hand and curled Clio's fingers around the pearl. "You're an island girl," she said. "Why didn't you just throw him out the window?"

Clio smiled. "Most of my life has been about not dis-appointing you. I sometimes think that this whole notion of being an island girl, this whole code of female honor, needs to be looked at a little more carefully. I sometimes think it has caused me a great deal of trouble. You taught me that an island girl is resilient, courageous, kind, generous. Island girls do not indulge in self-pity, or alimony, or pain-killers. Well, I suppose an aspirin now and then is all right. But it is a very hard thing to be, Aunt Emma." She sighed heavily. "I wanted to be an island girl, more than anything else. I wanted to please you."

To Clio's surprise, Emma looked at her with tears in her eyes. She took Clio in her arms, and for the first time that Emma could remember, that Clio could remember, Clio wept.

For four hundred dollars a month, Clio rented a small wooden house on the east end of the island of Moloka'i. It was in the district known as Kainalu, which was under the guardianship of the shark god. "I know it very well," Emma said when Clio told her. "And the god will look after you. I myself have seen it."

A few miles out of town, the red dirt and cactus and rough-barked cottonwood gave way to vine-draped valleys fragrant with guava and rose apple. Great forests of tree ferns, and *kukui* planted in remembrance of sacrificed chiefs, filled the valleys. Green streams ran over the *palis* that separated Kainalu from the isolated leper colony on the windward coast.

The cottage sat in a grove of banana and mango trees. From the front porch, Clio could see across Pailolo Channel to the island of Maui, the long ascent of sacred Haleakala, blue and lavender, lifting from the sea, rising into the clouds. Through the *plumeria* trees and milky plumbago was a small, rocky beach.

Deer came down from the mountain at night, seeking warmth in the eucalyptus behind the house, and she was awakened by their mournful barks. They sounded like melancholy dogs. The cry of the deer reminded her of a poem by Izumi Shikibu that Mabel used to recite to her when Clio was unable to sleep.

> *In this mountain-village*
> *Woken from sleep*
> *By the wind rustling in the rice-leaves,*
> *Deep in the night, the deer's*
> *Voice I hear.*

She swam in the morning and again in the early afternoon. She swam at sunset. She climbed to the *heiau*, a long twelve-mile hike, and she often walked upstream to the waterfall at Halawa, but it was in the ocean that she felt as if she were, each time and at last, the self her heart would have chosen had it been asked.

She would swim until she was tired, although not too tired to get back to the beach. She found a hole in the reef into the deep water at the edge of the channel. If she swam out far enough, she could see the big rock on the side of the mountain that marked the site of the shark god's burial place. Sometimes she was overcome by an inexplicable feeling of panic, as if there were too much beneath and around her. She feared that the ocean might suddenly curl her into a wave and fling her from the loneliness of earth into the loneliness of space, and she would hurry back through the reef as if the ocean were trying to catch her.

Although Clio had gone to Moloka'i, the isle of sorcery, because she loved it best of all the islands, the knowledge that Henry Kilohana, the man she had taken to the pond, was on the island made her feel elated and expectant, as if she had a secret. She did not try to find him, nor did she look for him in the small groups of men sitting on cars outside the firehouse, or at the feedstore, or at the basketball court at the public high school. She knew that on an island so small, where most people were either related or had known one another all their lives, she would find him.

And she did, one afternoon at Obayashi's store. She was buying cone sushi and Evian water. It had surprised her to find mineral water in a place where it was difficult to find a good lamb chop, and she had just asked Mr. Obayashi how it was that he came to stock the water when a man behind her put a packet of twenty-test fishing line and a jar of kimchee onto the wooden counter and said, "We use kimchee for fish bait here, if you want to come fishing one day."

"I have an order for your auntie," Mr. Obayashi said abruptly to him. "This is last-time credit."

"I'll take it to her," Henry said calmly.

Mr. Obayashi, wrinkled with age, walked with out-stretched arms to guide and steady him. He bumped into a dusty cardboard advertisement for Coppertone tanning lotion that had been there since Clio was a child. There were not many tourists on Molokaʻi; not much local call for skin-darkening products. With some effort, Mr. Oba-yashi lifted a box to the counter and pushed it toward Henry. The box contained canned food and soda. "For your auntie," said Mr. Obayashi. "Last time."

Henry nodded slowly, undismayed, his hands in his back pockets. "You going somewhere?" he asked Clio as he lifted the carton to his shoulder. He had a small black tattoo of a cross between his thumb and forefinger.

She had been hoping to stop at the library before it closed.

"No," she said.

Henry's aunt, Ginger Kilohana, lived with her grandson, Earl, in a rusted yellow school bus in the middle of a field. On the side of the bus someone had written in spray paint,

Stay Out of This Bus! Ginger had lived in the bus for twenty years. The tires of the bus, long flat, were hidden in weeds. Nearby was a muddy stream and a wooden outhouse with a roof of palm fronds. Ginger owned a fourteen-eightieths share of the land.

An outrigger canoe was pulled up under the palms at the mouth of the stream. No one had bothered to turn the canoe, and the hull was warped. The wood was so porous that rainwater seeped out before the boat could fill with water, and the mosquitoes had long since moved to the truck tires along the shallow streambed. The broken *ama*, the outrigger, lay buried in fallen palm branches and rotting coconuts.

The front door of the bus was broken, held open with a block of wood. Henry carried the box of food into the bus. Clio looked at the door. She was no longer called upon much to repair vehicles. Dix's roommate at school, fellow Squid-Mon Dicky Herbert, had been given an old Army tank by his father for his fifteenth birthday, and its restoration had been one of Clio's more interesting initiation requirements by the Squids.

Clio went to work. Ginger did not have a toolbox, so Clio had to use Henry's penknife and a can of oil.

"My father refuses to take Hawaiians as clients," Clio said, wiping her oily hands on the grass when she had finished. "But, as you can see, I do."

He laughed. "Hawaiians don't pay their lawyers. We promise you a pig, then we forget it's yours and eat it. We bring you a fish and then stay for dinner. That canoe has been lying there since I was in high school, rotting in the sun because the Kaanaipos said it was Mack's responsibility, and Mack said it was theirs."

He took two cans of beer from a dirty Styrofoam cooler under the bus and handed one to her.

This is a new idea, she thought. There is no romance

or longing in this view of the past. No nostalgia here. No sadness. No broken heart.

Clio came from a family whose lines of descent were scrupulously documented. Her husband, Tommy Haywood, had no family. But Henry Kilohana was related to almost everyone on the island in an easy, unrecorded way, sometimes without benefit of marriage, sometimes without benefit of blood-distance. It was impossible to keep track of Henry's relatives, and what is more, no one would think it very important to do so.

"How did you get that?" she asked, pointing to a line of white scar tissue across his knuckles. The backs of his hands were marked with hook punctures. Clio could see a piece of coral growing under the brown skin.

"My cousins and I used to pick fights with sailors in Waikiki."

It was Henry's cousins, Clio knew, whom her father was prosecuting in Honolulu.

He began to strip a palm branch. His black hair was held at the back of his neck with a rubber band. His nose did not broaden at the nostril, but was narrow, and even haughty. "You can't even call us the working class," he said. He began to weave the palm into a lariat. "The working class wants satellite dishes and motorboats, but Hawaiians don't want anything. Well, maybe a case of beer. Maybe a new pony." He smiled at her. "There used to be Hawaiian-language newspapers, and the women made mulberry bark cloth and quilts, the designs inspired by their dreams. But there was a turning away from everything. From the beautiful as well as the practical. They even stopped learning to read and write. My great-great-grandfather was an interpreter of omens for a chief, but my grandfather couldn't speak Hawaiian." He knotted the end of the palm lariat. "They began to die."

"One of the reasons I liked being married was that I didn't have to think," she said.

He laughed.

"About these things, I mean. About these islands."

"You think about them?" he asked. "My cousins believe the government is going to hand over a lighthouse to them. They want to secede. Rachel Kaanehe thinks she'll be crowned queen when the legislature settles her claim. The same legislature is building a hydroelectric plant in her backyard and she's worried about what she's going to wear to her coronation."

It was hard for Clio to know when he was teasing. He had the occasional humorlessness of someone who has had to struggle to get knowledge. He was both detached and furious. She wondered if he knew that Hawaiians were once put to death for sarcasm.

"All that we have left, as Hawaiians, are gestures. As a race, I mean. You know that. They're just using what they have."

"The Kilohanas?" she asked.

"All of us. Especially the Kilohanas, because they have the least of anyone."

"And my family?" she asked. "My aunt?"

"Maybe memory is a gesture, too," he said.

She stood there, thinking about it, and he smiled at her.

"How do you know how to fix buses?"

"Oh," she said. "From the time when I was trying to be a boy." She made herself smile. "How do you know about gestures?"

He handed her the little palm lariat and said, to her surprise, "You have a great conscience."

.   .   .

They stopped by the side of the road so that he could look at the surf.

Clio stayed behind in the pickup while he strolled slowly onto the beach to talk to the boys who sat against the banked sand patiently studying the movement of the wind and the waves. He pulled off his shirt and squatted down in the sand, his elbows on his knees. A man on the beach, his arms held tightly across his bare chest, had a large tattoo on his back, from neck to waist, of the Virgin Mary.

Clio knew that even though she was waiting, Henry would feel no need to hurry. The men on the beach would talk about a few things, the currents and tides, but not much more. Clio could hear their conversation as clearly as if she'd been hunched down with them on the sand. She had grown up listening to Dix and his friends, and it had always seemed to her that most of the important things that passed between boys had never been spoken. An exchange of information had occurred—she had been there to feel the transaction, if not to hear it—but very few words had been used. She'd been confused by it. She'd thought that intuition was a feminine, graceful trait, but the rough boys who communicated with a glance or a grunt or a nod were very intuitive.

Henry came to the truck and stood at the window, his T-shirt around his neck.

"No good," he said. "Waves are breaking to the left. Toward the rocks."

Clio nodded and looked at the water, trying to be as coolly nonchalant as one of the boys on the beach. It made her smile.

He got into the truck and started it, leaning out over his arm as he backed out of the brush. The rear tires caught in the sand, and the engine raced as he moved the truck back and forth, finding a sure place.

"Who was that man with the tattoo?" Clio asked.

"I went to grade school with him."

"I like his tattoo."

"He got it in prison. He designed it himself. For protection. A guy from Japan did it with razors and Magic Markers." The wheels pulled free of the sand and Henry drove slowly onto the beach road.

"Why was he in prison? Did he occupy a pool hall and claim it belonged to his grandfather?"

He did not answer at first, and she wondered if she had offended him.

"Two tourists were blown up in his marijuana field. He learned how to lay mines in Viet Nam," he said at last, smiling.

"Why did the tattoo protect him?"

"Because of the other men. He figured if he had the Mother of God on his back, they might think twice."

Clio was silent as she herself thought about it.

"I think you like local guys," he said, looking at her over his outstretched arm, his hand on the big steering wheel.

She looked at the smoothness of skin on his bare shoulder, the brownness of his skin, and the black hair on his arm and on his chest. She shuddered. Cheap thrill, she thought.

"Maybe I do," she said, forcing herself to look away.

He waited silently on the small porch while she picked limes from a tree in the yard. When she went into the kitchen, he sat on the floor in the front room and looked at her books, and the ferns that she had brought back from her walks.

She filled an abalone shell with red salt, and made fish and rice and *namasu*. She was pleased by his praise of her small collected things, and of the food, not because she thought that he might be right, but because he thought so. He did not say very much. She knew that it was not lack of interest, but temperament. He did not need to speak, or to be heard.

She looked at him and she thought, I cannot wait any longer.

She could count the times that he had touched her. He had brushed against her in the grove of Norfolk pine, and in town when he had helped her to put boxes of food in the back of the Jeep. He had touched her fingers when she gave him the shell of salt, and again when he gave it back to her.

She went to him and gave him her hand. She led him into the little room where she slept. He sat down on the bed. She pulled off her wet bathing suit and stood before him. He was very still, even when she put her hand on him.

"What is it that you want?" she asked. When he did not answer, she said, "You confuse me by not telling me."

He gently pushed her from him and lay her on the bed. He placed his scarred hands on her body. He still did not speak, but she could hear his breathing grow deeper and quicker. She listened carefully, as if each breath were a declaration.

She forced herself to lie still. There was sand between her legs and under her breasts, where it had settled on her damp skin. He held her knees as he lifted first one leg, then the other, to brush the sand from the bottom of her feet. There was the faint dry sound of sand falling to the floor.

He was on his knees behind her, his hands slow on her body. He lifted her hips, and pulled her to him. His brown fingers with their pink nails encircled her waist, the fingers separated, holding her. He took off his shirt, pulling it over his head, never releasing her, changing hands as he removed it. She did not know what he was going to do to her and this uncertainty was as arousing as the feel of his hands on her.

He leaned her back against him. She was cold and his body warmed her. He braced her against his heavy thighs, moving her back and forth. She could smell lime on his hands.

She thought of Mabel. We liked to swim the horses, Mabel used to say. I am his horse and he is swimming me. He is my horse and we are in the white water, the spume of the surf on my coat, mixed with the foam of my sweat, his hands in my wet mane. I am his horse. He is mine.

"When my cousin Leroy Kilohana was staying with me one summer, we found an *'aumakua* image inside a cave near Halawa. It was a foot long, with one pearl-shell eye. Human hair was pegged into its head with iron nails. We covered it with rocks and threw leaves and dry branches across the opening of the cave and ran like hell back down the mountain. We knew it was a sorcery image because we'd felt the lump of human flesh or shit or nail parings stuck in the opening at the back.

"Sometimes at night I dream about it. My father has a big poi-pounder, nearly two foot high, that he keeps behind the front door. He says it's his *'aumakua* and sometimes when he's drunk he squats over it as if he were going to sit on top of it and take it in like a woman would. He slaps his thigh like he is galloping, and pretends to ride it. The statue that we saw in the cave was not like the poi-pounder. It was not a symbol of procreation or food. It was a symbol of death."

He rose from the bed and stood at the porch door. Clio

watched him. His thick, strong legs, his heavy arms, seemed suddenly dear, as if the recognition of his imperfection made him more valuable to her.

"Sometimes when I walk in the forest, going *mauka*, going to the mountains, I want to see it again. I don't want to take it, only to look at it."

He stepped into the yellow moonlight. Clio was surprised that he'd told her about the cave—not its location, not even that it was on Moloka'i—but the story of finding it and the mystery of the memory of it, woven day to day, month to month, over those years. It was not that Henry believed in magic, although she knew that he did, and it was not that he feared that he'd be struck lame or blind or even dead if he betrayed the god, it was that the unseen, seen, image possessed the history of his expiring race in all its poignant, willful destruction. It was the Hawaiians who had sold all of the sandalwood trees, not the *haole* traders. It was the Kilohanas who were in jail, unable to post bail, too furious to accept the money raised by *haoles* on their behalf.

Clio came onto the porch. The channel glistened through the trees, and there was the sound of surf against the rocks, hurrying to meet the tide. Her *pareu* flapped behind her in the fresh breeze, like a wing. "You look like Hina, the moon goddess. You shine in the light," he said, smiling at her.

She went to him, between his knees, and he paid obeisance to the moon as she paid obeisance to him.

Henry's father, Packard Kilohana, lived in a cottage on the side of a hill, surrounded by surfboards sunk vertically into the ground. Clio thought that the history of surfboards could be learned just by walking around the fence. There were old *koa* boards, heavy and clumsy-looking, and the new short boards called Thrusters, and the thick epoxy boards from the sixties.

Packard Kilohana held open the screen door for them. He had a huge head, matted with gray hair. "I never cut my hair in twelve years," he said to Clio in greeting. "Not since the unhappy days I stopped chasing cows."

Ginger had told Clio that Packard was named after the car.

"The car?" Clio had asked. "He likes Packard cars?"

"No, honey, he was got in one."

Clio hadn't understood.

"You know, made love in one. His ma and pop."

A young German shepherd followed Packard Kilohana as he went to open a window. No matter how careful Packard was in his housekeeping, Clio knew, it would be impossible to keep the red dirt of west Moloka'i from drifting like smoke through the house. Even if he kept the windows and doors tightly shut, the dust would find its way inside, into his teeth and ears. Clio sneezed, just thinking of it.

He went to the back of the house and returned with a piece of coconut cream pie on a paper plate. He gave it to Clio and gestured to her to sit on the sofa. Henry walked to the back of the house.

"Laka kept me up all night," Packard said, pulling the black ruff of hair at the dog's neck. The dog looked at him, lovesick and patient. "I hear this barking, barking. I get up. Nothing. I go back to bed, she bark again. I come outside, and she is looking up at the sky, barking. You know what she saw?" Packard Kilohana had the same accent as Mabel, a combination of old English and Pidgin.

Clio shook her head. She finished the piece of pie. It was delicious.

"Shooting stars. She was barking at stars."

Clio touched the dog on her back and she looked around at Clio for a quick moment, black pupils rolling in the corners of her eyes. The dog turned back to Packard, who laughed at her.

There were trophies on the big television set. Cowboy hats encircled with dried flowers, and whips and spurs, hung from nails on the walls. In the corner on a wooden stand was a Mexican hand-tooled saddle, black with years of sweat. Clio thought of the bridles and boots in Tommy's house in Malibu; chaps that would never be worn, ropes that would never be thrown.

The stone poi-pounder was in its place behind the door. A ragged pile of pornographic magazines was next to the sofa. A pillow was propped against the wooden arm of the sofa, and Clio wondered if Packard had been reading the magazines when they arrived.

Henry came into the room and handed her a can of Mountain Dew.

"I think I knew your auntie," Packard said as Clio put the paper plate on the floor. "But I'm not sure I got the right lady." Clio watched the dog lick the plate clean, pushing it across the floor with her big tongue. "Long time, was she married with the manager at Nalakaa Ranch? I was the cow boss there one time. Was she nimble and fat? I'm trying to recall her."

Clio noticed that he was staring at her legs. She wondered if he meant Emma, even though Emma was tall and slender. "I never knew Auntie Emma's husband," she said. Out of politeness rather than an attempt to be understood, she had slipped into Pidgin. Packard would understand her if she spoke in a more formal way, but to talk Pidgin was a sign of acceptance for both of them. It meant that she was a child of the land, as was he—not a newcomer, not a white, not a *haole*. Pidgin made them equal for a moment.

"It was long time ago." He shook his head in apology. "You and me might even be cousins," he said with a laugh. His teeth were crooked and stained. His eyes were heavy-lidded, and red from too much sun and drink.

Clio wondered if it were possible that they were cousins. She liked that she did not know anything about Henry. She did not want to know. Aunt Ginger had tried to whisper things to her: his mother had been killed in a car at the bottom of the hill when he was a boy; he found her body in the *kiawe* trees on his way home. His girlfriend lived in Maunaloa, down the hill from Packard. His cousin Leroy was better-looking than Henry, but not so nice. Leroy didn't like *haoles*. Packard Kilohana molested his niece. Clio had tried to stop Ginger when she told her these things over six-packs of beer, Ginger not troubling to separate the gossip from the true. "Love 'em and leave 'em," Ginger had said. But Ginger had not mentioned that they were related.

Henry stood at the screen door, looking down the narrow, slanting lanes of Maunaloa town, his hands in the back pockets of his jeans. The weight of his hands pulled the waistband low on his hips. Clio could see the black hair at the small of his back. Below his waist, there was the faintest change in the color of his skin. She felt herself flush with desire.

"My boy is handsome," Packard said with a smile. "No *huhu*, Henry," he called to him: Don't be angry, Henry.

"I was wondering how the break is at Long Beach." He turned away from the door. He was restless. "We're going now, Pop. You need anything?"

Packard slid his dimpled hands behind the loose bib of his denim overalls, as if he'd been caught misbehaving. He looked like a big brown baby and it was hard for Clio to imagine him on the back of a horse, one of the last *paniolos*.

He did not have the lined, calloused skin of a man who had spent his life in the sun and wind, and Clio wondered if it were because he had grown stout since the days he had won his trophies.

He walked them to the door, moving with the deliberation of someone who has lived around big animals. "You say 'How's it' to your ma," he said, confused about her relation to Emma. He put his hand on her shoulder.

"I will," she said.

"Was your auntie one of those Clarke girls?"

"Yes," Clio said, pleased.

"Do you take after her?" he asked. For an instant, Clio could see recognition in his eyes. He was trying to remember Emma, out of nostalgia as well as a wish to please, but he could not do it.

"I don't think I do," Clio said. "I wish I did."

He laughed. "For what?"

"She was lovely."

He slapped his thigh and Clio expected to see dust rise in the air around him. "Isn't that something!" he said to Henry.

"Goodbye, Pop."

"Adios," said Packard. He took Clio's empty soda can from her hand. They went onto the porch. He gave them some bananas that were leaning against the wooden porch rail. The dog stood close to him, pressed against his legs, whimpering happily as he pulled her ears.

As there was no telephone in the cottage, Clio called Emma to give her the number at the pay phone in Obayashi's store. "Don't just call in an emergency," Clio had said. "We can talk about anything. Even genealogies."

Emma called once, a week after Clio left Honolulu, to

tell Clio that everyone was looking for her. "You'd think you'd robbed a bank," Emma said. "What did you do?"

"I don't know," Clio said, bewildered. "I just left. Perhaps that's it."

"Yes," Emma said. "They worry if you leave. They have all the defensiveness of the provincial. They *are* provincial. They wonder if you might know something they don't know. That frightens them. There's a package here for you, too. From a Ms. Mimi Sands. Shall I open it?"

"What about Claire? She left, too, but no one holds it against her."

"But she's come back as a duchess and someone who's lived in Europe. They like that. You know how some people are prurient about sex, or money? I've often thought that island people are prurient about the outside world."

"So all I have to do is come back a duchess? That sounds easy enough to do."

"But you'd have to be Claire."

"Oh," Clio said.

"Your father called."

"My father?"

"And Dix came by with a bag of lichees and a good book on Hawaiian furniture. All twenty pieces of it. He stayed only a few minutes. He was so restless he kept hitting his head on the branches of the *hau* tree. I thought he wanted money, which I'd have found for him, but he wanted to know where you were, too."

"I should leave more often."

"My mother thinks that you're here, of course. That's one advantage. She thinks you're here at Hale Moku repairing the outboard so that you can take her by sea to Rosemount Plantation. She asked me this morning when you'd have the boat ready. Do you ever think how beautiful the women must have been? Those lovely *hapa-haole* girls with their thick black hair and green eyes in the Worth ball gowns they ordered from Paris. Going to dance at Rosemount in white satin gowns. They wore white to show off their brown shoulders. The only trouble was those slippers. The ones you liked to dance in when you were a child. They had trouble dancing in shoes."

"How did you know I used to dance in the slippers? You never told me how you knew. I thought Lester had told you."

Emma laughed. "I myself have seen it."

"You watched me?"

"I saw you once, by accident. The door was open. That is my memory. Or perhaps I dreamed it. It's all a dream, Clio."

"Yes, it is all a dream. I'd be happy to take Grandmother to Rosemount Plantation, even if it's overgrown and deserted. Like Sleeping Beauty's castle. We're used to that."

"Perhaps you *could* take her," Emma said. "Perhaps she's right and we are the mad ones. It all exists in the imagination, anyway. Memory and expectation. Reality is the least important aspect."

"I worry about that," Clio said. "The unimportance of it."

"Steamy called, too. I gave him the number at Obayashi's. He's thinking of going to Waimea with Claire and he wanted to know what you thought. 'Clio will kill me,' is what he said, to be exact." She paused. "They all want something from you, Clio."

"Except Henry. Henry is the only one who doesn't want something."

"I think that's how it works, Clio. People wanting things, I mean. They're supposed to want something. It's not unreasonable to want something."

"But I don't want anything from them."

"That's not true. You do ask for something."

"I do?"

"You ask to be left alone."

"That shouldn't be too hard. For others, I mean."

"And what about me?"

"You?"

"Do I ask for something?"

"Oh, you are the worst of all."

"Well, there's the irony then. That you think I'm the worst of all." There was regret in Emma's voice.

"You all give me too much power," Clio said. "Me, of all people. Grandmother even thinks I can summon back the dances at Rosemount Plantation."

"Well, you can."

"By taking her there?"

"By letting her believe that it exists."

"I do. I do let her believe it. And still it's not enough. *That* is irony."

"Perhaps I'm wrong then. Perhaps she shouldn't be encouraged."

Clio laughed. "I'm going fishing tomorrow with Henry. He is a fisherman."

"Well, I've opened your package while we talked and Ms. Mimi Sands has sent you what looks like a child's uniform. I can't quite make it out. Could it be a girl's scouting uniform?"

"Yes, it could."

"Shall I mail it to you? Is it something that you need?"

"No. Not yet."

"I'll speak to you soon, then."

"Emma?"

"Yes, child?"

"I didn't mean to offend you. About the past and what

you have hoped to do. When I said that you wanted more than anyone."

"No, Clio, never. You have never offended me."

A few hours later, Obayashi's granddaughter came from the store to say that there was another call for Clio.

Mr. Obayashi looked up irritably when Clio came up the wooden stairs of the store. There was a smell of tobacco smoke from the pipes of the men sitting in the yard, and the acrid fumes of mosquito punk, and the peppery aroma of fried chicken cooking in the back of the store. Clio decided to buy some of the chicken to take home for supper.

"Stay plenty time," Obayashi said, shaking his head as if it were Clio's fault that the caller had been kept waiting so long. It had taken ten minutes for Clio and Obayashi's granddaughter to run back to the store.

Clio reached for the phone, out of breath. Obayashi's fingers had grown rigid around the receiver and he could not let go of it. Perhaps that is why he is angry with me, she thought. His hand is paralyzed with age and disease and he is embarrassed that I see it. As she helped him to unwind his fingers, she wondered who would be calling at seven in the evening on a windy day on Moloka'i, wondered who had been willing to wait nearly twenty minutes to speak to her. She hoped that nothing had happened to her grandmother, or to Emma. Mr. Obayashi's short-legged *poi* dog watched intently as Clio prized the phone from Mr. Obayashi's grip. The dog's long pointed ears twitched with interest. Except for Packard's dog, all of the dogs on Moloka'i looked alike. They, too, were related. She yanked the phone away from Mr. Obayashi.

"Hello?"

"This really is not a good idea, babe. Not a good idea at all."

"What isn't?"

"I just want you to know that I don't approve of what you're doing. This is not the way to do it. All wrong, babe. I waited that night at the Outrigger 'til nine o'clock. I thought something had happened to you. Lucky for you, your brother was there and we had dinner with Claire. He has a movie he wants me to do."

Clio could suddenly see the force of all things efficacious that would be brought to bear on her.

"His script's not bad," Tommy said, momentarily distracted by the thought of his career. "I'm thinking of doing it."

She was so angry at them, her husband and her brother, so furious, that she began to tremble. "What does this have to do with me? Why are you calling me?"

The old woman cooking *makizushi* on a hot plate had stopped to listen. Mr. Obayashi turned his back to Clio and noisily rearranged a blue glass pyramid of Vicks VapoRub jars. Flies lighted on a long rectangle of pineapple upside-down cake on a piece of waxed paper, but Mr. Obayashi was too upset to notice them. Perhaps he was thinking of the caller's telephone bill. Clio wondered if she could reach far enough with her hand to chase away the flies.

"It has a lot to do with you, but that's not why I've been holding for forty fucking minutes. Not to have a story conference, I can tell you. Not to discuss plots. Not this plot. This is the stupidest thing you've ever done. By far. No contest. I'm obsessed with this, and I don't like it. I'm coming to get you. Tomorrow. Claire says there's a plane every few hours."

Clio looked around the store. Mr. Obayashi's granddaughter sat on top of the white ice-cream freezer, banging her thin legs against the side. Clio thought it must be cold, sitting there. The girl stared at her and ate blue shave-ice from a paper cone. Blue was vanilla. Clio wanted one. The color of the syrup had never corresponded to the color of the fruit, or even to the taste of the fruit. Pineapple was pink, guava was green.

"Why," she asked, "would you want someone who doesn't want you?"

"You want to know? I make allowances, that's why. I'm adjustable. I like having you around. I can deal with your bad behavior. It's worth it to me. I believe in this family. Even if you don't. We know how you feel about families, for Christ's sake."

"That's just *my* family," she said in exasperation, "not all families." She realized that he had drawn her into a conversation. "Listen, Tommy, I'm going to say goodbye now. Don't call me again. I'm going home now and eat fried chicken. Then I'm going to find a lawyer."

"What do you want?" he shouted. "You want to live in Beverly Hills? Okay! You want to drive the Bentley? Okay! You want to work? Fine. You want to have a kid? Maybe."

"I'm hanging up now." There was the sudden loud sound of rain on the tin roof. It reminded her of the sound of rain at Nu'uanu.

Gently, sneakily, with both hands, she placed the heavy receiver back into its cradle. She could hear Tommy shouting her name as she hooked the receiver in place. Mr. Obayashi frowned as she severed the magical connection across the rough channel to Honolulu.

She worried that the phone would suddenly ring again, disturbing the dusty stillness of Obayashi's store before she could get to the road. She knew that Mr. Obayashi would be shocked if she refused to take the call. The girl was gone from her seat on the freezer. Clio forgot about the chicken and the other small things she'd meant to buy, *kiawe* honey and a spool of thread. She left without thanking Obayashi and his wife, and set out for home like a thief.

Through the sound of the rain and the tumble of rising stream water at the side of the road she heard the sharp ring of the telephone. She wondered if it would soon be too dark to pick the Surinam cherries she'd noticed on the way, if the rain had already torn the pleated red berries from their stems. She began to run.

The rain fell on her head and shoulders and splashed up the back of her calves, cooling her. Just offshore, along the narrow shoals, the last streams of light clung like spirits hesitant to abandon the land. She could see the lights of west Maui shining across the channel. The trees were dark in the rain, the bark stained black, the leaves heavy in the last light. She watched the rain move through the fields, the grass bowing beneath it. The stones by the side of the road soaked up the light, and the darkness was cool upon her face.

She had read that morning that many new species of insects and reptiles, even fish and birds, were discovered each year, and she wanted to tell Emma. Emma kept a catalogue of the species that had disappeared from the Hawaiian Islands. In the last ten years, thirteen species of Hawaiian plants had become extinct, more than in any other place on earth. The *'ahinahina*, the silversword; and the lovely spiderflower; and two species of *Phyllostegia*, both named after the amateur botanists in Emma's family who had discovered them. Emma herself had a fern named in her honor. Clio and Emma found it one morning at Kawaikoi Stream in Koke'e and they carried it back down the mountain as if they'd been bearing an idol. And of course, Clio thought, we were.

She could see Ginger's bus in the field. A light bulb attached to a twisted piece of metal hanger was swinging wildly in the wind, like a fish caught on a line. The bus looked like a ship outrunning a storm.

A dog barked, sticking its head through a shattered window of the bus. A boy ran to her across the field. It was Ginger's grandson, Earl. He stopped abruptly, almost on top of her, his face close to hers, and jerked her hand roughly. Clio could see Ginger standing in the door of the bus with a broomstick. She gestured with the broom, as if to shoo Clio away. Earl's palm was hot and dirty. Clio wondered if he'd been holding candy, or pennies. He was eating a strip of *pipi kaula*, beef jerky, and it smelled rancid.

She heard the waves as they broke against the rocks of the king's fish pond, and the lizards singing in the palms. The deer were on the mountain, and stars rushed through the dripping trees. She looked around her. All things were rustling with spirits. She ran through the field to home.

When Henry came a few hours later to bring her a fish, she was lying on top of the bed listening for the sixth time to Coleman Hawkins and Ben Webster play "It Never Entered My Mind." It was one of the first songs that Lester had played for her at Wisteria House.

Henry looked at her and took the fish into the kitchen.

He came back into the room, drying his hands, and sat in a chair at the foot of the bed.

Clio reached over to play the song again. The air seemed to tremble with the rise and fall of the music.

"I spoke to my cousin Leroy," he said. "There's a demonstration in Honolulu in a few days. The Human Reactor is coming. A protest against the missile tests on Kahoʻolawe."

"The Human Reactor?"

Henry smiled. "He's from Hiroshima. He travels to different countries for peace. He's radioactive."

Clio smiled, too. She lifted her hips from the bed and pulled down the top sheet and slid under it.

"Leroy says no one's going to fire missiles on people in boats, not even the United States Navy." He paused. "I'm not going. I'm sick of gestures."

"Do you remember in high school the lecture on Appearance and Reality?" she asked. "It was very misleading, wasn't it? It made me believe there was a distinction between the two. Reality was true and Appearance was false. But Appearance is just as real as Reality, sometimes even more real. Appearance *is* Reality." She stopped for a moment. "My father, I now see, has always known this. I suppose my own mother has, too. Tommy knows it. My grandmother. It means that they can do whatever they want. If nothing is real, then nothing matters."

"If appearance is reality," Henry said, "everything is real."

"Come here beside me," she said, smiling.

His hair smelled like tar soap and woodsmoke. "I've been very happy here," she said. She looked at his scars. When he was a boy, a lure had ripped from the mouth of a billfish and caught in the thin curl of his ear. There were scars at the corners of his eyes, one from a bar fight, the other from a fight in the Army.

"When are you going?" he asked after a while.

"Soon."

"No more hiding in the forest?"

She shook her head. She could tell from the change in his breathing that he was falling asleep.

She did not move, but held him and thought about Earl and Ginger in the cold, dirty bus and Packard up on the hill making banana cream pies and reading sex magazines. She thought about her mother. She wondered if Kitty had clipped the Biwa pearls from her trousseau nightgown with her gold manicure scissors when she tired of it, the lime green of the silk no longer suiting her. Or had she simply dropped the nightgown on the floor of her dressing room for her maid to take away, to take home and snip off the little pearls herself? When Clio married Tommy Haywood, Kitty had sent her a silver tray and a book, *The Great Estates of Australia*, which had photographs of Kitty's house in it. Although the book was a rather formal and un-imaginative wedding gift, especially from one's mother, Clio was happy to have it. She had had trouble remembering how her mother lived; the rooms in which Kitty received friends or worked on her scrapbooks as she sang along with the music from *Camelot*. I have had trouble remembering, Clio thought, because I have tried to forget.

Most nights Kitty would wait patiently for Clio—so uncharacteristic of Kitty, who never waited for anything —until Clio was no longer able to hide beneath the weight of the day. Then Kitty would ease herself in her lithe, careless way into Clio's bed, sliding the pillow under her pale head, not caring that she had pulled it from under Clio's head. Clio would say, "Go away, Mother, I cannot bear the sadness of thinking about you," but Kitty would fold her hands daintily, commandingly, across her chest, and say, "Let me tell you about my day, Clio."

I have missed her, Clio thought. Despite my efforts, I have missed her. Not my mother, I do not know my mother and I don't think I would have liked her much if I did, but I have missed, as people do, having a mother. And my father. My father. I have missed them both. I have missed them very much.

. . .

Ginger made her a lei of white honeysuckle. Clio knew it had taken many hours to pick the tiny blossoms, and she was pleased by Ginger's gift. Earl jumped up and down and pulled Clio's hands, asking her when she was coming back to Moloka'i. She told him that she didn't know; soon. She could tell that he didn't believe her.

The smell of the honeysuckle was strong inside the small plane. She watched from the window as the dry land of west Moloka'i disappeared beneath her. She could see the houses on the hill of Maunaloa town. For a moment, she was startled to see two frightened giraffes running in the shadow of the plane, until she remembered that developers had opened a Safari Land.

She had been very happy on Moloka'i. The drive into Kaunakaka'i town to buy the Honolulu newspapers, usually two days late if they were there at all, and the hours spent drinking warm beer in the Mid-Nite Inn as she read them, were far more satisfying than having many things to read, in many restaurants, even with cold beer. There was, she had discovered, a serenity in the diminution of choice. On Moloka'i, she had read with concentration every single article in the old editions of the *Star Bulletin*, not once through, but many times, and when she'd been able to find a mainland melon—a soft, too ripe melon—she had eaten it with as much pleasure as if it had been one of Mr. Kageshiro's prize-winning fruit.

Mabel was in the moon-viewing pavilion. She looked up when she heard them on the gravel path and waved her calligraphy brush, and black ink flew across the room.

They drank the tea that Tadashi had left for them in a black iron pot. They ate miso soup and dumplings. Mabel greedily gulped down the broth and held out her lacquer bowl for more.

Clio said, "We live in a matriarchy, Emma, don't we? Not just here in this house, but throughout these islands. There is the Charlotte Ranch. And the island of Niʻihau, bought by a woman a hundred years ago. And Miss Caroline and Miss Geneva Fairnsworth. I used to think it was because all of the men were killed early, like my grandfather, or because they went off, like your husband. There were so many accidents."

"Your grandfather was spearfishing with Lester at Polihale, down toward Na Pali, when he drowned. He grew confused," Mabel said. "He began to swim to the bottom, you know, away from the light, into the depths. Lester tried to save him."

"Rapture of the deep," Emma said, laying down her chopsticks.

"What?" Mabel asked.

"Rapture of the deep!"

"Yes, I believe that is what it is called," Mabel said quietly.

"Hunting accidents and drownings and road accidents," Clio said. "My mother's first husband fell into Kaikea Canyon trying to pick ginger for her. But it isn't only death or misfortune that has taken away the men. It is time. The women are strong; they live long. Only ten years ago, when your aunt, who was then eighty, came into town to make her calls, she was escorted by outriders, handsome men on horseback with rifles, their hats wreathed in flowers, ferns tied at the necks and fetlocks of their big horses."

"She was known as Coconut," Mabel said dismissively. "She saved her infant son, he's dead now, from the tidal wave of '34 by climbing a coconut tree. It was she who did that, not me. People thought it was me, but it wasn't. She was washed out of the tree three times and washed back. It's funny," she said, pausing. "She never much liked that son."

"We were called 'Miss' even if we were married, as if we were young girls," Emma said, pouring broth into her mother's bowl.

"Or spinsters," Mabel said.

"Except my mother, of course," Clio said. "My mother was never called 'Miss,' was she?"

Emma smiled. "She married young. She didn't stay on the ranch."

"I met Henry Kilohana's father on Molokai'i," Clio said. "An old cowboy."

Emma looked up slowly. "An old cowboy? Are there young ones?"

"I've been thinking since meeting him how important it is not to sentimentalize those things that are disappearing from the world. It leads to kitsch."

"Did he give you a piece of pie?" Emma asked. Her face was flushed.

Clio laughed with surprise. "You *do* know him! I thought you must have come across him."

"Yes, I came across him."

"He lives in Maunaloa in a cottage with a fence made of surfboards."

"He used to say I was the only one who could dance the hula *Pua Kukui*." To Clio's surprise, Emma rose and began to move her hips in a slow circle, her arms bending like the branches of the *kukui* tree as she danced the old cowboy love song. "You're caught by my lasso," she sang.

Clio watched her, enchanted. "I didn't know that you knew him."

"It's all right, Clio," Emma said as she suddenly sat down. "It is all right that he didn't remember me." She was blushing.

Clio looked at her. She wanted to lie to her, to say that Packard had remembered her very well, but she could not do it—not because she was morally fastidious, but because she knew that she could not fool Emma.

"He was the most beautiful man I'd ever seen. I could tell he was coming from the sound of his bell spurs jingling in the wet grass. I'd have moved in with him, in that little house up there on the hill, if he'd have had me. He was married and I was married. I was different then, of course. I was younger and nicer-looking, but I don't mean that. I mean that I was interested in the present. Not like now." She paused. "I liked the way he made love to me. He was very gentle, very untried." She spoke as if she had just awakened from sleep. "His hands were so rough and broken, the skin so split and calloused, that he at first refused to touch me. I had to take his hands and place them on my hips and my knees. My breasts. I once pulled a cactus spine out of his arm with my teeth and I would have swallowed the little spear with love had he not made me spit it into his hand. I wanted everything, even his injuries."

She rose and walked back and forth along the narrow verandah. She was grave with memory, and sorrow.

"Why did you never tell me?" Clio asked quietly, her eyes full of tears.

"*That* is why I didn't go with Fitzroy to Tahiti. I did choose love, Clio. I chose Packard and I chose the right thing. I know that. I knew it then, even if he didn't choose me." She spoke in a rush, pale with regret. "I only went to him three times. My body was red with dust."

"It is a strange thing to say, but I am happy for you." Clio glanced at her grandmother. Mabel's head was turned toward them and she was frowning with the effort to hear, but she was not listening to them.

"Hi, Cliome!" a voice suddenly called. "I hope we're not bothering you girls!"

Clio looked into the garden. Tommy Haywood and Claire Clarke and Dix Lynott were walking across the lawn. Claire's arms were linked with the men, and their arms pressed against her breasts.

The woman, speechless, watched as Dix came lightly up the wooden steps. He kissed Mabel on the forehead, and sat back on his bare heels on the tatami.

"You have to take your shoes off," Claire said to Tommy. "My grandmother thinks we're in Japan."

She placed her shoes on the stairs and sat on the mat next to Dix.

Tommy pulled off his boots with effort and threw them impatiently onto the grass, nearly hitting Tadashi as she came across the lawn, weighed down by a tray heavy with saké cups and bottles.

"Oh, sorry, babe," Tommy said to Tadashi. Tommy turned to Clio and winked. "I'm glad I didn't have to come

to Moloka'i to get you," he said, hoisting himself onto the
edge of the verandah. "Claire told me you were here."
He swung his legs over the side. His feet in their socks
swept across Mr. Kageshiro's orchids, grown dense in the
slatted shade of Mabel's pavilion. Clio started to warn him
that he might break the stems, but, to her surprise, she
stopped herself. She could think of nothing to say.

Emma poured the warm saké into cups and handed
them round, first serving the men. "I didn't know you
admired *waka*," she said to Dix. He was politely trying to
read Mabel's incomprehensible calligraphy.

"Admired who?" Claire asked as she reached out to
tuck some hair behind Dix's ear. "Who's Waka?" Dix's
ear turned as pink as if Claire's fingers had singed him,
and he shook his head to escape her fingers.

Claire turned petulantly to Tommy. "Will you blow on
my saké to cool it?"

"It is supposed to be hot," Mabel said innocently.

"Thank you, Grans," said Claire. "What would we do
without you?"

"How is that cunning girl Charmian?" Mabel asked Dix,
taking his hand. "Have you finished the repairs on your
little boat? It is my understanding they do very good repairs
at the Honolulu Iron Works. Your wife must be vexed not
to be at sea."

Clio looked at Emma. Mabel thought that Dix was Jack
London. Dix very courteously agreed that it was vexing
not to be at sea.

Tommy slid awkwardly across the mat to Clio. "I was
going to have to use my big guns, babe. I was ready to get
serious." He was showing all of his tolerance and he was
pleased with himself. "I'm glad you finally got some sense
in you. Why didn't you come right to the hotel?"

"I am trying to get away from you," Clio said, speaking

for the first time. "Not to you. I thought you knew that. I am never living with you again."

"Listen, what I know and what I know are two different things."

Clio wondered if Emma had heard him. She realized that he embarrassed her. She looked at Emma, but Emma was gazing at her hands, frowning. "Perhaps we should talk about this another time," Clio said quietly. "When we are alone."

"There's nothing to talk about." He drank some saké and wiped his mouth with his hand.

"Well, we'll leave it to the lawyers then. Always a dangerous thing, it seems to me, but if that is what you want—"

"You don't get it, Clio, do you? We're leaving for L.A. Tuesday. I've been offered a couple of movies. I have to get back. I've already stayed too long." He stretched on his side on the tatami, his head resting in his hand. "I'm not giving you up, babe." He smiled.

"Who is there with you, Clio?" Mabel asked loudly. "Is that Mr. Haywood? How astonishing of him to come here!"

"But why?" Clio whispered to him.

"I finally get everything just right and you want to fuck it up," he said, spinning the saké cup in his hand. She wondered for an instant if he would break the fifteenth-century ceramic cup. "Do you know how much fun the press would have with this? Jesus."

"You know, the horrible thing, horrible for you, I know, is that I'm not trying to fuck it up. I'm not trying to do anything to you," she said, sliding her hands behind her knees. She was trembling and she didn't want him to see it.

"It's simple," he said. "Here's the deal. I'll send a car.

Someone to help you with your stuff. Better yet, leave everything here. There's shops at Ala Moana. You don't need much, anyway. That's one of the things I like about you. No cotton balls. No electric hair rollers. No makeup in the sink. You're clean. I mean, besides pissing in the tub."

She wondered if she should thank him.

"I've been staying with your mom and dad," he said. "I was getting bothered at the Kahala. Too many people knew I was in town, but I'll move back to the hotel tomorrow."

"You've been staying with Burta?"

"We're all going to my house at Waimea," Claire said. "Why don't you come, Aunt Emma? I'm sure Mother'd be happy to see you. Well, maybe not happy. Mother is never happy."

Dix carefully rolled up Mabel's scroll, weary of pretending to make sense of it, and Mabel patted his head contentedly.

"Grandmother has the ugliest hands I've ever seen," Claire said, staring at Mabel's swollen fingers.

"In Buddhism," Mabel said kindly, "ugliness is not denied or expunged. It is taken inside and made beautiful."

Claire stretched across the mat to a tray of sashimi, cupping her hand under the piece of fish so that the soy sauce would not drop onto the mat, and put the fish into Tommy's mouth. "How can you be a Buddhist, Grans? You're not Japanese."

"What kind of fish is this?" Tommy asked, spitting the sashimi into his hand. He dropped the sashimi into his saké cup.

"We're going to Waimea to work on Dix's screenplay. It's really great, but it needs a little work." Claire held out another piece of fish for Tommy. "Mamie says she's desperate to see you, Clio."

"It's not a bad script," Tommy said, waving away the fish. "A couple of college kids hide out in the mountains behind Oakland in full combat gear. They can't deal with our corrupt society. They'd rather hide out in the mountains than live in a country that oppresses them."

Clio looked at Tommy. "I had no idea you were so stupid," she said.

"What, babe?"

"How is Mamie?" Mabel asked Claire. "I am so fond of her. Forgive me, but Mamie was always my favorite grandchild."

Claire made a face at Clio.

"Her school is doing well," Emma said, speaking for the first time in a long while. "Mrs. Pi'ilima at the museum tells me that Mamie and her friend have sixty children now."

"Her friend, Frank Harimoto?" Claire asked mischievously. "Her friend the gardener, you mean."

"Yes," Emma said.

"I know all about her friend!" Mabel said sharply. "I am interested in her school, not her love life."

Clio looked at Emma. They had not known that Mabel knew about Mamie and Frank Harimoto. Emma shook her head in admiration, and Clio smiled.

Claire was reluctant to give up. "Did you know that Mamie has sold some of the old things she and Lily Shields used to collect? Remember that junk?" She turned to Emma. "It was very valuable. Can you imagine? She sold some Hawaiian artifacts to keep the school going. Sold them to people from the mainland." She looked around to see if she were having an effect. "It's bad enough that she's living with the gardener; now she's selling things. Never a good idea to sell. That's what Nando always says."

"I'm so pleased that your mother has decided not to sell the plantation," Emma said calmly.

Clio looked at Emma, wondering if she were up to her own mischief.

"She has?" Claire was surprised. "Mother's not selling?"

"Following your advice, we thought," Emma said, sipping her saké. She looked at Claire over the rim of her cup.

"My advice?" Claire asked, frowning. "My advice?"

"You'll help with the script," Tommy said to Clio. "It could use some of your spelling. No offense, Dix!" he shouted over his shoulder. "The car will be here in the morning."

Clio saw the blossoms on the cup-of-gold vine, closing with nightfall. The flowers, like little golden chalices, smelled like ripe apricots. The petals were furling so quickly that she could see them move. She wanted to drink from them. She turned to Tommy and Claire, knowing that they had the greatest gift for harm. They were the most dangerous, the most careless. "I admire what Mamie is doing," she said to Claire. "Mamie has something that moves her. Like Emma. I think it is clever of her to use the past, to sell the past, for the things that she needs now."

She jumped up and went down the stairs into the garden. The cup-of-gold flowers had closed. It was too late to sip from them. She could hear the ocean. No longer stricken with light and heat, it was crisp again, and strong. She went into the garden, and stood there, poised, not breathing. "I think it is time that you left," she called out to them.

"What is it, Emma?" Mabel demanded to know. She began to whimper.

"My mother is tired," Emma said. She rose and took

the scroll from Dix and rolled it up briskly and tied it with
its brocade ribbon.

"Are you tired, Grans?" Claire asked sarcastically.

Tommy stood with deliberate slowness and stretched,
striking his hands against the cherry-wood ceiling beams.
"Thanks for the saké," he said, lowering his arms, pretending that he had not hurt himself. It was the first time
that he had spoken to Emma. She did not answer him.

Dix said, "We should go, anyway. It's late." He was
embarrassed.

"You're kidding, right?" Tommy suddenly shouted into
the garden at Clio.

Claire reached out and fixed the collar of his shirt. "Yes,"
she said, soothingly. "She's kidding you."

Mabel leaned forward, smiling, her head cocked like a
wading bird, adrift once again, no longer listening to them.

Claire jumped onto the grass holding a shoe in each
hand. Her skirt scalloped around her as she disappeared
across the lawn. "Bye, Grans," she called back. "Bye,
Emma."

Dix gave Mabel an awkward kiss on the side of her
head, in her hair, and kissed Clio standing lightly on the
grass, and then he, too, disappeared into the darkness.

Tommy hopped across the lawn, struggling with a boot.
"Tomorrow, Clio!" he shouted, and he was gone.

"He doesn't believe me," Clio said, looking up at
Emma.

"They never do," Emma said.

"They never do?" Clio began to laugh.

"Not even when they're crazy about you."

"Not even then?"

"No. Especially not then." Emma paused. "Thank good-
ness he's not crazy about you."

Emma eased Mabel's heavy chair down the stairs that
the Japanese architect had sent from Nara, and they went

through the hospitable darkness to the house, bumping against each other in their new intimacy, the intimacy of women who have spoken about love.

Clio went early the next morning to the house in Nuʻuanu. She walked through the garden to the lanai. Although the front door was never locked, she did not want to go inside that house.

Clio wondered if Burta and Tommy might be on the lanai, perhaps sharing a papaya, but no one was there.

She saw Steamy. He was on the lawn, crouched over, searching for something in the grass. He was not wearing his glasses. "Don't tell me," she said. "You took them off, and when you awoke, both the girl and the glasses were gone."

Steamy shook his head. His eyes were red and he looked as if he were in pain. "That was the last time, Clio. And that's not going to happen anymore. Contacts." He pointed to his eyes. "Only I've lost one."

"You'll have to change your name. You can't be Steamy anymore."

"I can't?" he asked in disappointment.

"No," she said. "What is your real name, anyway? I've forgotten."

"Cliome."

"That's my name. Didn't Burta name you something like Earl? Or Junior? I think she named you Buddy."

"What is my name? I don't remember. You've confused me now. You always confuse me," he said fretfully. "The lens just popped out. I've only had them two days." He dropped to the wet grass and sat in a tiny circle, his legs pulled to his chest. He was afraid to put down his feet. He looked at her. "What are you doing here?"

"I'm looking for Tommy," she said.

"How incredibly weird! He's looking for you! He went to get you. He said he was moving to a hotel. Mom didn't want him to leave. She didn't know he was going to get you. She'd have been even more upset." He shuddered, imagining Burta's fury.

"I thought Burta was hoping for a reconciliation," Clio said, teasing him.

"Nope, not anymore. She figures she can have him without you. Sorry. Claire's looking for him, too. She's finally going to Waimea. Her husband—is he a king or something?—she said he called and told her he'd stop her allowance if she didn't go to her mother's."

To Clio's surprise, she felt sorry for Claire. "All these men threatening women. You're not like that with your girlfriend, are you, Steamy? Do you tell her you'll stop her allowance? Do you beat her up?"

"I don't have a girlfriend," he said, squinting up at her. "I want someone different. Someone like you. I'm tired of girls who say they prefer trees to humans. Or butterflies. It's so easy to like butterflies. The last girl I went out with believed in unicorns."

Clio looked back at the house.

"You're not listening," he said.

"I was just wondering if I should wait," she said.

"Are you going back to Tommy?"

"Steamy." She put her hand on his shoulder. "What's the matter with you?"

"I told you. You confuse me. You brought me up. I practically lived in your room until you ran away. It was terrible here without you."

She turned to the forest. "I would have died if I'd stayed. I thought I was dying, here in this house."

"Why didn't you take me with you?"

"Oh! How could I? I didn't know if Emma would even have me!"

"Is it because of Dad? Because you don't like Dad? Because he is the half that we share? Is that why you left me behind?"

"You think that my own mother was any better?"

"I sometimes think you are like your mother. You know, moving on all the time."

"I haven't moved fast enough, or far enough," she said, her eyes filling with tears. "What a terrible thing for you to say."

"I liked your mother! She was pretty and never paid any attention to us. It makes me nervous when grown-ups pay attention to me."

"But we're grown-ups."

Steamy frowned. "You are, maybe. Not me. Maybe you could adopt me."

"I don't think so."

"Is it against the law or something?"

"I don't want to adopt you, Steamy."

"Are you going to stay here? I mean, in Hawai'i?"

She did not answer him. She did not know the answer.

"I mean, if you did stay, maybe we could get a house together or an apartment or something. I'm about ready to move out of here, anyway."

"Perhaps I will live on Moloka'i."

"Moloka'i? They don't even have television, do they? You'd be so lonely."

She shook her head.

"What do you mean? You met someone? You actually met someone on Moloka'i?"

She was hesitant to tell him about Henry. She realized that she did not want to tell him because she did not want to forfeit his love. I want all the love that I can get, she thought. I am still in the Love Contest.

"Anyone I know?" he asked stiffly.

"No," she said.

He let go of his knees and stared at his palms.

"I'll help you find your lens and then I'll go," she said. She took a breath. "His name is Henry Kilohana. He is a fisherman."

"You don't have to. Help me, I mean."

"I want to help you."

He looked around absently. "I'm named after Father. I just remembered."

As she bent over to help him look, there was a sudden yell from the house. They both looked up, startled.

"What the hell is going on? Doing some weeding?" Burta shouted.

"He can't see," Clio said, straightening her back. "He lost his new lens."

"You don't need to tell me my responsibilities! I asked Steamy a question," Burta said, forcing herself to speak more quietly. "Not you, girlie." She enunciated with slow precision, her teeth together. She prodded Steamy with the tip of her sandal.

Clio stepped toward her. "If you say one more thing to him, or if you touch him again, I will kill you."

Burta was so astonished that she could not speak.

Steamy slowly stretched his legs in the grass, and stared up at Clio, his mouth open.

Clio put out her hand. "Get up." She pulled him to his feet. "I suppose now is as good a time as any," she said to Burta. "I've waited too long as it is. I know now that I'm the only one who can do it."

There was something so determined, so competent in her voice that Steamy stepped between the two women. Clio put her hand on his chest, and her hand lifted and fell with his breath. She was surprised that he was panting. "I could use Mr. Yama's mango pole," she said, looking around the garden. "There's a penknife on my key chain. I could hold your head in one of your birdbaths."

"You're nuts! That's why your husband threw you out!" Burta said harshly.

"No, she isn't," Steamy said, pushing away Clio's hand. "She's not nuts."

"Oh, you!" Burta turned to him. "You idiot!"

"I wouldn't, Burta," Clio said. "Not in front of me. Not ever. I could probably kill you with just my hands."

Burta shook with anger. "Your mother was a bitch, too. You're just the same! No wonder no one ever wanted you. At least she had money."

Clio, who had turned to look once more at the forest, turned back, and calmly put her hands around Burta's neck.

Lynott came onto the lanai, a martini in his hand. "Burta, your show is on television! Sweetheart?" He waved hello to Clio, then pointed to the face of his watch.

Burta hesitated. She looked back and forth between Clio and Lynott. Clio smiled and let her go. Burta wiped the corners of her lips, her mouth held wide so as not to smear her dark red lipstick. Her hands were shaking. "Don't you ever come here again. Don't dare come here!" She strode unsteadily toward the lanai.

"Your show's just starting!" Lynott called. "You're just in time." He paused. "You look funny, sweetheart. Are you all right?"

"I want to go with you this time," Steamy said to Clio. "Don't leave me here again."

"You'll be fine, Steamy. You were always fine."

"There's my contact!" he said in surprise, bending down to pluck it from the grass. There was a dark circle where the dew had soaked through the seat of his trousers. He held the lens proudly between his fingers. "You know what I was thinking just then? It reminded me of the time I cut my head. You bandaged it with stuff from the forest. Do you remember?"

"I remember. You were fine. Then and now."

"You're not disappointed?"

"Disappointed?"

"In me. In all of us."

Clio turned to nod goodbye to the ancestor figures on the lanai. She knew that she would not see them again. She looked at the silver *kukui* trees on the hill. The sound of the stream was lighter than usual. It was going to rain. I did not run into the forest, she thought.

"No, I'm not disappointed," she said and kissed him goodbye.

"There is someone here," Tadashi said as Clio came in the kitchen door. "On the lanai."

"A man?"

Tadashi nodded and pointed to the garden. Clio had hoped to rest before seeing Tommy. She wiped her face and hands with a towel and went out the kitchen door.

Sitting on the lanai with Emma and Mabel was a man, as Tadashi had said. They were listening to *Lucia di Lammermoor*, Mabel's favorite opera. The man lifted his dark head when he saw Clio, and rose to greet her.

"We've been waiting for you. You're here at last," Emma said.

Clio stared at Henry. He smiled at her, amused by her surprise.

"He hasn't much interest in the past!" Mabel shouted. "Isn't it grand?"

They laughed. "We have been talking about Moloka'i," Emma said. "Henry says that it has changed very little. I never much liked Moloka'i. Did I ever tell you that, Clio?

Oh, I saw its beauty, but it was too Hawaiian for me. Tell me," Emma asked Henry, "is the General Hospital still there? My father gave that to Moloka'i."

"Everything is the same, although Moloka'i Ranch is now owned by people from New Zealand. The men are angry because they brought in ranch hands from Mexico."

"I remember your mother," Emma said. "She was good on a horse."

"My father said she was the best he ever saw," Henry said.

Emma looked at Clio. "I used to hope that Clio would write down the story of these islands. Our story, and your story, Henry. But now it seems so foolhardy an idea that I wonder how I could ever have imagined such a thing. I am going to change. I am going to do it differently. How could I have spent my life this way? And to enlist Clio in behalf of the past! Write it down for whom?"

"For me," Clio said quickly. "That was our understanding, Aunt Emma. You allowed me to live at Wisteria House, and in exchange, I learned what you had to teach me. I was happy to learn it." Something in Emma's voice made Clio feel alarmed.

"Letters, songs, name-chants. Lists of extinct birds! What does it all signify? You two should sign up to go to the moon."

"Well, Paris, maybe," Clio said. "Paris would be nice."

"Does he play 'Net of the Moon'?" Mabel asked, taking Clio's hand.

"You know, Clio," Emma said before Clio could answer, "that committee to protest the Navy's missile testing on Kaho'olawe has been in touch with me. They've asked if I'll accompany them. They need support. As someone interested in saving ancient sites, they thought I might be of assistance." She paused. "This would be about the future. For a change."

Clio looked at her in surprise. "A protest will make no difference to the government, Emma. They've been using Kahoʻolawe as a bomb site for years. Kahoʻolawe itself has been abandoned for a century. It is hardly hallowed land."

"Will you answer me, Clio?" Mabel asked querulously. "Does he play 'Net of the Moon' or do I have to wait for Kageshiro to come?"

"The channel is very rough this time of year. There are sudden storms. It's a meaningless demonstration. There are better things for you to do than circle Kahoʻolawe in a bad sea for hours," Clio said.

Emma looked at her. "I've spent years doing just the sort of other things you mean. So have you. Raising money and spending money and recording oral histories and restoring buildings, and that, as you know, has made very little difference."

"It has mattered to us," Clio said.

"I don't think the boy has eaten," Mabel said loudly.

Clio looked at Henry. She was suddenly weary. She wanted to be alone with him. She could think of nothing but putting her hand on his skin, her mouth on his skin. She dared not stare at him too long, lest Emma see her desire. Emma would not disapprove, she knew, but Clio was protective of her passion. It was one of the first things she'd ever thought of as her own, and she meant to keep it her own for as long as she could.

"Are you hungry, young man?" Mabel shouted over the opera. "Kageshiro is late."

"Will you stay here with us?" Clio asked him. "I live in the cottage in the garden."

He nodded. She could feel that he, too, was full of desire.

They rose together.

"I believe that I knew your father," Emma said quickly, gazing up at him. "He taught me to lasso." She smiled. "It sounds funny now, but he did."

"I always wanted him to teach me," Henry said, "but he never had time."

"There you are," Emma said.

"Perhaps you could teach him," Clio said to Emma.

"Perhaps I could."

"I am very hungry," Mabel said. "Will you bring him to us as soon as he is ready?"

"It sounds as if you're going to eat me," he said.

"We have returned to the ways of our ancestors after all," Emma said, laughing.

She lay on the bed and watched him take off his shirt. He looked out of place amidst the rich bed hangings. His presence made the room seem too feminine.

He looked at the sorcery sculpture that Emma had given to Clio the summer she left her job in the camera store. Bits of dried flesh and the blood of human sacrifice were still lodged in the god's saw-toothed helmet, and Clio was surprised to see him touch it so easily. He noticed her expression. "It's not voodoo, Clio," he said with a smile.

"So I'm discovering."

He went into the sitting room.

"It is so unlike Emma to join a demonstration," she said. She could not see him from the bed. "She won't even lend her name to a committee. This is very odd of her. It's all because of your father."

"I'll go with her," he said from the other room. "My father?"

"I'll go, too," she said.

"No," he said, coming into the room. "It's a small boat."

He stood at the side of the bed. His bare arms and chest

were dark against the bed. His hair rested heavily on the back of his neck. The wind had risen, and she could hear the jasmine vines brush against the screen.

He bent over the bed and lifted her hips. He pulled down her skirt and underpants, and took off her shirt. He lay her arms on the pillows above her head. He parted her legs.

He looked at her as if he were looking at a woman for the first time. Perhaps he was. She closed her eyes, barely able to lie still beneath his scrutiny, unable to watch him while he looked at her. He began to speak to her, telling her what he saw. Clio had learned to wait to discover what it was that he thought, what it was that he wanted. It sometimes seemed to her that they made love in order to talk.

The jasmine moved back and forth across the screen. She could hear the birds settling in their nests. There was the shuffle of an animal looking for some small live thing to eat, a mongoose perhaps, on his evening round. It trotted up and down the path outside the window. She wondered if she would ever be able to stop listening.

He held her open with his fingers. She flushed with shame and desire.

"I could have guessed it," a voice said. "Actually, I knew all along."

Henry slowly turned his head. He had never seen him before. He gazed impassively at him, waiting patiently as if it were Tommy who needed to explain himself.

He took his hand from her vagina. He gave her her shirt and watched as she put it on. It was inside out and it bunched under her arms. He pulled it over her bare lap, covering her.

"What do you want?" she asked. She had meant to speak with force, but she could only whisper. "Why are you here?"

"I came to get you." His eyes flickered for a moment to the sorcery idol. "What the fuck do you think?" He rested his hand on the base of the sculpture.

Henry rose, his pants unbuttoned at the waist. "There's nothing for you here," he said, standing at the foot of the bed.

Tommy turned as if he had just realized that there was another man in the room. He lifted the sorcery god from its pedestal and held it loosely in one hand. A scrap of ancient *kapa* cloth, dry and brittle, fell to the floor. "Want to bet?"

Clio slid off the bed. The T-shirt reached only to her waist, but she seemed not to know it.

"Is this all about Morocco?" he suddenly yelled. "Is that it? Man, I told you: I believe in adult education. It was just that once. Did it ever happen before? No. And it won't happen again. Women do things just as bad to men. Sometimes worse things. It fucking evens out."

She wondered what it was that women did to men that was worse than beating them. Perhaps he means murder, she thought. It was a curious scorecard that he was keeping. "If I beat you up and leave you bleeding in the Sunrise Suite at the Kahala Hilton, we'll be even? We could stay together?"

"Even?" He laughed. "I didn't say that. I don't think it works quite that way. Sorry." He passed the idol from hand to hand, and she realized that he was nervous, and that his nervousness made him dangerous. I wouldn't be able to beat him senseless, she thought. I am not strong enough. That is why it doesn't work that way. It never has, and it never will.

"Put your clothes on," he said in disgust. He picked up her skirt from the floor and threw it in her face.

Henry stepped toward him and Tommy took the god in two hands and struck him in the head.

There was blood on Henry's face, dark against his skin, and Tommy looked startled. Henry gazed at him with interest. Then he grabbed him tightly around the chest. Tommy dropped the sorcery god with the force of his embrace. There was a smell of sweat and expensive tanning oil. Tommy's silk shirt was dark with perspiration. There was blood on Henry's chest, and on his arms.

As she bent to pick up the sculpture, to safeguard it, Tommy kicked out at her in fury. She looked up in surprise and she saw that Henry was no longer interested in making it easy for him. He was no longer curious, no longer amused that Tommy would be so reckless as to try to fight him. Clio saw that he was angry. He meant to hurt him.

He shoved him out the open door onto the porch. Tommy fell to his knees and Henry bent low and picked him up with one hand and hit him across the face.

Tommy put his hand to his face. He was bleeding, and he stared at the blood in amazement. "He cut my face!" he said, shocked. "He cut my face!" He looked up at Clio, as if for help, wiping the blood and mucous from his face with his sleeve. "I knew it! I knew you were fucking someone. I knew it all the time. You deserve each other. Fucking island." He spit blood.

"You knew nothing," she said.

"Cunt."

Clio whispered, "Take him away from here. Take him away!"

Tommy tried to stand, but he could not get to his feet. Henry lifted him and pushed him ahead of him, and Tommy fell onto the grass.

She closed the door and turned off the lights, afraid of being seen, not by Emma, not even by Tommy, but by someone, some stranger, who meant her harm. She ran from room to room, into the kitchen, into the bathroom, full of fear and elation. There was a quarter moon, like a clean fingernail, low in the sky, but she did not see it.

Henry let himself in quietly. "I thought you were gone," he said as she darted to him through the darkness. "The lights were out."

"Gone?" she whispered in astonishment.

He held her to his bare chest and she kissed his eyes and his hands. There was blood on his hands. He was breathing heavily.

She held herself apart from him, to see him.

In the pavilion, Mabel had started *Lucia* again, playing it very loud.

She leaned into his chest. "Forgive me," she said. "No more Love Contests."

The boat was very small, as he had said. The life preservers were stuffed beneath the console. There was a radio so that Henry could talk to the other boats. His cousin Leroy was on a blue sampan. One of the fishing boats had been chartered by the Human Reactor, who had come from Hiroshima after all.

The Coast Guard had dispatched a cutter and it was so close that Clio could see the faces of the young sailors as they watched idly from the sides. They looked sunburned, and a little bored.

The island of Kaho'olawe, bare of vegetation, disappeared with each new sweep of water, and Clio, like the sailors, wondered why they were there.

Emma stood at the wheel with Henry. "All cultures end eventually, Henry," she shouted, turning to smile at Clio.

Henry, intent on keeping the small boat steady, did not answer. Emma turned again to Clio and beckoned to her with a gesture that seemed to take in the sky and bleak

Kahoʻolawe, and even the pink-faced, sullen boys on the cutter.

"I wonder what a Human Reactor looks like?" Emma called gaily to Clio.

Clio looked at her, surprised by her sudden anger at Emma. She wondered for a moment if she were jealous. Perhaps she did not wish to share Henry, the presence of Henry, even with Emma. But she knew that it was not jealousy. It was Emma's change of heart. It was an insult to Clio, who had lived in her service for years. She believes that all the time in the world is ahead of her, thought Clio, and I believe that all time is behind me.

"I used to shoot deer on Kahoʻolawe," Emma said, shouting over the sound of the outboard and the sound of the sea.

Henry nodded. "It was good hunting there."

The two of them! Clio thought.

Another boat came alongside. An old Hawaiian charter captain was at the wheel, a Kona fisherman named Pupule.

He waved to Henry.

Henry waved back at him.

In the front of Pupule's boat stood a small Japanese man in a yellow slicker and black gloves. He, too, waved.

Emma looked at him, then turned to Clio, smiling in amusement. "Do you think he wears that oilskin to contain his rays?"

Clio smiled and nodded, distracted. She had been watching the cutter, suddenly near enough to be either purposeful or careless. Henry, too, had noticed the closeness of the boat. She wondered if the Coast Guard were preparing to lower sailors into their boat. Perhaps they were going to be arrested.

And then the Coast Guard boat rammed them from behind.

With a startled smile, Emma stumbled against the rail.

She turned to Clio, and put out her hand, and fell into the sea.

Henry grabbed a rope from the deck, and a life preserver, and, pointing off the bow, pushed the line and the vest into Clio's outstretched hands.

Clio could see driftwood and seaweed, foam and wrack, all with sudden clarity, but she could not see Emma.

The boat rolled from side to side. Henry idled the engine, fearful of hitting Emma, or the other boats, rocking, too, in confusion. He turned the boat in small, slow circles. On the other boat, Pupule climbed to the fishing tower. His boat swayed so wildly that his outrigger poles seemed to touch the sea. The man in the yellow coat huddled in the cabin.

A rescue boat was lowered from the cutter. It, too, rolled in the rough sea, and the helmsman raced the engine, trying to outrun a swell, making a sudden deep wake that rushed upon the smaller boats. A wave washed over them, and Clio was swept into the sea.

The waves broke without regret, without pleasure. Salt burned in her nose and throat. She lay on her back and tried to breathe, tried to find the bright sky and black Kahoʻolawe. The sea lifted her high, and dropped her with a roar.

Someone called her name.

It is my grandfather, she thought. My grandfather who drowned one winter evening of rapture of the deep.

But it was not her grandfather.

It is Kimo Danforth, my mother's husband, who fell to the bottom of the canyon, the flowers for my mother clutched in his fist. It is Miss Stant, with her broken heart and her straw bag full of stolen shirts. It is Uncle McCully, who drowned in a tidal wave looking for Mamie.

But it was none of them.

She could hear the women and the unheeding children and the reckless warriors and fishermen, lost at sea, all of them calling to her.

But she was wrong. It was none of these. It was Henry. It was Henry, calling her name.

She fought hard against the water god. When the sailors tried to pull her into their boat, she resisted with such ferocity that she broke her collarbone in the struggle. She thought that she was bodysurfing with the Hawaiian boys at Makapu'u Point. "Where is my fin?" she asked. "I've lost my fin." The young sailors finally lied to her, telling her they had her fin in the boat. Only then did Clio stop struggling and allow them to lift her from the lamenting sea.

Emma was taken by the god, as she had known she would be were he ever given the chance, and her body, because of this, was never recovered.

In her generosity and wisdom, Emma bequeathed all of her treasure to Mamie Clarke and Frank Harimoto to dispose of as they saw fit in the furtherance of educating the young of Hawai'i in the ways of the people.

Wisteria House was, despite Emma's wishes, not hers to compel, as the city, a few weeks after her disappearance at sea, claimed the land for the new sports arena, which they announced would be named the Fitzroy Aloha Center in honor of her extravagant gift.

To Clio, Emma gave the house called Hale Moku and her charts and genealogies and books. She also gave to Clio the guardianship of her mother, Miss Mabel Clarke.

Clio had to sell some of the rarer of Emma's papers at auction, and the two feather capes that had once belonged to Ka'ahumanu, the queen who changed the islands forever when she refused to obey the *kapu* that forbade her eating with her favorite chieftains. Clio tried to ask Mabel's permission before selling the capes, but Mabel had waved her away.

She insisted that Clio sleep on a futon at the foot of her bed. Clio lay on the mat and watched the lizards on the ceiling; her 'aumakua, Emma's 'aumakua.

She listened to the lizards and wondered if she had become a listener out of sympathy with her grandmother. But Clio knew that she had been listening all of her life. It was what she did best. She had listened to the ceaseless, glancing stream; and to the clicking of her mother's white suede high heels as she left Hale Moku. She had listened to the deer on the mountain; and she had listened to Emma, most of all she had listened to Emma: "Two steep and wild mountain ranges called *palis* embrace the lovely valley known as Nu'uanu. It was from Nu'uanu, the first resting place of the gods, that life spread throughout these islands, Clio. The *'e'epa* people, the gnomes, lived there. The *menehune* constructed a temple, a *heiau*, not far from your mother's house, for the children adopted by the gods. I like to think that we are descended from those children."

Clio wondered if Emma were right, if they were the descendants of those first blessed orphans, endowed with their powers of magic. Clio had once tried to open a breadfruit tree like the sorceress Papa to hide at the heart of the tree, but the tree had refused to open for her. Emma had said that the tree did not obey because Clio had not fully learned the words to the tree-opening chant. Clio learned them and tried again, and when the tree still did not open, she did not tell Emma.

"We must put up a stone for Emma, who has no grave," Mabel said one night.

Mabel continued to suffer from *kadami no yoru*, a darkness of the heart. She worried that her grief would cause her transubstantiation to be postponed, at least until she could achieve a Buddhist state of egolessness.

"Emma wanted to be buried near a *pua kenikeni* tree," Clio said, watching a lizard eat a termite. "She said so many times." She turned on her side to ease the ache of her shoulder.

"Is there still a *pua kenikeni* grove near the mill?"

"There is one, I know, near Hau'ula."

Clio wondered if Emma's body had floated, like the blue glass balls that came to shore, from warm current to cold and back again, from the livid, dense waters of their islands to the cold, gray waters of Japan.

"Too built up," Mabel said. "We will make one here. We will have everyone to stay. We will open the house again and consecrate the land and plant a grove of *pua kenikeni*. Frank Harimoto and Mamie will come, and Claire and Dix, and all of our friends."

"Claire and Dix are in Los Angeles."

"Fine."

Clio heard Tadashi leave her bed in the next room. The wooden floorboards moaned at the lightest touch, and day and night Clio listened to Tadashi's restless movements as she moved through the house.

"Have you Emma's genealogies and name-chants with you?" Mabel asked fretfully. "Do you have them?"

"Yes," Clio said.

Mabel sighed and turned heavily in her bed.

Clio longed to sleep. She had not been able to sleep more than a few hours each night. Although her shoulder no longer gave her great pain, it was difficult to rest.

"She worked so hard on them," Mabel whispered. "It was her gift to me. She thought I'd given up my own life for the past. That is why she would not go with her husband when he asked her to leave. To go would mean that I had been wrong not to go."

Clio listened as a branch of the big monkeypod tree rubbed up and down the rain gutter. It sounded as if the house were being cut open with a dull knife. Maybe that is why Emma didn't go to Tahiti, Clio thought. Maybe.

"Do you think you will continue her work?"

Clio did not answer.

"You think it is too late?"

Clio did think that it was too late.

"To save it? To save the past? Too late for me?"

Clio hesitated. "For you?"

"For me to help you," Mabel said timidly.

Clio was so tired, so exhausted by all of them, that she could not answer.

"Is it too ironic?" Mabel asked.

"A little," Clio said. Tears ran into her hair and into her mouth.

"There is a line in one of Hitomaro's love poems that torments me: *How can I find my girl, wandering on ways I do not know?*"

Clio listened as Tadashi moved haltingly down the dark hall, her hand trailing tentatively along the wainscotting so that she would not slip and fall. Tadashi's tiny feet, safe within their cloven socks, slid over the wooden floor.

Clio rose from her mat.

"Clio? Child?" Mabel whispered. "Where are you?"

She went to his room, the room that her mother had lived in as a girl. He was reading, and he looked up at her.

"We could swim," he said quietly.

"No," she said. "Not swim. I don't want to swim yet."

They went lightly through the rooms, not hurrying, finding their way through the house. She could smell the dust of Hale Moku in his hair. He did not let go of her hand, lest she stumble over a calabash, or a root, or a rock on the beach.

He undressed her at the water's edge. The waves leapt at her feet. He does not undress me, she thought, as he undressed me when they pulled me from the sea. He is no longer mindful of my pain and my grief. He is touching me without sorrow, at last.

The ocean was invisible. Clio could hear it tossing restlessly in the darkness. The black branches of the palm trees brushed against the black sky, sweeping the pallid stars, making her dizzy. He held her, out of the path of stars, out of the current, and, for a little while, she stopped listening.

I myself have seen it.

A NOTE ON THE TYPE

This book was set in Granjon, a type named in compliment to Robert Granjon but neither a copy of a classic face nor an entirely original creation. George W. Jones based his designs on the type used by Claude Garamond (c. 1480–1561) in his beautiful French books. Granjon more closely resembles Garamond's own type than does any of the various modern types that bear his name.

Robert Granjon began his career as a type cutter in 1523. The boldest and most original designer of his time, he was one of the first to practice the trade of type founder apart from that of printer. Between 1557 and 1562 Granjon printed about twenty books in types designed by himself, following, after the fashion, the cursive handwriting of the time. These types, usually known as *caractères de civilité*, he himself called *lettres françaises*, as especially appropriate to his own country.

Composed by PennSet, Inc.,
Bloomsburg, Pennsylvania
Printed and bound by The Haddon Craftsmen,
Scranton, Pennsylvania
Designed by Brooke Zimmer